Never Again

Warnings

There are warnings enough—that first cold night in August
When Andromeda swings up in the East and crickets are silent!
The early dusk of September, heavy dew in the garden,
And blurring eyes, and aches, and names forgotten.
Never again, never again the summer of strength and beauty.
Friends waver and vanish—O chill north wind of warning!
Look long, love deep while you may.
Too soon December.

– Katharine Day Barnes

Never Again

Heather Starsong

Never Again
Copyright © 2015 Heather Starsong (www.heatherstarsong.com)

"Do Not Go Gentle into That Good Night" by Dylan Thomas, from *The Poems of Dylan Thomas*, copyright © 1952 by Dylan Thomas. Reprinted by permission of New Directions Publishing Corp.

Edited by Robin Wilkinson
Cover art by Stephen Clay Elliott
Design and layout by Ann Erwin

Author: Heather Starsong
Title: *Never Again*

Description: Second edition | Boulder, CO: Dancing Aspen Press
Subjects: Fiction, Youth & Aging, Family Relationships, Romance, Alien contact, Women's literature

Identifiers: ISBN Trade Paperback #978-0-9975450-6-7
          ISBN eBook #978-0-9975450-7-4
Library of Congress Control Number: 201594917
First Edition: August 2015

Table of Contents

Prologue

It is not unusual for an old woman to remember being young. But it is strange for a young woman to remember being old. As I did.

This thought comes to me as I lie face down in the midst of my little vegetable garden, having snagged my cane, lost my balance, and fallen. I am not hurt, but shaken. The tilled earth is soft, and it feels like too much effort to get up just now.

My head is turned to the side. From this position my garden is upside down. I have a worm's eye view around the roots of bushy lettuces, the orange tops of carrots under their ferny leaves, tomato plants towering over me, hung with bright fruit. There are weeds everywhere.

It's all undone, all the work I did in my garden when I was still young, before I went up the mountain. It's hard to believe that only four days ago I walked freely there, high above tree line, ran lightly, leaping from rock to rock.

I turn my head. Dizziness spins through me and my eyes go dark. I am in the spaceship, the Elirians around me, touching me with their strange, seven-fingered hands, transforming my body.

Greg comes running. "Mom, what happened? Are you okay?"

I open my eyes. I'm not in the spaceship; I'm in my garden. "I'm fine," I say. "Just resting."

Greg bends over me. "What the hell are you doing? You shouldn't be trying to work in your garden yet. You just got home from the hospital yesterday."

He is frowning, his lips pressed together. I guess I'm hard to care for. The change was so sudden I forget I can't move easily anymore, can't squat to tend my garden, that I must lean on my cane and be careful.

Greg lifts me to my feet. I smell the faint tang of his sweat. In spite of his impatience, he is gentle, supporting me with his strong arm as he helps me into the house and settles me in my rocking chair. I lean my head back and close my eyes.

I know they are far, far away now, across the galaxies, but still they seem near. I remember the soft touch of their radiant fur, see their luminous eyes, hear their melodious voices singing, *Write your story.*

It seems a small thing to do in the face of great need. But now they are gone, I would do whatever they ask. After all, they are far older and wiser than I.

I am too weary to write now, but I can start remembering. It all began when I climbed the mountain on my birthday.

Chapter 1

The Special Place

The path was steep, crisscrossed by roots of tall evergreens that towered above me on either side. Early morning sun slanted through the trees, dappling the path and casting long shadows ahead of me. Using my stick for balance, I climbed with difficulty, my knees stiff and aching. My toe snagged on a rock and I stumbled forward. As I caught myself and straightened, my heart wavered, skipped a beat, stopped for a moment, then raced. I leaned on my stick, almost blacking out. At last the familiar dizzying feeling passed.

I took a deep breath. Crisp, cool air, smelling of pine needles and moist earth. Another step up, then another. I can make it, I told myself, I will. Just this one more time.

Each year on my birthday, I had made it somehow, never knowing if I could, up the long side of the mountain, passing from wonder to wonder, to my special place. That year, the year 2011, it was my eightieth birthday.

My heart was still uneven, racing in short bursts as I continued to climb, watching carefully now for rocks and roots. A shiver of fear ran though me. Only a few days ago my cardiologist had warned me I was at high risk for heart attack when it raced like that. Was I crazy to try to climb so high and far?

Behind me I heard laughter and shouts, and then in a moment I was surrounded by little boys in blue Cub Scout uniforms. They had arrived in the parking lot just as I was leaving, bursting out of their van and scattering like seeds exploding out of a dry seedpod. I had turned back to watch them, laughing with delight. Those little boys jumped and ran, punched each other, shouted, ran back and forth across the parking lot as if running were nothing, jumped as if they had to, as if it were an essential part of their being. The two young men accompanying them were calling them together as I started up the trail.

Now they surged by me, still running, jumping over the rocks and roots. I laughed again; I couldn't help it. They were so exuberant, so alive! At the same time a sob caught in my throat. I used to jump like that, run, dance.

One young man kept up with the boys; the other slowed and walked beside me.

"Beautiful day," he said smiling down at me.

I pulled myself together. "It is indeed," I responded. How handsome he was, his tanned young face under a wide-brimmed hat, his clear eyes.

"How far are you going?" he asked.

"As far as my legs will carry me."

"Have a good one." He quickened his steps and moved on, and soon the whole group was out of sight around a bend in the trail.

Alone on the path, I stopped and questioned myself again. Maybe I should just go a little way, sit by Silver Lake a while, and then go home. Not push it.

But if I didn't go this year... Sudden tears stung my eyes. If I didn't go this year, then I would never go again. I'd give up, tell myself I was too old.

Never walk again in the beauty of the high country, never go again to that magical place I loved beyond all reason, never again dip in the icy crystal stream, lie on the soft tundra, the stern, jagged peaks around me, the deep sky above?

Wind moved through the pines, a soft soughing sound that felt like the voice of my sorrow.

I'd already lost so much. If I lost this, too, would life still be worth living? Would I just shrivel?

No.

With an impatient gesture, I rubbed a tear off my cheek, took a firm grip on my staff, and started walking again. I must not give up.

One more steep part and the trail leveled out, opening into a view of Silver Lake and the peaks above. There was still snow up there, even this late in the summer, white against the deep blue of the sky. I tilted my face up. No blue anywhere so deep as the blue of Rocky Mountain sky.

When the trail branched, I followed the sign that said "Sapphire Lake, 2 miles." My heart had steadied, going back to its normal ka-thunk, ka-thunk, and my legs were losing their stiffness, finding their rhythm. I'm okay, I thought with a surge of joy. I'll make it.

I knew this trail. I had walked it every summer for more than forty years. Each rock and tree, each turn in the path, each new vista greeted me with the welcome of a long-beloved friend. The path ran for almost a mile along the side of Silver Lake, wide, smooth, and mostly level, leading through ancient evergreens with a mantle of moss and flowers at their feet. Little rivulets trickled out of rocky crevices and crossed the path. Here and there the glimmer of the lake shone through spaces between the trees. On the other side of the path, I noticed a tall lightning-blackened tree standing among the live ones. An image flickered through my mind from a dream that had waked me two nights before. There was a forest like the one I was walking through now.

I stepped to the side of the trail, leaned on my staff, and closed my eyes. The dream filtered back, at first in scattered images, then in its entirety.

I was floating in the sky, disembodied. Far below I could see Earth, blue, marbled with white clouds. A voice somewhere near or within me said, *It is time to return to Earth.*

No.

It is time. When the voice spoke again, I felt a pull from Earth. I resisted, then surrendered and began to fall, slowly, slowly, drifting between stars. At last I came to rest on a mountaintop, taking on the translucent shape of a human body. A path opened before me and I followed it, my body becoming more substantial as the path led me always downward over tundra and rocks, past lakes and streams, until I came to a forest. There in the trees near the trail stood a tall, black-robed figure, his face hidden by a deep hood. He opened his black cloak, and I went into it. Darkness, peace. Wrapped in his embrace, I knew he would be there when I needed him. He was my way home.

When he unfolded his cloak I saw that the path led to an opening in the forest. Below in the valley was a village. I could see people moving around their houses, fenced gardens, beasts in the fields. I walked a short way, then turned back to Death, for so I knew him to be. He nodded to me and I went on my way, reassured.

It was a good dream. I stood awhile longer letting its comfort wash over me, then glanced up at the black tree that reminded me of Death. "I'm glad you're there, but I'm not ready yet," I told it as I stepped back onto the trail. "I want a few more years to walk in these beautiful mountains."

As I went on, I thought of the first time I had walked this trail. I had recently left behind the wreckage of my first marriage and moved to Colorado with my two teenage children and a new husband, Jon. Jon and I found this trail in late summer. I remembered how happy I had felt, deeply in love, walking hand in hand with him. Little did I know then.

Soon I reached a place where the trail divided again, the left fork looping back around the lake, the right going up. Up I went, my steps quickening, my spirit soaring. The trail grew steeper, still leading through the forest. It crossed a small bridge over a creek that rushed down from above, its voice loud among the quiet trees. Farther on, two big ponderosas, one on each side of the trail, made a gateway for the ending of the forest and framed a dramatic view of the peaks and the waterfall spilling down the precipice below Sapphire Lake. I paused to look through, remembering the first time I had come there, how awed I had been. I still was.

Now I climbed along the edge of a wide valley. The river from Sapphire Lake flowed down the center, shining in the sunlight. I walked in wonder, beauty all around me—the sparkle of sunlight on pine needles, the seed-heavy grasses bending in the wind, the bright wildflowers. I stopped to trace the lacy gray-green pattern of lichen on a rock by the side of the trail. Farther on, I pressed my nose against the trunk of a ponderosa. It smelled like butterscotch. I pulled off a bubble of sap and walked on, sniffing it on my fingertips.

At a sharp turn in the path, I came to a rocky outcropping with micro worlds of tiny flowers and mosses in its crevices. A resting place.

I was hot. I dropped my pack and wiggled out of my gray cloak. That cloak, deep-hooded, made of tightly-woven Welsh wool, imbued with the smoke of many campfires, was a treasured possession. I always carried it with me, even though it was heavy, as it could keep out a light rain, or a chill wind, or serve as a blanket when I rested on the ground. You never knew what might arise in the mountains.

Now I folded it and tucked it under the flap of my pack, then sat, legs straight in front of me. My knee braces, tubes of supportive elastic, always bunched up and pinched me when I walked. I straightened them, pushed my wispy white hair back under my hat, took a drink from my water bottle. I mustn't stop long, I told myself. I need to reach my special place before noon to have time to enjoy it and still be on my way down before the thunderstorms come.

Just before the last steep ascent to Sapphire Lake, a little path leads off the trail to the bottom of the waterfall. I followed it, stepping over brush the forest rangers had put there to conceal it, down through the trees, squishing through the marshy place at the edge. The cascade poured out of the lake high above, rushing, roaring, sparkling in many channels around islands of flowers, past my feet and on down into the valley.

Once long ago, twenty years or more it must have been, I had come there alone, crossed that turbulent waterfall, barefoot, almost knee deep, bracing myself with my stick against the tumult of the current, my skirt hems soaked, then scrambled up the almost-vertical rocky slope on the other side, on all fours at times, to come to the lake. Ah, long gone that agile woman who would dare such challenge. It seemed impossible that she could be the same woman as I, standing at the water's edge, stiff-kneed and cautious.

I stood a while, drinking in the sweet air off the tumbling water, then turned back on the hidden path to the main trail. The last bit before the lake was the steepest part. I used to just stride up it, I thought, impatient with myself as I stopped halfway to catch my breath, my heart pounding, my knees aching. If only my knees didn't hurt. Never mind. I can still do it. It just takes a little longer.

The very last part before the lake was rocky, rising in big, irregular steps. I set my staff carefully, but as I tried to maneuver an especially high step, my leg buckled and I fell forward, banging my knee sharply on the edge of the rock above. I gasped and crouched there a moment in shock, then, dragging my injured leg behind me, crawled on two hands and one knee to the side of the trail. There a spreading fir shaded a soft patch of earth. I leaned against its trunk, drawing my wounded knee up against my chest. I felt nauseated, shaky, near tears, and my breath came in little short bursts. Putting my attention there, I worked to slow it. Long inhale, exhale.

My long, denim skirt was torn. Gingerly, I moved it aside. No blood. The knee brace had protected me from scrapes, but my knee throbbed from the impact.

Maybe you won't make it today, a voice within me commented. After all, you're eighty and this is the second time you've stumbled. You have to admit you're not so steady on your feet as you used to be.

My heart took off in a series of series of rapid beats, and I had a moment of panic. I moved my leg, stretching it out and bringing it back to my chest. I'll be all right, I answered the inner voice. It's not broken. In my pack, I found my water bottle and a pouch with ibuprofen. Three magic little orange tablets. They always helped.

After resting a little longer, I pulled myself to my feet, holding onto the tree trunk. My staff still lay among the rocks in the trail. Carefully, testing my leg with each step, I walked to it, glad no one had come along and tripped over it while I was recovering.

I climbed the rest of the rocky place on all fours, and so came at last to Sapphire Lake, 11,500 feet above sea level.

There was a place I always rested, just above the lake on a bit of grassy slope. I slipped off my pack, stretched out my legs, and breathed in the view. High, rocky peaks with patches of snow towered above me. Below me, the lake shimmered in the morning sunlight. A light wind rippled its surface and colors flowed across it, green, blue, even purple in the shadows.

After nibbling on some trail mix, I lay down on my back. My body ached with relief. I let my spirit float into the sky, following the white puffy clouds coming over the peaks on the west and drifted, thinking of my special place.

I couldn't remember what year I first discovered it. It was on my birthday, long ago. Coming down from a solo hike to the pass, I saw a valley far below with a stream running through. I had only begun at that time to dare venture off the trail.

After a long scramble down the steep side of the mountain, I followed the stream toward its source, past a small waterfall dividing around purple-pink flowers, and came to a place of pure magic.

For more than an hour, I lingered there, dipping in the icy stream, sitting watching its flow, thinking of the year past, the year ahead. Peace within and without. Clarity.

After that it became a ritual to go alone on my birthday, dip in the stream to clear the past year, and dream the next. I had only missed once, the year I had a hip replacement.

A group of people passing, talking loudly, roused me from my memories. As I opened my eyes and looked up, I saw the sun glint off something silver high in the sky above the southern peaks. It hung there, shining like a tiny star—but it was daylight. It must be a plane, I thought, frowning, trying to see more clearly. But a plane would move, and this bit of silver sun glint hovered motionless over the highest peak. For a long, still moment I stared at it. Then it was gone, just gone, like a light turned out. I rubbed my eyes and sat up.

What in the world was that? I looked again at the place where it had been. Nothing. Only the deep blue of the sky.

I rubbed my eyes again and looked at my watch. Already 10:30. I should get going, I told myself. My special place is still far above. I stood slowly, still wondering what I had seen.

The trail was steeper after I left Sapphire Lake. I slowed my pace, steadied my breath. Not far above the lake were two large rocks by the stream's edge. I paused and time shifted. I saw myself sitting there with my daughter, Lisa, the weekend before she left for college. She'd asked me what I wanted for my birthday.

"Walk with me. A day in the mountains."

We sat there by the stream. I don't remember what we spoke of, only her exquisite young beauty and the aching poignancy of her imminent departure.

Farther on, a huge boulder, high as a house, rose up out of a grassy meadow spangled with wildflowers. Years ago, when he was still in his teens, my son, Greg, walked this trail with me. I smiled, remembering how he'd run to climb that boulder, agile as a monkey. I could almost see him standing on the top as he did that day, grinning down at me.

I walked on, thinking of my children. Lisa and Greg, only a year apart, born of my first marriage when I was very young. Then Robin, child of my second marriage, born when Lisa and Greg were almost grown. All three were blessing.

Higher up, at a turn in the trail, a view opened to a gigantic rock jutting out of the mountain high above. The trail switched back and forth across its face with plunging views of the valley and lake below. I had climbed that high only a few times. Twenty-five years ago, in the chaos of my divorce from Jon, I left home impulsively in the middle of the afternoon, drove to the trailhead and ran up this trail, ran past where I now stood and on, up and up. Storms ricocheted amongst the peaks. I gloried in them. Thunder crashed and rain soaked me. As I dashed up the rockface on the switchbacks, I met hikers running down, ponchos flapping.

A man leaping from rock to rock shouted as he passed me, "You're going the wrong way!"

"No, I'm not!" I shouted back. No outer storm could match my raging spirit. At the last minute, when thunder and lightning became almost simultaneous, caution prevailed. I ducked under a rocky overhang and sat sipping hot tea from my small thermos until the worst had passed.

Now I looked longingly at the great rockface, the high zigzag trail. How I would love to go there today, to stand in the wind at the top. I doubted I ever would again.

The trail curved and climbed through another wooded area with wide open places under the trees. At a steep incline, the makers of the trail had for some reason sent it across the stream, curved it around, and sent it back across the stream. The bridges were only two logs lashed together. I came to the first. The logs were wet with spray, perhaps slippery. How many times I had danced across or stopped in the center to exult in the rushing water. But now—I took a step forward, then drew back. The bridge was too narrow, the fall of water three feet below too swift, the rocks it swirled around too menacing. There was another path I knew. Back down the trail, a little way off among the trees, a steep scramble would bring me back to the main track above the second crossing. There was brush across that path, too, but I made my way around it and climbed up on all fours. I stumbled to my knees when I reached the top, breathless, my heart racing in the crazy runaway beat of tachycardia. "Hush," I said, laying my hand over my heart. But it took a long time for it to hush, and longer still for the beat to settle. So I had to rest again.

It was becoming harder to get going after a rest. My legs stiffened so quickly. I got up slowly. Not much farther now. The trail left the stream and climbed, curving around a steep fall to a valley below.

A vertical slab of gray rock jutted out of the uphill side of the trail. I remembered the time Jon and I had walked there with Robin when he was seven or eight years old. I sat leaning against that slab of rock while he and Jon played, throwing stones over the edge of the precipice, watching how far they bounced and rolled.

Jon had been a devoted father, adoring his young son, lavishing him with loving attention, supporting him in all he endeavored. A devoted husband, until—

With a swift kick I sent a stone flying down the steep bank.

And before Jon there was Dan, who courted me with poetry and kisses and married me when I was barely out of high school, too young to know any better.

Another kick, and a second stone clattered down after the first.

Perfidious husbands.

As I stepped to the edge to watch the stones still tumbling far below, the earth under my foot crumbled and fell away. For a breathless moment I teetered there, before I caught my balance and pulled back. I leaned against the rockface on the other side of the trail, my heart pounding wildly.

"Careful, woman!" I muttered aloud. "Sure, there's a few other rocks I'd like to send down after Dan's and Jon's, but not my body."

I rested there until my breath quieted, the rock warm against my back, then went on up the trail. Slower now. My injured knee was complaining and the pack was heavy on my shoulders. Or maybe it wasn't the pack but the weight of anger, grief, the long years of loneliness.

Here. This is the place. The path wandered off the trail to the right, faint in the grass. I looked up and down. No one was coming. Once beyond an open space and a stand of stunted evergreens I would be out of sight. I hurried to the evergreens. They had grown thicker since I had last been there. It was a struggle to push though them, but I finally found a way and emerged on the other side, scratched and breathless.

Over the years, it had become a ritual to take off my boots here and go barefoot the rest of the way, partly because bare feet would be less damaging to the fragile tundra, partly because the delicacy of the tundra felt so delicious underfoot, and there were marshy places to walk through, cool mud even more luscious. There was also the sense I was on holy ground, and like Moses before the burning bush, must take off my shoes.

Before me the terrain dropped away to the valley below. Autumn colors had already touched the grasses. They rippled in the light breeze, green, gold, rust. Across the valley I saw the stream I had followed all the way from Sapphire Lake and the rounded hump of the huge boulder that sheltered my special place. I was close.

As I bent to unlace my boots, my heart stopped, did a double beat, stopped again. I blacked out for a moment. When I came around, my head spun. I laid my hand on my heart. "Hush." The beat was settling, but my heart ached.

A cloud passed over the sun. The clouds were bigger now, still white but edged with gray.

I stuffed my socks into the toes of my boots and tied the lacings together for a handle. I must keep going, I said to myself.

No! the voice within me warned. Go back. You've already gone too far.

But, my spirit cried, I can't go back now. It's only a little farther. I'm almost there.

The inner voice was silent. I got to my feet, staff in one hand, boots dangling by their laces in the other, and started slowly down the side of the valley. I could see the boulder clearly. It did not look far, but I always forgot how the clear air of the high country deceives, making things distant seem close. It took me a long time to cross the valley, bare feet tasting mossy grass, cool mud and water, smooth, warm surface of rock. Finally I came to the stream, to the waterfall dividing around vivid purple-pink flowers. One last climb.

Clouds had gathered as I crossed the valley, but the sun broke through when I reached my special place. It shone on the surface of a deep pool rippling in the curve of the stream and on the vivid green grass and tiny wildflowers at its edge. All was sheltered by the huge, rounded boulder that had guided me across the valley. Sunlight glinted off tiny bits of mica embedded in its surface, and gray-green lichen sketched their delicate patterns across it. At the top of the boulder, where the mountainside folded around it, one lone, ancient krumholz tree curved low to the ground, creating a cave beneath its twisted boughs. All around, the jagged peaks rose up. I stood still, gazing. Always the wonder of this place surpassed my remembering.

Gently I stepped forward, found that one particular hollow in the ground where it was perfect to rest, and eased myself down. I slipped off my pack, pulled off the pinching knee braces, and stretched out on my back. My head whirled and my heart pounded. But I had made it.

After a while I sat up. It was time to consider what I must let go of from the year before. For many years it had been the same—I must let go of complaining and resisting my limitations. Every year I let go of that and then, alas, still fought the encroachments of aging in the year that followed.

Oh, it's hard to know—what is the line between accepting and giving up?

Dan often quoted from a poem by Dylan Thomas:

> Do not go gentle into that good night.
> … Rage, rage against the dying of the light.

I did not think I wanted to rage when that time came. I thought it would be more graceful to go peacefully. But if so, I'd need to practice. Who knew when that time would come?

I stood up and slipped out of my clothes. Standing naked at the edge of the pool, I prayed, "Pure waters, cleanse me of fighting against what I cannot change."

I lowered myself, hands on the rocks at the edge, and put my feet in the water. It was very cold. I drew my feet out again. If only the sun would stay out. I knew I would have to move quickly or I would lose sensation in my feet before I could dip my whole body. In then. A few steps to the deep place. Complete submersion. Ice cold baptism. I came up with a gasp, scrambled to the shore, and stood wet, naked, and exulting in the warm sun.

If that doesn't cleanse me, I don't know what will.

I wrapped myself in my bathing cloth and sat down again. My heart was steady. I laughed. My cardiologist would never have recommended high-altitude, icy plunges for arrhythmia.

It was time to think of my intentions for the next year. In the past, my intentions had been about projects I wanted to accomplish in the coming year. Now all the affairs of my life seemed far away, down the long path I had climbed, down the long canyon I had driven up that morning. Nothing seemed to draw me as I sat there, high above it all.

A cloud darkened the sun and I shivered. No intention came to me. Focus on my massage practice? There are plenty of massage therapists in Boulder. I shouldn't be teaching yoga; I can't model the postures accurately anymore. It's become hard to keep my garden up. I never last at tango more than an hour. Is it worth dressing up and going out? My family? My husbands are long gone, my children all grown and immersed in their own families and careers.

I drew my cloth more tightly around me. It tore. It was old, blue with patterns of big white flowers. Jon had bought it for me in Hawaii more than thirty years before and I had carried it on every hike since to wrap myself after icy plunges in high lakes and streams. It was dear to me, imbued with the songs of all the waters I had dipped in summer after summer. When it wore out in the middle, I cut it in half, sewed the sound ends together, and trimmed off the worn. It had lasted another ten years, but now...

Too many memories. All the way up the trail— And there were a myriad more not connected to the path I had just walked. More still. Memories I couldn't remember. Often the children related some incident in our shared past that was vivid to them, and I had no recollection of it. But I knew those memories still lived, somewhere in the unreachable regions of my mind.

It was too much. I couldn't hold any more. My life had been too full.

It had not been an easy life. It was like the wild mountains around me, ecstasy in the high places, despair in dark ravines at the bottom of sheer cliffs. Not often the wide, level path beside Silver Lake.

Too many memories. They weighed me down like the pack I had carried up the mountain. No, heavier. Much heavier. Like an immense manuscript hanging over me, riffled by the thumb of God, a blur of endless pages falling on me, page upon page, pressing me into the ground.

Bowed by the weight, I drew my knees to my chest, bent my head, and sank down, down into myself until I came to that nubbin of courage that always brought me back.

I straightened. "Come on," I said aloud. "It's been a lot, but you're not done yet. And only you can shape what remains."

An intention. Perhaps at age eighty it should change, become less about accomplishments, more about a way of being.

Slowly it came. "May I live gracefully with my limitations. May I accept aging as part of my life, a part to be lived richly and fully and with gratitude."

I sighed. It was good. I got up, threw off my bathing cloth, and plunged again to set the intention.

The wind was a little rougher, prickling my wet flesh when I emerged. I dried off, spread my bathing cloth on the grass, and dressed quickly, snuggling into my gray cloak. Such a delicious sensation, warm clothes over cold skin.

I ate lunch, savoring the flavors of cheese and bread, the warm richness of a ripe tomato from my garden, the thick, smooth texture of dark chocolate, hot tea from my small green thermos. Leaning back against the boulder, I rested my eyes on the mountainside across from me, the steep rise of it, the rocky outcroppings, the varied colors of the vegetation.

Suddenly I sat up straight. There it was again, high in the sky, catching the sunlight. This time I thought I could make out the shape of a silver disc. And it had moved. Now it hung over the northern peaks. A shiver of wonder ran through me, a sensation of inexplicable expectancy. A cloud blew across, obliterating the silver disc. I stood up, fixing my eyes on the place where it had been. But more clouds blew in, swift and gray, piling up, hiding the tops of the peaks.

Finally I turned away. I should start back soon, I told myself, but I need to lie down a little first. Still marveling, I curled up in my cloak and nestled into the soft grass at the base of the boulder. I meant to rest only a few minutes, but I fell asleep.

Raindrops on my face waked me. The sky was dark. Thunder rumbled behind the peaks. I sat up bemused, the shreds of a dream drifting away. Wind whipped around me.

A gust caught my bathing cloth and flipped it into the stream.

"No!" I cried, leaping up, grabbing for it. Too late. The current swept it away down the waterfall that divided around pink flowers, bending now in the wind. I stared after it, stricken with loss. As if all my years of walking free in the mountains were swept away with that worn blue cloth.

Lightning made a jagged path through the dark sky, the crack of thunder swift after it.

Oops, I thought. I should have been out of here long ago. Still more concerned for my possessions than myself, I snatched up my knee braces and socks and stuffed them into my pack. The rain became a torrent. Another jag of lightning, boom of thunder. I looked around wildly for shelter. The krum tree. I grabbed my boots and pack and made a dash up the side of the boulder. The rock was wet. I slipped and fell flat, face down. For a moment I couldn't move in an agony of paralyzed breathlessness. Flash and crash came together. I gathered myself and made one last desperate scramble for the shelter of the krum tree.

Searing light exploded through my body.

ʕ ʔ

It was dark when I opened my eyes. My head was turned to the side. Something sharp pressed into my cheek. I saw stars and the black shapes of peaks shutting out the stars. The images whirled. I closed my eyes and spun away.

When I opened them again, the stars had moved, new ones wheeling up out of the valley. The valley. Where was I? Something sharp pressed into my cheek. I sought to move my hand to push it away. Nothing happened. I could not find my hand. I struggled. I could not move, not my hand, not my legs. Panic surged through me. I tried again. No movement. In my struggle, I became fully conscious. I was prone, splayed out, the surface under me hard. Rock. And I was cold, bitterly cold. I looked again at the stars, the shape of the peaks that blocked the stars, and knew where I was.

I'm in my special place, I realized. It's night. And I'm cold. I can't move. I struggled again and managed a slight movement of my head. Pain seared through me like lightning. Lightning! There was a storm. Memory sifted back. The last scramble toward the krum tree, the simultaneous blaze and crash.

I gave up struggling then, immobilized by terror, eyes fixed on the stars over the valley. Cold sank into me. After a long time I tried again.

No response to the desperate signals I sent my frozen body. Think, I told myself fiercely. I'm still alive. I'm not completely paralyzed. I can breathe. My heart is still beating.

As if summoned by my thought, my heart began to race, faster and faster until everything went dark.

The stars had moved again the next time I opened my eyes. The stars move, I thought. The night passes. Morning will come with sun to warm me.

Will I live till then? The question cleared my mind. I have been struck by lightning and paralyzed. I have no idea what other damage may have been done. No one knows where I am. There will be no rescue.

I am cold. I think—yes, I'm soaked. It was raining hard. I can't move to warm myself. Fear, grief, longing surged up, twisted and thrashed in my immobile body. I'm not ready. Not done. There's something else I must do. Is there? Already too many memories. No! I don't want to die yet.

Panic silenced all. When I could breathe again, grief came. Will I really die? Leave this dear old body that has served me so well? Never dance again? Never see my family again? My children—Lisa so far away, Greg, Robin, my grandchildren. Never hold little Colin in my lap again?

Must I leave this beautiful Earth? Never watch the sun rise again and feel its first warmth on my face? Delight in the ripple of wind in aspen leaves? Never feel tundra under my bare feet again?

Never again.

Sobs tore through me, shaking me, but still my arms and legs lay numb and heavy on the side of the boulder. I wept until I had no breath left. Cold pressed into me. Deathly cold. My heart hammered, raced, stopped, hammered, ached, raced.

Darkness.

Chapter 2

The Elirians

Warmth touched me. Consciousness quivered up from dark, frigid depths.

Clara. A voice sang my name. Never had I heard such a voice. Rich with overtones, it created a symphony in two syllables.

My eyes flew open. It was still night. The stars had not moved.

Clara. The music of my name came again, but I did not hear it with my ears. The night was silent. Somehow my name sang inside me. Warmth penetrated me. I wanted to weep with relief, but I was still frozen.

A hand touched my brow, delicately, lightly. Heat poured through the fingers, making tunnels of light in the fierce, black headache.

Then I heard other voices singing within me, each voice a little different. Unearthly harmony, like the music of the spheres, the stars dancing their vast circles in the depths of the universe. Their resonance was warmth in me, healing, life returning.

A high, clear voice sang softly. *We were almost too late.*

A deeper voice resonated within me. *She still lives, but is very cold. Come on the other side of her.*

A curved shape blocked my view of the stars. Softness touched my face. More warmth flowed into me.

Clara, can you hear us? It was the first voice.

I struggled to breathe, to speak, and felt concern pour over me.

No, no. Don't try to speak that way. Just with your heart.

My heart? My heart was still beating. It did an extra flip-flop to let me know, then took off in a dizzying flurry of beats that almost sent me into blackness again.

She hears us, the higher voice sang. Its sweetness poured through me, melting the ice in my limbs.

The deep voice. *Don't ask her to speak. Her heart is too weak.*

I slipped in and out of awareness. The music of their voices rippled in me, softening my cold paralysis.

Clara. The first voice separated from their symphony. *We're going to take you up.* The source of warmth bent over me, enfolding me with softness. Arms came under me and turned me. I looked up into deep, luminous eyes, the color shifting in them, blue, green, purple, like Sapphire Lake in the wind. *Don't be afraid. You are safe.*

The arms lifted me and folded me into a fetal position, folded me although moments before I had been splayed out on the cold rock, stiff as a dead starfish left behind by the tide. It seemed that more arms came around me, holding me close, securely. I felt the beating of a heart. We rose and kept on rising with smooth, effortless motion. My face was buried against the warmth of the one who carried me. The beings that accompanied us sang as we rose, but now I no longer heard words, only the unearthly beauty of their song.

Still we rose. I became curious, turned in the arms that held me, and looked out. My stomach plunged. I was in the sky. Far below, the peaks tilted as if we flew over the curve of the Earth. The arms tightened around me and words emerged from the song. *You are safe. We are almost there.*

Trembling, I turned away from the abyss and nestled deeper into the comforting arms. Then I realized I had moved. I held still a moment, not daring to believe it. A tentative message to my hand. My fingers wiggled. Relief! I slid my hand into the enfolding softness. Fur? Was it fur? But so fine. It felt as if it held an electric charge of warmth. Each hair shone with a delicate light. Wonder filled me. Have I died after all?

No. I remembered the cold rock, the still night, the stars. I had been in my special place when these strange beings found me.

Our motion ceased. We hovered, then moved again. We were inside something, away from the chill of the night. I kept my face buried in the soft fur.

The song had stilled as we moved inside. Now the music had words again, and there were new voices, weaving with the three I knew. All were song, strange, haunting beauty.

Does she live?

She lives, but we must tend her quickly. She is deathly cold.

Her heart is unstable.

That's for sure, I thought.

A ripple of what seemed like the music of laughter spilled over me.

She hears us. That is good.

Lay her here, a bell-like voice sang.

The arms moved to lay me down, and I clung, my fingers clutching at the warmth that had brought me back from death.

Melody poured over me with the words, *You are safe. Do not fear. We are here with you.*

Their song was love and beauty embracing me. How could I fear? I loosened my grip on the delicate fur and felt myself gently laid down on a surface so soft I felt nothing but warmth, blessed warmth. The last remnants of frozen paralysis slipped from my limbs. I wiggled my toes and wept.

Ah! The song around me softened. Compassion enveloped me. A gentle hand touched my chest. My heart thumped, skipped, and settled. Slowly I opened my eyes and looked up into the luminous eyes of the one who had carried me and was still close beside me. *You are safe,* it sang to me, and I understood that safe meant loved.

Turning my head slowly, I found myself in a dome-shaped room with large windows spaced around its arc, black night and stars beyond. Silvery light emanated from the curved walls. Five strange creatures floated around me. They were round, about five feet in diameter, covered with fine fur. It was silver, but iridescent, rippling with delicate color as they moved, each a little different. One was primarily blue, another pale pink, another purple, another golden. The one who was steadying my heart was silver touched with deep rose. They had no legs; they floated or hovered or rested lightly on the floor of the room, the soft surface they had laid me on. Arms emerged from the center of them, jointless, fluid, tapering at the ends into many-fingered hands. Many arms. No faces, only eyes. Such eyes! Wide set, slightly tilted up at the outer corners. Bottomless, sparkling, light filled, containing all the colors of sky and water.

The silver-pink being picked up the edge of my sodden cloak. *There's water in her fur,* it sang in its high, sweet voice. *That makes her cold.*

It did. Though the music of their voices warmed me from within, and though my paralysis had melted, the wet clothes chilled me.

All the beings seemed to speak at once, a melodic weaving of concern. They seemed to communicate not only with their inner song, but with the movement of their fur. Many hands touched me, seeking, asking.

That is not fur. Not part of her.

See, she has none here. A gentle hand touched my cold bare foot.

We must find how to warm her.

Her heart.

I started to speak aloud, "I can take them off," then stopped, appalled. On Earth I had often been told I had a lovely voice, but that same voice, breaking into the resonance of their weaving songs, seemed a raucous croak.

No, no, the high, sweet voice sang inside me. *That is too hard for you. Just speak to us with your heart.*

My heart pounded and ached. *I think I have to use my mind,* I thought to them.

Mind? The song went up in question.

The wet things are my clothes. When they are dry they warm me, but not when they are wet, I explained with my thought. *I can take them off.*

Clothes? The word was strange to them. But they understood. Many hands lifted me and drew off my wet clothes. I lay naked on the soft, warm floor, my skin still cold, goosebumped.

Do you have a blanket? I asked silently.

Blanket? Another question.

I sent them an image, and understood that they did not know of such a thing. Why should they with their radiant fur?

There was a burst of singing, a flurry of hands moving, fur flying, hands weaving. So fast! In a moment I was lifted again and wrapped in a blanket woven of iridescent silver. It radiated the light of their fur and was warm, so warm.

Rest now, the rose being sang to me. It laid a gentle hand on my chest. *I will hold your heart.*

⮫ ⮪

Sunlight pouring in the big windows woke me. Outside the sky was blue. At first I thought I was looking out my bedroom window, waking from a strange dream, then realized that my little house was surrounded by trees and there were no trees in my view. My entire body ached, but I could move. I turned my head and looked into the strange, mutable eyes of the silver-rose being who still sat beside me, its hand resting lightly over my heart.

I closed my eyes. Fear rippled through me. It's a dream, I told myself. You're not quite awake yet. Open your eyes again. You'll see the cottonwood with the sun shining in its leaves.

Clara? The music of my name, unearthly.

I stiffened, my eyes still closed. The long hike, the storm, the cold rock, the life-giving warmth, the flight through the night sky—one by one the images rose behind my closed lids. Then another image came, the tiny silver speck I had seen in the sky the day before. Knowing I would not see the cottonwood tree, I slowly opened my eyes again. The silver-rose being was still there, watching me, its hand still keeping my heart blessedly steady.

It isn't a dream. Or it is, and I can't wake.

Across the room a door opened into another room, a wall of switches, lights, objects that were clearly part of an instrument panel. The other four beings hovered in front of it.

Realization came slowly. An instrument panel and outside nothing but sky. I was dying and have been rescued by these beings from another world. I must be inside the silver speck I saw above the peaks. There's blue sky and sunlight outside, so we're probably still in the Earth's atmosphere. Not too far away. Not too far! My stomach turned as I remembered looking down on the tilting peaks the night before.

I stirred and realized I was naked, covered only by the silver blanket. Vaguely I remembered the strange beings taking off my sodden clothes the night before. Clutching the blanket around me, I tried to sit. Pain shot through all my limbs, and I fell back, helpless.

No, lie still, the silver-rose being sang within me. *You are still wounded.* It rested its hand over my heart again and quieted the beat that had begun to race with my effort.

I lay under its hand, stiff with fear. It was all too strange. I was on a spaceship far, far from home. Wounded, I did not know how badly. And naked. Utterly vulnerable. Where were my clothes?

The silver-rose being turned toward the instrument room, then back to me. A moment later the pale pink being floated over and laid my clothes beside me. I turned to touch them, my long denim skirt, my long-sleeved shirt, my cotton underpants, my gray cloak. They were dry and clean, neatly folded. My mind whirled. They had all been soaked. How could my heavy wool cloak be dry so soon?

I rolled to my side, reaching for my skirt, struggled briefly, then gave up again, gasping in pain.

Ah, both beings sang in concern and compassion. *Let us help you.* They lifted me with their many arms and dressed me gently, tenderly, then wrapped me in the silver blanket and laid me back on the warm, soft floor, my cloak beside me. All the while they sang, and their song vibrated through my tissues, easing the pain. Enfolded in their loving care, resonating with their song, I felt my body soften and my fear slip away.

The pale pink one floated away, but the silver-rose one stayed beside me.

I lay quiet, fingering the textures of my cloak and the silver blanket, the cloak rough, earthy wool, the silver blanket silken-fine, radiant, unearthly. Gradually I slowed my breath. How sweet the air, imbued with a strange, fresh fragrance. It was visible, circling the room in blended rainbow colors. The colors entered me with each breath, liquid light, soothing, nourishing. With each breath, more of the pain slipped from my limbs.

I turned again to the being beside me. It had been watching me, giving me time to find myself. *You knew I wanted my clothes,* I said to it, remembering to use my thought. You knew I was afraid.

Yes. A single note.

A quiver of fear ran through me again. *What else do you know about me… everything?*

No. We do not know everything, only what you tell us now. We do not search you without your permission.

What … Who are you?

The being took its hand off my heart for a moment to touch its own heart, then laid its hand on my heart again.

I am Kiria of Eliria. In no way can words on a page convey the melodic depth of that name as Kiria first sang it to me.

Eliria? I asked.

Home. Kiria sang then. The song whirled me through galaxies to a faraway planet circling a distant sun. It was a moist, verdant planet, entirely covered in trees, vines, flowers with shapes and colors utterly strange to me, woven through by streams and lakes. Round, iridescent beings in many colors floated amid the foliage, like large flowers themselves. Kiria's song ached with longing for the faraway beauty of her home.

My fear was totally gone now. I was lost in wonder. *Why have you come so far?* I asked.

Hearing my thought, the other four beings floated out of the instrument room and gathered around me. *We will tell you. And we ask your help. But first you must know our names.*

The pale pink one sang with the high, sweet voice. *I am Lillilia of Eliria.* It touched its heart and then mine.

I am Merilea of Eliria. The purple one was the one with the deep voice. It also touched its heart and then laid its gentle hand beside the hands of Lillilia and Kiria.

Tirini of Eliria, the golden one.

Rosiri of Eliria, the blue one.

Gathered around me, their hands on my heart, they sang me their story.

The entire universe is held together by an energetic web that wraps and connects every sun, every planet, every asteroid. The web holds us all in balance. Each sun and each planet has its role to play in maintaining the balance. But for the last several millennia the planet Earth has become more and more discordant, so much that it has begun to twist the web.

There are many intelligent beings on the planets of the universe. Even though we are far apart in different galaxies, we have learned to communicate along the energetic web lines and have formed a council. Each planet and each intelligent race of beings, has its gifts. Our gifts are healing song and the ability to see into the nature of things, to find their essence.

You must have other gifts, I thought to them, *to build this ship that has carried you so far.*

We did not build the ship. Tirini's deep green eyes sparkled with flecks of gold. *Our spaceships are gifts of the planet Akara. We have no metal on Eliria, nor do we have the kind of intelligence to create a spaceship. But once the Akarans have created it, we can know its form and how to operate it.*

They sang together again. *We are all concerned about planet Earth. Over the years different planets have sent emissaries to Earth. They have taken on human form and attempted to shift the chaos into balance. Many have been killed by the Earthlings. Others have gotten caught in the tangle of discord and lost their way, forgotten where they came from, forgotten their ulada.*

Ulada? I questioned.

The song of the Elirians paused. Their wide eyes met, creating an energetic web over me as I lay under their gentle hands. Then their song resumed.

Your ulada is your life's purpose, your destiny. It calls you to rise out of your planet and serve the balance. It can be very simple. An ulada on Eliria can be that one of us tend a certain tree so it holds its sound in the song of Eliria. Such an ulada may last only a short while, until the tree is strong. Or an ulada can be huge, like the one that calls us here.

I shivered in awe. *Why have you come?* I asked again.

To study humans. The emissaries of the other planets have not failed. As we circle your planet we can see those they have touched, like points of light in the darkness. But the emissaries, those that have lived to return to the council, say it is difficult for those humans to hold the light, entangled as they are in Earth's discordance. Now the council has asked the Elirians to bring their gifts to Earth. Twenty-five of us have risen from Eliria, called to that ulada. We are in five spaceships over different parts of the Earth. We have just arrived.

Their song ended and they sat silent around me. I thought of all the years I had joined with others fighting the destruction of our planet, its creatures and wild places—marching, protesting, collecting signatures, knocking on doors. Finally I had given up in despair as the power of greed-backed money and insane denial seemed to sweep away all our efforts. My grief for the lostness of humankind, the violence, the devastation, welled up in me.

The Elirians, still touching my heart, felt my sorrow. *Ah!* they sang to me.

How can I help? I asked them.

We must learn about human bodies, they sang together. *The emissaries before us have taken on human form and learned to function in it, but have not really understood it. We hope that if we can learn how your form shapes your being, perhaps we can help to bring humans back to their essence. Earth has not always been out of balance. It was once one of our wisest and most beautiful planets. Long ago.*

Their song settled into silence. A tremor of fear ran through me. *You would like to study me?*

Yes, Merilea answered. *If you are willing. We cannot without your permission. If you are not willing, we will take you back and watch over you until your people find you.*

I wanted to help them. They had saved my life, and never had I felt so tenderly cared for as I had since they found me. I realized I loved them. I was enchanted with the incongruity of their round, fluffy forms and the ancient wisdom in their deep eyes. I felt I could listen to the sweetness of their voices forever. And they had come to assist my beloved Earth.

I am willing, I told them. But I was afraid, clinging to my life so newly given back. *How will you study me? Will you need to cut me open?* I sent them an image of a hip replacement surgery from a YouTube video.

No! No! Their fur flattened, their eyes went wide with shock.

No, Kiria sang alone, rose-tinted fur fluttering. *We touch you with our fingers. We can read all of you that way.*

Merilea's eyes were dark gray with traces of purple, like deep water flowing in the shadow of a cliff. *You were willing to let us cut you open?*

Well, I would be dead by now if you hadn't found me.

The others murmured, *Ah, the light is strong in her.*

Do I need to take my clothes off? In spite of myself I was anxious about that.

No, Kiria answered, *we can touch you through your clothes.*

But I'm not a very good specimen, I apologized. *I'm old and a lot of me isn't working properly anymore.*

We will mend what does not work well, Lillilia sang.

How will you know what to mend if you don't know human bodies?

Kiria stroked my cheek with one delicate finger. Her eyes were gray, green, blue, shot with light, like sun shining deep into the ocean. *We see your essence.*

I caught my breath. What would it be like to embody my essence?

You want to study me now?

When you are ready.

Knowing I was plunging into unfathomed depths, I looked into their wondrous eyes. *I am ready.*

They shifted around me. I could see now that each of them had five arms, and their hands had seven fingers, five in the middle and a thumb on each side. Twenty-five wise, many-fingered hands came to rest on my body, light and warm, touching me from head to foot. Their song began, their voices interweaving. I drifted away.

⁂

It seemed forever that I dreamed, floating on their song, feeling their delicate touch like liquid light penetrating every part of my body. When at last their song faded into silence, I opened my eyes. Rose-orange sunset poured in the big windows. I breathed deep of the rainbow air and stretched. Nothing hurt. My entire body glowed with well-being and peace. Never in all my life had I felt like that. Even at times when I was young and in the best of health, there had always been some nagging discomfort somewhere. Now there was nothing but joyous ease and vitality in every cell.

The five Elirians sat around me, their hands resting serenely in their fur. They had no faces, no mouth to turn up, no nose to wrinkle, no brow to furrow or smooth; their eyes expressed it all. They smiled at me.

Thank you, Rosiri sang within me. *You are the first human we have touched, and we have learned much from you. Even though you dreamed, you told us about the parts of you as we touched them. Are all humans so complex?*

I sat up—so easily!—drawing the silver blanket around me, and they shifted to let me become part of their circle.

We all have individual differences, of course, I answered, *but our organs are the same, except for those that differ between male and female.*

Male and female? The council spoke of that, but we don't understand it. Tell us of male and female, Merilea asked.

I am female. I was accustomed now to simply thinking my conversation with them. After that one embarrassing croak, I had no desire to try to speak again. And just thinking was so easy. They understood me without my having to struggle to find the right words. Often an image said it more fully than any words could convey. I sent them an image of a naked man, explaining that the part on the front of him that I did not have fit into the open space between my legs to make children. They were puzzled, so I went on to elaborate on the reproductive system, menstruation, intercourse, birthing, nursing, raising children. I could not help that the images I sent were burdened with my love and grief, joy and pain.

Ah! they murmured.

I shifted my position a little, leaning on my hand. As I did, I glanced down at it and had a moment of confusion. There was something strange…

But Lillilia was asking, *You have pain to bring out your child, and to bleed every moon?* Caught up in the question, I forgot about my hand.

Yes, I answered, *I've often wondered who thought that up. You didn't put that part back, did you? The bleeding, when you fixed things inside me?*

They looked around at each other. *No, we didn't find that in you,* Tirini answered.

I was relieved. *That's good. It stops when we get older.*

Male and female. It is very strange, Kiria marveled. *There is conflict between you? We felt your pain.*

Often. Attraction, for how else would we reproduce? But also, yes, conflict. Dominion of male over female. I have been lucky in my part of the world, but in many places the females are like slaves to the males.

That is the duality the emissaries spoke of, Rosiri mused.

How do you reproduce? I asked. *Don't you have male and female?*

No, they sang together. *We are of Eliria. When an ulada calls us, we rise out of her. When our ulada is complete we sink back into her. We are Eliria, born of her, returning to her. We need no male nor female.*

Even though I now knew they were neither male nor female, I thought of them as female, with their sensitive touch and their soft, fluffy bodies.

I had difficulty at first knowing who was speaking, as they had no lips to move and their song sounded within me rather than coming from any direction, but gradually I learned to distinguish their voices. Lillilia's was high and sweet like a flute, Kiria's rich and full like a cello. Tirini's voice had the bright clarity of bells, Rosiri's the haunting quality of an oboe. Merilea's was the lowest voice, like a bass fiddle grounding their harmony when they sang together. But no comparison to earthly instruments or any earthly sound could begin to capture the wondrous, soaring beauty of their song from the stars.

They inquired about each part of me, each system, each organ. As I told them about human bodies, I learned more about theirs. They had no need of ears because they communicated telepathically and received sounds through their fur. Since they levitated, they had no need for legs. No need for lungs or digestive system because they drew in all their nourishment from light through their eyes, and from the atmosphere of their planet through their fur. The air I breathed in their spaceship had come all the way from Eliria, constantly renewed by being passed through a reservoir of Elirian essence in the instrument room. I noticed that I had felt no hunger or thirst since I began breathing that air.

They had only three organs: their fur; their heart, which seemed to hold the functions of both brain and heart; and their eyes. Arms, eyes, fur, all were directly connected to their heart.

They were very concerned that my brain and heart were separate.

Are all humans that way? Rosiri asked. Her eyes were deep blue, sparkling like a wind-rippled lake.

Yes, I answered

The brain and the heart separate, Kiria mused. *That is another duality.*

What if the heart guides you one way and the brain guides you differently? Tirini asked.

It often happens.

They rippled their fur in distress. *No wonder there is so much trouble on planet Earth,* Kiria exclaimed, *if one being cannot even agree with itself.*

My sorrow for my kind arose again. *It can be worse than that,* I told them. *Some of us shut down the guidance of our heart and listen only to our brain.*

But the brain does not know love, Merilea sang in her rich, low voice. *We searched it. We found love only in your heart. The brain is like the instrument panel on our ship. But yours is shadowed with something that upsets your heart. We did not know how to heal that.*

If only you could!

What is it? Rosiri asked.

I don't know. I've been trying for many years to learn what it is, how to clear it. Many of us have. We have had great teachers in the past who have guided us. Maybe some of them were the emissaries you spoke of. But it is hard. We understand, but still we fall back. It is twisted thought patterns, fear mostly, I think, that shadows us. Other humans may tell you differently, but whatever it is, it causes us to hurt ourselves and each other and create the discordance that you feel across all the galaxies.

I could not tell them more, as sorrow overwhelmed me. They gathered close around me, enfolding me in their fur, and sang to me, *Ah.*

Kiria placed her hand on my heart, and the song quieted as she searched me. *I think,* she sang, *it is love in the heart that can heal the fear in the brain. You have much love in your heart, a strong light. You can heal.*

Night had gathered outside the big windows.

Come now, Merilea sang. It is night. *You are tired. You must rest now so your body can receive our healing.*

Each one held me against her heart. Then Lillilia wrapped me in the silver blanket and laid me down like a small child. It was true, I was very tired. Curled up on the soft floor, lulled by their song I drifted into sleep.

❧ ❧

When I woke, the sky outside the windows was blue, touched with the pink of sunrise. I nestled in the silver blanket. It was a wondrous thing, warm yet light, shining with the soft radiance of Elirian fur. After a while, the sun came around to shine through the nearest window into my face, and I got up, stood, and stretched. How exquisite the feel of my body. Light, limber, no pain. What a miracle!

Gathering the blanket around myself, I went to a window and looked down. Far below, enfolded in blue haze, I saw the curve of Earth. The Elirians came to me, embracing me with their many arms.

Good morning, I greeted them.

Their song of good morning was like sunrise.

Today we must return you to Earth, Kiria sang. *Your people are searching for you.*

I clung to Kiria, feeling torn. The glimpse of Earth had called me, but I could not bear to leave the magical dream of this spaceship with its rainbow air and these five wondrous beings with deep eyes.

I hate to leave you, I told them. *Will you come to Earth? Will you become emissaries? Such love as you are would be most welcome there.*

No. There was sadness in their answering song. *That is not our ulada. We could not survive for long on Earth. We are here to discover the essence of human beings and carry what we discover back to the council. Stronger ones will come. Do not fear. The balance will shift.*

We will gather up many of your people to study and learn from them, Merilea explained. *If they are willing. We will take those about to die and renew their life in thanks for what they teach us, as we have done for you. We saw your light as you came up the mountain and felt the trouble in your heart, though we did not know the lightning would take you.*

But you must be careful, I interrupted in sudden fear for them. *Don't let anyone see you. They may shoot you down, or capture you to study you. Our methods are not so gentle as yours.*

No fear, Tirini assured me. *The Akarans protected us. We can shield our ship in an instant so that it cannot be seen by human eyes. We have sensors that can move us more swiftly than any Earth missile. We are safe.*

When our work is finished, Lillilia sang, *we will return to the council and then to Eliria. Home!*

They all sang then, their voices weaving in a song so sweet and haunting that I knew it to be the song of Eliria. It swelled around me until I felt my heart would break with its beauty. When it ended, we rested together in silence.

It is so far away, I thought after a while. *Won't it take you thousands of years to get home?*

Rosiri's eyes took on a faraway look. *No,* she sang. *On a thread of the web, we fold time. It will take no time.*

One more thing. Lillilia floated into the instrument room and returned with something in her seven-fingered hand. She gave it to me. I stared in shock at the two pieces of metal that had held my hip together. *It was not of your essence,* she explained.

I put my hand on my left hip, searching through my skirt for the deep indentation of the surgical scar. It wasn't there.

You have new bones. Lillilia's eyes smiled. They were soft blue-gray with wisps of pink like the sky at dawn. I slid the two pieces into the left pocket of my skirt, close against the new bones.

Tirini turned to the instrument room. *We will go down now.* Her gold-tinted fur rippled as she touched the instrument panel, lightly, in quick sequence with her many hands.

I folded the silver blanket, laid it on the floor, and put on my gray cloak.

Kiria guided me to a window to watch our descent, dropping through the deep blue sky, the mountains rising to meet us. Far below, nestled between the peaks, I saw my valley with the stream running through, a shining ribbon in the morning sun. Then we were down, hovering a few feet above a lichen-covered rock at the head of the valley, upstream from my special place.

A door slid open in the silver wall. Tirini came and held me close against her heart. *I must stay with the ship. All blessing to you, Clara. May you complete your ulada in joy and come to rest in the bosom of your Earth.*

The other four floated down with me. My bare feet touched smooth rock with a thrill of recognition. I turned to look back at the ship, a silver disc hovering above us.

The vibrant ease of my body seemed to belong with that magical ship and its circling rainbow light. But now I stood, bewildered, an old woman with my feet on a rock of planet Earth.

I sent them my thought. *It will be strange to go back to my old life in this new body. What must I do?*

They gazed at me a long time in silence. A wordless song wove between them. Then the words came. *Your light is strong. You have given it to many over the years. Your ulada is almost complete. Let your light shine.*

Their song shifted, filled with tenderness. *Our love is with you. You can call on us anytime and we will answer. We are with you always, even across the galaxies. Love knows no distance.*

One at a time they embraced me, holding me close against their hearts. Still singing, they floated back into their ship. The silver door slid closed and the ship rose up. For a moment the sun glinted off it, dazzling my eyes, and then it was gone.

Chapter 3

Return

I sank down onto the wide, smooth rock, bone of the valley, rounded by long-ago glaciers. I have been in the presence of perfect love, I thought. How can my imperfect self bear such love? How can I go again among humans where love is twisted, tainted? How can I not? I lay with my face on the smooth rock. The sun shone down on me.

My gray cloak was too warm. I rolled over, took it off, and sat on it, my knees pulled up to my chest. It was still early morning and the valley was quiet except for the bubble of water pouring out of many springs around me, forming a stream. I breathed in the smells of earth and water and the cold, fresh scent of wind off the snowfields above me. Nearby, a marmot chirped, another answered.

Back in my own world, I could barely comprehend, or even believe in, the experiences of the last two nights and the day between in which all my pain had been taken away. Yet I could feel the weight of the two metal pieces in my pocket challenging my unbelief. I rested my hand over my heart. It beat quietly and steadily.

I stood. So easy to stand! No need to push off the rock with my hands. No ache in the knees. Joy flooded me. I squatted. Then jumped straight up from the squat into the air, landed lightly, painlessly, on the smooth rock. Health and strength sang through every cell of my body. I tilted my head back and shouted, "Thank you!" into the sky. I jumped again, whirled, spun down onto the rock and up, effortlessly. "Thank you," I breathed, knowing they could hear.

A wisp of melody wound through my heart. Humming it softly, I picked up my cloak and started walking down the valley, earth under my bare feet, morning sun in my face. I walked slowly, ecstatic to be alive, following the growing stream, wading through marshes and wide, shallow pools reflecting the blue sky and peaks above, the hem of my skirt wet. All around me the high, spare clarity of the tundra.

A bend in the stream, and I had returned to my special place. People had been there. The grass was trampled; there were muddy boot prints on the rocks at the water's edge. I felt a rush of territorial anger. How dare anyone come to my private place? Then I remembered Kiria saying, *Your people are searching for you.*

Of course. And how glad I would have been to have them come for me on that terrible night when I lay dying, before the Elirians found me. Someone had gathered my boots and pack, tucked my poncho around them, and laid my staff beside them. Whoever did that must have expected me to return. I squatted down beside my pack and looked inside. Wet knee braces and socks. I spread them on the grass. My water bottle. The water was cold and refreshing, the first thing that had passed my lips since the Elirians found me.

As I tilted my head back for a second draft, my eyes moved to the top of the boulder. I choked, gasped. The lightning had struck the krum tree. Heart pounding, I climbed up to it and knelt amidst its ashes and shattered branches. The thick, curving trunk was split, black in its long burn. There was nothing left of the cave where I had often taken shelter. Had I reached it, even the Elirians could not have saved me.

I stroked the black scar. "You took the hit for me," I whispered. "I live and you are destroyed." I imagined my body lying charred on the rock under the arc of the scorched trunk. It so easily could have been. If I had not slipped. The terror of that night came back and clutched me. Kneeling on the soft bit of earth that had once been the floor of my sheltering cave, I clung to the burned trunk, waiting for the waves of panic to subside. Gradually I became aware of the sound of the stream. A dip, I thought. Perhaps a dip will steady me.

Back down by the stream, I unbuttoned my skirt and let it fall. As I slipped my underpants down and lifted my foot to step out of them, I froze, standing on one leg like a stork, staring at my inner thigh. The wrinkled diagonal folds I was accustomed to seeing there, angling down from my groin to my knee, were gone. Instead I saw smooth, taut flesh, lightly tanned. A quiver of shock ran through me. I stumbled, coming to both feet, my panties around my ankles, and bent to look at my legs. No longer dry, scaly skin, scars of old scratches and falls, swollen knees, but straight, unblemished limbs.

My hands were shaking so hard it was difficult to unbutton my shirt. I threw it away from me and looked down. A lean, scarless belly. A patch of bright, curly hair where there had been only straggly gray strands. I brushed my breasts and gasped. They tilted upward. I reached back to touch my buttocks. Firm and round. I held out my arms. The flab that had hung loose from my upper arms was replaced by the clean lines of well-developed muscle.

Dizzy with shock, I closed my eyes and touched my face. My once drooping cheeks were smooth and lifted. For a long time I stood at the edge of the moving water, covering my face, my mind unable to grasp what my eyes and hands had perceived.

At last I dropped my hands and looked down at my body. It was the beautiful, perfectly formed body of a young woman, streaked with ashes where I had touched myself with fingers stained from the remains of the krum tree.

I began pacing around, speaking aloud to the water, the rocks, the lichen, anything that could hear my voice and help me remember I was back on Earth. "They made me young. Young. But I'm not young. I'm old. I'm eighty. I didn't know they did that. I thought they just healed what was wrong inside. What was outside wasn't wrong, just old."

I touched myself again, stroking the smooth, firm lines, leaving more streaks of ash on my flawless skin.

All the intensity of the last two days swept through me—the weight of memories, the night of pain, encroaching death, the wonder of the Elirians, my miraculous healing, the death of the tree I loved, and now this momentous change. I dropped down into the grass and curled up in a ball. My old body gone. Gone. Sloughed off like a snakeskin. Yes, it had been frail and faulty, but it was mine. I loved being healed of my pain and stiffness, it was wonderful that my heart was steady, I was glad to be alive, but I didn't want to be young again.

The grass was soft and cool under my cheek. When did it happen? I asked myself. It must have been when they sang to me and healed everything inside. I felt the inside changes. Why didn't I notice the outside? Because I was wearing my hiking clothes that cover me completely to protect my aging skin from the sun.

Then I remembered the moment on the spaceship when I looked down at my hand and thought something was strange. I drew my hand out from where it was curled against my chest and looked at it. No gnarly knuckles, brown spots, purple veins. Smooth and young. That's what I had seen but had been too fascinated by our conversation to attend to.

All the time I was there I was absorbed in the miracle of the Elirians and their spaceship. No thought to look at myself. But now…

What does my face look like? I wondered. I sat up and moved to the edge of the pool to look in. For a fleeting moment I saw Kiria's eyes looking up at me. Then a light breeze ruffled the surface and erased them. I drew back, chilled by the strangeness of seeing her eyes when I sought to see my own.

"I was going to dip," I reminded myself. "That would be a good idea. I'm all over soot." I stood and brought my hands together at my heart. I never dipped without a prayer, but now I had no idea what to ask of the stream. Finally I prayed, "Wash away the ashes," and plunged in.

My emotions were like a lava lamp, only swirling faster—joy, fear, grief, feelings I had no name for—one color after another predominating. As I came up, waist deep in the icy, flowing water, I felt anew the incredible vitality of my body. I shouted, gathering up water in my hands, tossing it over my head, letting it fall down on me, sparkling in the sunshine. Clearly my body loved being young. But even the feet of a young body can go numb.

When I scrambled out, morning sun shone warm on me. Some of my confusion had been washed away with the ashes. I saw the muddy footprints on the rocks and squatted down to wash them away.

People are looking for me, I remembered. What time is it? What day? Where's my watch? I rummaged in my pile of clothes and found it in the zipper pocket of my shirt where I always put it when I undressed to dip. I must have put it there two days ago. Two days? It seemed centuries since the old woman I had been climbed laboriously up the side of the mountain.

The watch said nine o'clock. They were looking for me. Robin must have called and found I wasn't home. When? How long had they been looking? I thought of Robin and felt how anxious he would be.

I should go down. But then? I would have to relate to people and I didn't know who I was anymore. My special place shone in perfect beauty and it was still early in the day. I'll stay a little while, I decided. Some yoga on the soft tundra might help me find myself.

I was soon lost in the wonder of my body, how I could bend forward with no pull or ache in my sacrum, how all my postures flowed with more ease and flexibility than I had ever experienced. I tried a wheel, a posture I had been unable to do for years, dropped back into it with perfect control, and pressed my hips up toward the sky, exulting.

The warmth of the sun dimmed. Clouds emerged over the peaks. They were white with only touches of gray, but a ripple of fear streaked through me. I arced up out of the wheel and stood.

"No," I whispered. "I'm not staying too long this time."

I took a deep breath to calm myself. One more dip and then I go. An intention? I felt so strange to myself that I didn't know what to choose. The intention I'd made two days ago no longer fit; my limitations had been lifted. What will that mean? Confusion threatened again, but I realized I had a new concept. "May I find the *ulada* for this new life given me and carry it out with integrity," I prayed, and plunged one more time.

My bathing cloth was gone, so I dried myself with my skirt. Only when I saw streaks of ash on my skin again did I realize the skirt was sooty, not beautifully clean as it had been when Lillilia brought it to me. I never asked them how they got my clothes dry and clean so quickly. Even my heavy gray cloak. Perhaps they saw the essence of my clothes, too.

I shook the ashes out of my skirt and shirt and dressed, glancing anxiously at the sky. Mostly blue, but clouds were forming. After another drink from my water bottle, I gathered up my scattered belongings, socks into the toes of my boots, hat on my head, knee braces—I didn't think I'd need them—into the top of the pack. Gray cloak tucked under the flap. Boot laces tied together. With one last look around, I strapped on my pack, picked up my boots and staff, and set off.

As I walked down beside the waterfall that divided around pink flowers the color of Kiria, I looked for my bathing cloth. The bright blue should be easy to spot amid the muted colors of the tundra. Farther down there was still no sign of it, and the stream bank soon became crowded with willows, impassable. Let it go, I thought sadly. It was old and torn and now it's gone. Like my old body.

My mood quickly shifted as I crossed the valley. It was so easy to bound from rock to rock, so delightful to leap across marshy places, to squat to smell a tiny flower, to run up the last steep slope to where the stunted evergreens hid me from the main trail.

I parted the evergreens and looked through. No one in sight. I sprinted across the open space, and was sitting at the edge of the trail snugging up my bootlaces when two young men with big backpacks strode up toward me. They glanced curiously at me and slowed their pace. I looked up at them from under the brim of my blue hat.

"Good morning," I said.

They stopped and looked down at me. "Morning," the one with the green hat answered. A slow smile spread across his face. The other one, with a red hat, was smiling, too. He had bright brown eyes and was very attractive.

I tilted my head back, looked into his eyes, and returned his smile. An electric zing danced between us. Shocked, I bent my head.

He stepped closer. "Which way are you going?" he asked.

"Down," I answered.

"That's too bad," he said. "I was thinking it might be nice to walk with you a way."

I jumped to my feet, grabbed my staff. "Have a good hike," I said, and fled down the trail.

"None of that!" I admonished my wanton eyes as I dashed headlong downward. "*Absolutely* none of that. I may have a young body, but I'm not young. I know where that kind of thing leads."

I was running, easily, lightly, even leaping over roots and rocky places. As my shock subsided, the lava lamp swirled again, and I relaxed into the delight of my motion. I came to the two stream crossings and didn't hesitate a moment. It was easy to balance, dancing across. At the second one, the one that had daunted me on the way up, I stopped in the middle of the log bridge and drank in the sparkle of the water rushing under me.

Down and down. Thunder rumbled faintly behind me and I tensed. But it was far above, the sky still mostly blue. I ran, dropping again into the joy of it. At the rocky place just below Sapphire Lake, where I had fallen on the way up, I swung my stick in front of me, and pivoted around it, dancing from rock to rock. So easy! I ran on, lightfooted, past the people in front of me going down.

At the gateway between the two big ponderosas, I turned and looked back, as I always did, cherishing the last glimpse of the waterfall, the snowy peaks. I can come again soon, I told myself with a sudden rush of gladness. I'm strong now. This does not have to be my last hike of the year.

Thunder rumbled louder. It was dark over the peaks now and lightning flashed. I hurried into the shelter of the trees. Before long it began to rain. I had stopped to put on my cloak, when I heard male voices on the trail behind me. Instinctively, I veered off the path and dropped into a hollow in the ground behind some low bushes. I peered out as they passed. Eight men, five in the lead with big packs, strode down the trail, heads bent in the rain. My breath caught when I saw the next two. Robin and Greg. The eighth man walked a little behind them.

"I'm sorry," he was saying. "I know how you must feel. But we just can't risk it. There's been two lightning deaths up there already this summer. We'll go back up as soon as the storms clear."

Robin and Greg looked grim, their legs spattered with mud, their faces pale. My heart ached for them. I should have run out and let them know I was safe, but still I hid, afraid to show myself. Would they even recognize me?

That must be the mountain rescue team with them. They were looking for an eighty-year-old woman. My long skirt and cloak covered my body, but my face—I still didn't know what it looked like, but after my experience with the young man in the red hat, I was pretty sure it didn't look eighty. And they would want to know where I'd been while they searched for me for two days. What could I say? They would never believe the truth.

I hadn't thought of that part.

As soon as the men passed, I slipped from my hiding place and followed them, keeping just out of sight. My mind scrambled, exploring one impossible story after another. I didn't want to begin my new *ulada* by lying. But I couldn't speak of the Elirians, not to the mountain rescue team. If they did believe me, they might tell others and a search would begin. Maybe the Elirians weren't so safe as Tirini thought. I couldn't bear to think of my delicate saviors in the hands of cold science or the military.

But they wouldn't believe me. They would think I was crazy. I couldn't tell them.

The rain dwindled. Ahead of me, Robin and Greg and the man walking with them stopped where the trail reached the end of Silver Lake, not far from the parking lot. I drew back behind a stand of trees. Greg touched Robin's shoulder.

"We're going to hang here for a bit," he said to the man walking with them.

"Okay," their companion answered. He was a big man with a blond beard. "But don't go back up. We've got coffee and food in the truck." He bumped fists with Greg and strode off toward the parking lot.

Robin sank down on a wet log and bent his head into his hand. Greg sat beside him.

"We should have searched more around where her stuff was," Robin said. "She's gotta be up there."

"We combed every inch of that valley yesterday, and the stream."

"She might have gone up. There might be a cave or something."

"Those slopes are practically vertical. She couldn't have gone up there. You know how she weaves around, hanging onto that stick of hers. It's a wonder she got as far as she did."

"She walks okay once she gets going."

"True. But, Rob, she didn't have her shoes or her stick."

"Then where is she?"

"I don't know, but I think she's gone. Think of it this way, it's how she always said she wanted to die, in the mountains, under the sky. That was an incredible place where we found her pack."

Robin kept his head down. "I just don't think she's dead."

I couldn't hold back any longer then. I stepped out from behind the trees. "Greg, Robin, I'm here."

They leaped up and spun around. "Mom!"

I ran into their arms. They held me tight, my face against Greg's shoulder. Their questions poured over me.

"Where were you?"

"What happened?"

"Are you okay?"

"I'm okay."

Greg moved me away from him, holding my shoulders. My hood fell back. They stared at me. Greg's hands tightened on my shoulders. His eyes grew huge. I looked up at him, holding my breath.

"Mom-m?" he finally blurted out, his voice breaking in the middle of the syllable like a young child's.

"Yes," I answered.

Robin's face was washed with wonder. He touched my cheek. "You're alive."

"Yes."

"You look... like you did when I was a kid," Greg stammered. "Fifty years ago."

Shaken by his words, I lowered myself onto the log.

Greg sat down beside me. "Mom? Are you okay?"

"Yes." It seemed to be all I could say.

Robin sat down on my other side and took my hand.

Greg bent to look in my face. "What happened to you?" His words tumbled over each other. "You're all changed. Young! How could…? What happened? We've been searching for you for two days. We thought you were dead. Where were you?"

"I don't know." It was true. I didn't know where I had been, high above the Earth.

The big blond man came loping up the trail. "Hey, Greg, Rob, come on down now. We've got soup hot. You'll feel better—"

He broke off, his jaw dropped, when he saw me.

Greg pulled my hood back up, hiding my face. "Hey, Pete. We found her. She was walking down the trail behind us."

Pete came up to me. "Clara Norwood?"

I stood up, my staff in my hand. With my other hand I folded my hood over half my face. "Yes."

"Are you all right?"

"Yes," I said again. It was hard to talk. I could see he was a caring man, but he was so big, so male.

"Where the hell were you? We've taken this mountain apart the last two days, found your pack and boots and walking stick—" He looked me over. "I see you have them. Where were you?"

"I don't know."

"You don't know?" He pushed back his hat and rubbed his brow. "Well, I'm sure glad to see you alive and on your feet. Let's go down to the truck and tell the team you're safe. We have an EMT who can check you out, and some food." He glanced at me curiously. "You look in pretty good shape, but I'll bet you're hungry after being up there for three days. Come on."

He led the way down the trail toward the parking lot. Greg started after him. Robin touched Greg's shoulder. "Maybe we shouldn't."

Greg stopped and they looked at each other. "We've got to say goodbye to the guys and thank them," Greg said. "They've spent two days searching with us. It'll be okay. Just keep your hood up, Mom. We'll make it brief."

I followed them, doubting it would be okay. The hood wouldn't hide my face for long. I needed a veil.

The truck was an RV of sorts, with a small kitchen, some chairs, and a couch that was probably a pull-out bed. It was crowded with men and their smells. I kept my head turned away from them, my hood folded across my face. There were exclamations and cheers at my retrieval, a tumult of male voices. I was introduced to them all, but could only remember a few names—Matt with a thatch of dark hair, Chad bald and burly, Herb small and wiry with a red beard, and Pete.

I found myself seated on the hard couch. The truck was warm. "Can I take your cloak?" Matt asked.

"No, no thanks." But when I turned my head up to answer him, my hood slipped out of my hand and fell back. There was a moment of stunned silence, then uproar.

"I thought we were looking for your mother."

"She said she was Clara Norwood."

"Why did you tell us it was your mom?"

"More like your little sister."

"Doesn't look like the picture."

"If this is some kind of a joke—"

I straightened my shoulders. I'll have to get used to this, I told myself. I mustn't let them scare me.

"Stop!" Greg raised his voice and the men were silent, boring me with their eyes. I tightened my jaw and returned their gaze.

Greg spoke into the silence. "Rob and I are as confused as you are. She's changed since we last saw her. We don't know what happened to her, but we know she's our mother. So the search is over. She's alive and well enough to walk out. That's the good news."

"Let her speak," Matt said. "Let's hear her story."

I spread my hands, wordless. My sons sat down on either side of me, touching me, comforting me with their nearness.

"It's okay, Mom," Greg said. "Tell us. What happened?"

I began, resolved to tell as much truth as possible. I told them how I always went to my special place on my birthday, how it was my eightieth two days ago.

"Eightieth!" Herb exclaimed.

"Let her talk," Robin said sharply.

I continued, telling how I had climbed slowly but finally reached my place, how the storm had come up suddenly, how I had dashed for the krum tree and fallen, waked in the night paralyzed, thought I was dying.

"We saw where you fell," Herb said. "There were muddy skid marks, blood on the rock."

Blood? I didn't know I had bled.

"It's a good thing you didn't make it to the krum tree," Pete said.

"I know. I saw it this morning when I came back. I loved that tree."

Matt nodded. "It was an old one."

"So," Pete said. "The lightning struck the tree and you were close enough that it hit you, too. Temporary paralysis is sometimes an effect. Those storms can move in fast. The story makes sense so far. Then what? We searched everywhere and couldn't find you. You said 'when I came back this morning.' Came back from where?"

"I don't know."

The men were silent. Pete's jaw was clenched.

"What happened between the time you thought you were dying in the night and this morning? It's okay." Matt leaned forward to touch my knee. "Just tell us what you remember."

"I had strange dreams." I felt lightheaded. Perhaps that really was true. Perhaps it was all a dream after all. I looked down and saw my hand in Robin's. Smooth and young. It wasn't a dream. When I looked up again, the men were staring at me, silent, waiting. Matt's eyes were kind, Chad's hard. I took a breath and continued.

"Then this morning I found myself at the head of the valley, at the source of the stream. I had never been there before. I walked down the stream and came to where I had fallen, saw the tree. Someone had put my pack and boots under my poncho."

"That was Rob," Greg said. "He was sure you were coming back."

I looked at Robin. He'd been holding back tears ever since my return. "Thank you. I was glad to have them coming down."

Robin didn't reply, just squeezed my hand.

"You walked all that distance barefoot?" Chad raised one eyebrow. His question had the condescending tone of men who believe women to be inferior.

"The tundra is soft," I told him.

"You have ashes on your skirt," he said, jutting his chin out. "Fires are forbidden except in designated campgrounds. Were you making a fire?"

"No," I answered. "I was sitting with the krum tree."

"Why would you do that?" Chad asked.

That tone again. Ire rose in me. I lifted my chin. "I doubt you would understand."

"For a whole day and a night you don't remember anything?" Pete demanded.

I struggled with my desire to be truthful and my need to protect the Elirians. "Only strange dreams."

"Stop grilling her," Greg said fiercely. "She can't remember. What's likely is that when the paralysis passed, she wandered off somewhere. Lightning can cause amnesia, too, I would guess."

"It can," Matt said. He touched me again. "Clara, I'm an EMT. I'd like to take your pulse and blood pressure. Just to see how you're doing. Okay?"

I nodded. I remember the pumping on my arm, the fingers on my wrist. I think, as men go, Matt was gentle, but his touch seemed rough and crude compared to the wise hands of the Elirians.

"One hundred over sixty. Pulse sixty-five," Matt said. "She's good."

I gathered myself and stood. "Thank you very much for searching for me," I said to the men crowded around me. "I'd like to go home now." I picked up my pack and staff.

There was a bustle of movement and talk. The men stood, hugged each other, slapped each other's backs, and began climbing out of the truck. Herb turned off the stove and covered the soup pot. In all the excitement, food had been completely forgotten. I started for the door, but Chad blocked my path.

"There's more to your story."

I met his eyes. "I've told you what I can."

He towered over me. I lifted my chin and held his eyes.

Finally he turned away and left the truck. I experienced a moment of triumph at facing him down. Rude man. Three men were talking, blocking the door. Deciding to wait until the way was clear, I stood in the back of the truck listening to the men's voices outside as they moved away.

"That's the weirdest thing I ever—"

"Eighty years old, my ass."

"She seemed pretty confused."

"Lightning can do some strange things, but..."

Near the front of the truck, Matt drew Robin aside. I heard him say, "She looks okay and her blood pressure is fine, but if she were my mom, I'd stop by the hospital and get her checked out. A lightning strike is serious. And there was blood on the rock."

Robin nodded. He turned back and saw me, took my arm. "Come on, Mama."

We stepped out of the truck into late afternoon and drizzling rain. A few of the men were still standing outside talking with Greg.

"Thanks again," I said to them as Robin and I walked by.

"Sure thing."

"Glad you could walk out."

"Stay away from lightning, you hear?"

Greg shook hands all around and then joined us as we walked to Robin's car. I looked across the parking lot and was relieved to see my old Subaru in the corner where I'd left it.

"Oh, good," I said. "My car's still here. I was afraid they'd tow it when I didn't come back."

"Pete tagged it so they wouldn't," Greg said.

Robin unlocked his car and turned to me. "Mama, I want to stop at the hospital on the way home and get you checked out."

"I'm fine," I said. "I don't want to go to the hospital. I want to go home." The idea of the hospital horrified me. In spite of the strength and vitality I'd felt on the mountain, I also felt raw and new like a butterfly just out of the chrysalis. I knew the hospital scene; I'd been there enough times when my heart had run out of control. I didn't feel I could stand the questions, the lights, all the hook-ups.

"Matt thought we should take you," Robin insisted. "We don't know what the lightning did. And you had amnesia. I'm kind of worried."

"Maybe Rob's right," Greg said. "If you're okay, they'll release you. If not, it would be good to know what's going on and have you taken care of. We'll hang with you."

I didn't answer. It didn't feel like the right moment, standing there in the drizzle, to tell them about the Elirians and what they had done for me—if I ever could.

Robin got in his car and started the engine. "I'll meet you at the hospital."

"Right." Greg took my arm and led me to my car. "I'll drive. Where're the keys?"

They were in the pocket of my pack where I always kept them. I pushed the button on the key chain, and unlocked all the doors with one click. Even though I'd owned my car for more than a decade, I still marveled at that, the electronic world I could never quite believe in or feel I belonged to.

I let out a sigh as we drove away. "That was an ordeal."

"Sorry, Mom." Greg patted my knee. "I didn't know they'd grill you like that. But it's not surprising they'd want your story. They worked hard looking for you. They're all good guys, except for Chad. He's kind of a jerk. But you handled him well. You may look like a spring chicken, but you're still a feisty old woman inside."

He turned to look at me, sudden tears in his eyes. "God, I'm glad you're alive!"

I touched his hand. "I am, too. I'm so grateful you recognized me. I was afraid you wouldn't."

"Of course we would. You're our mom." He gave me another glance. "Though every time I look at you, I feel like a kid again."

He focused on the road for a moment, taking a series of tight curves at a speed that made me clutch the door handle.

When the road straightened out, he asked, "What in the world happened to you? You climb the mountain, an old woman who can barely get around without her stick, get hit by lightning, and come back a blooming young beauty none the worse except for a few ashes on her skirt. By the way, you've got a smudge on your forehead."

I put my hand to my brow. Probably I'd dried my face with my skirt before I realized it had ashes on it. "I thought I'd rinsed it all off," I said.

"Not quite. So. None of the guys knew what to make of it all. Rob and I don't, either. Seems like you had some kind of miracle."

"I did. I'll tell you. But let's wait 'till we're home and Robin's with us."

"Okay." He pulled out his phone. "I've gotta call Margo and tell her you're okay. She and the kids have been real worried."

I looked away, trying not to be nervous about his dialing and driving, and leaned my head against the side of the car. I heard Greg say "Hi, honey, we found her," then drew into myself. I felt lost, separated from the clarity of the high country, separated from the love of the Elirians, most of all separated from myself. How can I be me with this young body? With eyes that *flirt*? What kind of trouble will I get into? What will my life be like now? I slipped my hand into the left pocket of my skirt. The metal pieces were still there close against the hip they'd once held together. How did they get those metal pieces out without cutting me open? It was too much. I let the questions drop away like leaves falling from an autumn tree, and yielded to the motion of the car as we swung down the canyon.

Greg finished talking and put his phone away. He glanced over at me. "Mom? How're you doing?"

"Okay. Just kind of bewildered."

"No wonder. You've been through a lot."

We arrived at the hospital. "This is ridiculous," I said to Greg. "The doctors are going to be as stumped as the rescue team. If I ever make it past the front desk. We should just go home."

Greg opened the car door for me. "Did you really get hit by lightning?"

"I really did."

"Then we should check you out."

"Another ordeal," I muttered as we crossed the parking lot.

Greg grinned. "I can't wait to see how you handle it."

Robin was waiting for us outside the emergency room. We walked in together. The woman behind the desk was solid, burdened with a big bust. She looked up at us over the top of her glasses.

"She was lost on the mountain for two days, struck by lightning," Greg explained me. "We think she's had some amnesia."

The woman eased herself out from behind her desk. "Sit here," she directed me. She took my pulse and blood pressure. "Vitals are good." She went back behind the desk. "Can I see your insurance card?"

"I don't have it with me," I said, standing. "I'm on Medicare. No supplemental."

"Medicare?" she said, accusation in her voice.

"Yes. You have me in your computer. I've been here plenty of times."

"What's your name?"

"Clara Norwood."

The woman focused on the computer screen, her fingers tapping the keys. I waited, my sons silent beside me.

"Clara Norwood?" She looked up at me again.

"That's right."

"Says here your birthday is August 30, 1931." She was glaring at me now.

"That's right," I said again.

"Come on," she said. "Who do you think you're kidding?"

Feisty old woman rose up in me. "I beg your pardon?"

"I need to see your ID," she insisted.

My voice was cold. "I told you, I don't have any ID on me. My identity is far too weighty to take with me when I go hiking."

Robin suppressed a snicker. "You must have your driver's license," he said.

"It's in my car."

"Shall I get it?"

"I don't think it would help," Greg said.

The woman swelled her formidable chest. "I can't admit you without ID."

"It's a good thing I'm not dying." I turned to Robin and Greg. After all, I was their mother. "I don't want to be here anyway. I want to go home. I'm fine. If anything comes up, I can go to the doctor."

"Right," Greg said. He tilted his head toward the door and we left.

Chapter 4

Now What?

Home. My good old Subaru safe in the garage. My dear little house. Just being there helped me feel more grounded.

We rummaged in the refrigerator and got out soup and salad stuff, corn tortillas and cheese, and sat down around the dining room table.

"Okay, Mom," Greg said. "Tell us. What happened to you?"

"I will." I hesitated. "But first tell me how you got here. Last I knew you were in Santa Fe. And, Robin, when did you find out I hadn't come home?"

"The same day you left," Robin answered. "I knew you were going hiking and didn't want a fuss for your birthday, but the kids wanted to bring you cake and presents, so I called when I thought you should be home. You didn't answer. Later I called again, and finally went over to your house, to find that your car was still gone. I got worried and drove up to the trailhead, and there it was. By that time it was dark and getting cold. I found park rangers at the campground and reported you missing. Then I called Greg."

"I got in the car and drove," Greg said, "got to Rob's about three a.m."

"I went back home and got my hiking stuff," Robin went on, "kept in touch with the rangers. But it was almost dawn before they got organized. Greg and I met them and we started the search. I didn't remember exactly where your special place was, but I knew it was along a stream, high up. We followed the stream out of Sapphire Lake, then stayed with it when the trail left it. It was hard going, marshy, a lot of willows."

"Then I found your bathing cloth," Greg added, "tangled in the willows at the edge of the stream. I recognized it. You've had that thing forever."

"My bathing cloth!" I exclaimed. "Where is it?"

"In my pack, I think." He looked over at me. "It's pretty torn up."

"Oh." I closed my eyes a moment, feeling again the pang of its loss.

Robin was continuing their story. I brought myself back. "Once we found your cloth," he said, "we knew we were on the right track. Some of the guys went downstream, looking for your body, and Greg and I and the others went up. I recognized your place from that time I went with you long ago, and there were your pack and boots and stick. We thought sure we'd find you then. We searched the whole valley, all day. Where were you?"

I took a spoonful of soup. "I was there today. For a little while. But when I saw people had been there, I came down, knowing you were looking for me. Where were you today?"

"Up higher," Greg said, "and on the other side of the trail, down toward Sapphire Lake. 'Till the storms came. I kept telling them we should go back to the valley, that you couldn't get very far without your stick. But now I think maybe you could." He looked at me sharply.

I nodded.

"Okay," he said. "Tell us. What were your strange dreams?"

I looked from one to the other. They were clearly brothers, sharing many of the features I had passed to them, alike in many ways, and also quite different from each other. Greg was the more extroverted. He'd made it big in the corporate world, then dropped out at age forty to homeschool his children and practice yoga and Buddhist meditation. He wore a faded green sweatshirt, frayed at the cuffs, and his brown hair, streaked with gray, fell in loose curls around his shoulders. He sat leaning back in his chair, his eyes, green like Dan's, watching me keenly.

Robin's eyes were pure blue like Jon's. He sat with his elbows on the table, his chin in his hands, leaning toward me. He was quieter than Greg, almost a generation younger, and so far following a more traditional path, working toward his Ph.D. at the university. He wore his hair cropped too close for curls and even his hiking clothes were neat and tailored.

Both waited expectantly.

Still I hesitated. "It's such a strange story. I don't know if you'll believe me."

"Can't be any stranger than what we're seeing." Greg straightened in his chair. "Come on, spill it."

So I told them my story—the lightning, the night I lay dying, the rescue, the spaceship, the strange, beautiful Elirians, their songs, their mission. The telling made it seem more like a dream than ever. I was so awed by the wonder of it that it was hard to find words to speak of the love I had felt, the ecstasy of my renewal, my return to Earth. I pulled the two pieces of metal out of my pocket and laid them on the table, and ended by telling them how I had discovered my young body when I undressed to dip in the stream.

We sat in silence.

"Whoa!" Greg said finally.

"I couldn't tell the mountain rescue people," I said, "because I didn't want anyone to start hunting them. You understand? We must keep this secret."

"That's not going to be so easy," Robin remarked, "because of how you look."

"I still don't know what my face looks like," I said. "I tried to see my reflection in the pool, but the wind ruffled the surface." I couldn't speak of seeing Kiria's eyes. Of all the strange experiences I'd been through, that moment seemed the strangest.

"Why don't you go look in the mirror?" Robin suggested.

I laughed as I got up from the table. "The obvious solution." But my heart pounded as I walked to the bathroom. I stopped outside the door, not sure I wanted to see my face. Do it, I prodded myself. So I went in, turned on the light, and faced the mirror.

The reflection that looked back at me was so different from the last one I had seen that I barely recognized myself. My white, wispy hair, so thin you could see pink scalp through in places, was now thick gold-brown curls. The flesh of my throat and face was smooth and firm, the line of my jaw clean, my skin lightly tanned, my cheeks and lips rosy with health. No moles, sags, turkey neck, dark shadows, no wrinkles except for a few laugh lines around my eyes. My eyes! The color was not so different. My eyes had always been a changeable blue-green-gray—sea-colored eyes, my father had called them—but now the color was deeper, more luminous. Their shape was only subtly shifted. They were bigger in my face, set a little wider, slightly tilted up at the outer corners. But the whole effect caused me to shiver. They had given me Elirian eyes.

Now I understood the image in the pool. It was not Kiria's eyes I had seen, but my own.

I was beautiful as I had never been. As a young woman I had been considered pretty, but any grace in my features had been marred by an expression of apologetic self-consciousness. The face that looked back at me now, despite the shock of my changed appearance, had the clear, quiet gaze of an old woman who had spent decades in daily meditation.

"Who am I?" I asked the mirror. My Elirian eyes looked back at me and my inner old woman answered, You know as well as you ever did.

But I can't go out into the world looking like this, I thought in sudden panic. No one will know me. How will I relate? I backed slowly away from my reflection until I bumped into the towel rack on the wall behind me.

"Mama?" It was Robin outside the door. "Are you okay?"

"Yeah." I opened the door and buried my face in Robin's shoulder. "It's just kind of overwhelming."

Robin held me tight. "I can understand that, but you'll get used to it. Come on back now and finish your supper."

By the time we were done eating, it had grown dark outside the dining room window and was raining softly. The smell of rain on warm pavement drifted into the room, a city smell.

"What about Lisa?" I asked. "Did you tell Lisa I was missing?"

"I called her yesterday morning," Greg said, "before we left Rob's. She was frantic that you were lost. I would have contacted her by now, but I can't get South America on my cell."

"Oh! Call her right away," I said. "Use my phone. But, Greg, don't tell her everything, just that you found me and I'm okay. I'll tell her the rest, I'll have to, when she comes for Christmas."

Greg got up and went to my office. Robin and I sat together at the table. "I called Alice on the way down," he said. "She was real relieved to hear you're okay." He reached out and cupped my cheek. "You look incredibly beautiful, Mama, but you always did, even before." I laid my hand over his. There was love to be found on Earth, as well as in the sky.

We could hear Greg in the next room. "Hey, Lisa. Just wanted to let you know. We found her. She was coming down the trail behind us this afternoon. She's okay. Actually she looks pretty good. Give us a call when you get this." He came back into the dining room. "I left a message. She never answers her phone."

I got up and began clearing the table. As we washed up, Greg asked, "They healed everything inside you?"

"Everything. I feel incredible. Look." I squatted in the middle of the kitchen. "Remember my knees?" I jumped up out of the squat as I had on the smooth rock at the head of the valley. "And how about this?" I dropped back into a high arched backbend, my fingertips only inches from my heels, then pushed off with my hands and came back to standing again.

Greg whistled. He knew what it took.

"My heart is stable. And I haven't had one hundred over sixty blood pressure for years."

"That's pretty cool," Greg commented.

"I'm glad, Mama," Robin said. "I hated to see you struggling." He let the dishwater out and began wiping the sink and counter.

Greg piled the last pot on the drainer. "I guess I don't need to worry about hurrying up here for your funeral in the near future."

I shivered as I put the tea kettle on. "That's kind of spooky. It may end up being the other way around. I might outlive you."

"Don't rush me," Greg said. "I've got a while yet."

When we were settled in the living room with our tea, I said, "I don't know what I'm going to do. My friends won't know me. How am I going to explain this?"

"I know," Greg suggested. "You lie low for a week or so, then say you've been to a spa, gotten a makeover, you know, the works. Face lift, hair color."

"Hair transplant," Robin put in. "Her hair's a lot thicker now."

They grinned at each other and started tossing it back and forth.

"Boob job."

"Mole removal."

"Cosmetic dentistry." I began to giggle.

"Liposuction."

"Wheat grass diet."

"High coffee enemas." My giggles became laughter.

"Tummy tuck. You probably don't need one of those," Greg said. "You've kept your figure pretty well and your body doesn't look so different in clothes. But, judging by your face, without them... " He raised an eyebrow. I blushed.

"You know, Mama," Robin said. "You have what everyone's always wanted—the wisdom of age and the strength and beauty of youth. You could set the world on its ear."

"But I don't want to set the world on its ear," I said. "I'm still an old woman inside. I've lived a full life. I just want to be quiet, do a little massage, work in my garden, dance sometimes."

"That could be a conflict," Greg said. "An identity crisis."

"It's already an identity crisis!" I exclaimed. "What am I going to do about basic stuff like ID? Look what happened at the hospital. You were right. It wouldn't have helped if Robin had gotten my driver's license. Oh—I must have left it in the car."

"Do you want me to get it?" Greg asked.

"I will." I rose easily. "You won't have to fetch things for me now." That felt good. I went out to the garage, soft rain on my head, and brought back the little purse that held my driver's license, a twenty-dollar bill, and my Golden Age card.

We gathered around to look at my license.

"There's a faint resemblance," Greg noted. "But I don't think it's going to work as a photo ID."

I sighed. "What am I going to do? I need a photo ID everywhere, to cash a check, to get on an airplane."

"Don't try to figure it out tonight," Greg said. "We've done enough for one day. You're found and home and well. And I'm pooped."

"You must be." I felt penitent, asking them to solve my problems after all they'd done. "You guys have been great, searching for me, helping me, everything. I'll make a bed up for you downstairs, Greg."

We all stood. Robin embraced me. "I should get on home. Alice will be wondering where I am, and tomorrow I need to get back to school."

Later, as he hugged me good night, Greg said, "What I was saying about identity crisis goes a little deeper, I think, than your driver's license."

I shivered with premonition. "I think it does."

Chapter 5

In a Young Body

I took Greg's advice and laid low for a week.

The first day, I puttered around putting away my hiking gear, marveling with every move how easy it was to bend, to pick up, to reach. My ambivalence at being young faded into the background, and joy flooded through me. I can dance again, I thought, without getting tired and having my knees ache. I bet I could dance all night the way those crazy young *tangueros* do. And I'll be able to hike higher than I have for a long time. I can go to the pass again, and the glacier, and all the other places I love that I haven't been to for years.

For the next few days, I tore into the garden and began clearing up years of neglect. I had kept it going, planting a few things in the spring, watering it, but mostly it had gone wild. Annuals had reseeded themselves—pink and purple cosmos, gold and orange calendulas, snapdragons of many colors, heavenly blue morning glories climbing the side of the garage, spilling down over the tomatoes. Perennials had spread—roses grown taller than I, clematis tumbling off its trellis, ice plant, violets and sweet woodruff everywhere underfoot. I weeded, pruned, fertilized, transplanted, put in bulbs for the next spring, turned the compost pile, and reveled in the beauty of flowers and the dark rich smell of earth. Best of all, I could squat while I worked and stand up easily to move to the next place.

I walked every day, sometimes around the lake, sometimes over the hills. Occasionally on my walks, I met acquaintances and stopped to chat with them. I could see on their faces a look I knew I had often worn when I met former clients in the grocery store. That look says as loud as words, I think I know you, but I just can't place you. I watched it with amusement and a pang of guilt, but didn't feel ready to reveal myself. So we'd exchange greetings, remark on the weather, and move on.

Within the week I was back in the high country. I hiked all the way to the pass, climbing the switchbacks on the rock face I had looked at with such longing on my birthday, and stood on the continental divide, my heart soaring in the wind. No storms came that day. On the way down, I stopped again in my special place and lingered until twilight.

Wherever I walked, I thought about the gift of my renewed life, especially about the gift of beauty. Beauty had been a huge issue for me all my life. Early on, I had formed the belief that I would be loved only if I were beautiful. This was reinforced by my devotion to fairy tales as a young girl, identifying with the beautiful princess awaiting her prince. I longed for a quality of love I had missed as an infant with an impatient mother who did not pick me up when I cried or understand how to nurture me. All my life I sought that mother love, futilely, through a man, a prince, who would cherish me and not abandon me. And I believed beauty was the key to win him.

As I aged, I mourned the appearance of each new blemish, the sagging of flesh, the deepening of wrinkles, and believed myself less and less lovable as my youthfulness faded. I had the sense to stay away from plastic surgery and soon discovered that too much makeup made me look like an old tart, but I spent a lot of money on wrinkle creams and was obsessive about keeping my figure. Friends told me age had made me more lovely, that my white hair was a like a halo around my face, that my eyes were radiant, but I never believed them.

Only in the last ten years had I broken the myth and accepted my aging face and body, my unmanageable wispy white hair—all of it.

Now I had the beauty I would have died for, and I didn't need it anymore. I'd made peace with my singleness and didn't want to attract a man. I was an old woman, done with all that.

Now the beauty I had been given felt somewhat dangerous. I wanted to hide it, diminish it. Beauty attracts, and I'd always fallen in love too easily with anyone who desired me. Off I'd go on the romance roller coaster. Only that roller coaster was not like the ones in amusement parks where you step off safely at the end of the ride. My roller coasters always crashed and broke my heart.

Would I be any wiser now?

There was the problem of the driver's license.

I was nervous about that and entertained various disaster scenarios. The officials at the driver's license bureau would never believe the makeover story. I could tell them I needed a new license because my old one had expired. But it hadn't, as they would discover as soon as they found me on their computer. They would arrest me for attempted identity theft.

Finally, in my second week home, I came up with a plan. I called the driver's license office and asked what to do if I lost my license. I would need my social security card, the man told me, and proof of my address. I'd have to take an eye test and pay twenty-five dollars. I might have to wait; the line was long.

Okay, I thought, that doesn't sound too hard. I gathered my courage, put a book in my purse and went. When I arrived, I took a number and sat down to wait in one of the rows of chairs. The book distracted me, which was fortunate, because I had plenty of time to be nervous. It was three hours before my number came up.

Heart pounding, I stepped up to the counter, my social security card and proof of address clutched in my hand. The clerk was pale, her lank dark hair pushed back behind her ear, her skin pocked. She didn't look at me. I explained my plight, and handed her my Social Security card and a bank statement with my address on it. She still didn't look at me. She looked at her computer.

"Clara Norwood?"

"Yes."

"Address: 7 Moss Rock Road, Boulder, 80304?" Her voice sounded like a recording.

"Yes."

"Birthdate August 30, 1931?"

I sucked in my breath. "Yes."

She still didn't look at me. "Place of birth Boston, Massachusetts, USA?"

"That's right."

She tapped away on her computer. I realized I was tense, biting my lower lip. I let my breath out quietly. It seemed I had lucked into a zombie clerk.

She ran me through the eye test, still without giving me a glance. "Sit over there." She gestured toward a row of chairs against the far wall. "They'll call you for your picture."

I sat as directed, pulled out my book, and held it in front of my face, repressing a rush of unruly giggles. The zombie clerk. She never even looked at me.

The stout mustached man taking the pictures did look at me. He looked me over from head to foot. I was glad I had dressed modestly.

"Stand right here," he directed, sweeping me with his glance again. He stroked his mustache. "Now smile."

My usual tactic for ID pictures was to keep a sober face, but he would have none of that. "No, no. Not such a serious look. I bet you have a fabulous smile. Come on."

I gave in and smiled.

"Beautiful. When you have a smile like that you shouldn't hold back. Pretty eyes." He was definitely hitting on me. He looked into his camera. "Perfect. Great picture." He left his camera and went behind his desk. "Here's your ID and your temporary license."

I walked up to his desk. His hand lingered on mine as he handed me the papers. "You're all set now. Your permanent license should arrive in the mail within two weeks. If it doesn't, come on back here and let me know, hear?"

"Thank you," I said coolly, turned, and left. Outside in my car I let the giggles loose and all my nervousness with them. I laughed until tears ran down my cheeks. One not looking and the other looking at the wrong thing, neither had seen the incongruity between my face and my birth date.

My voice mail and email were loaded with calls and letters. Apparently there had been a report in the local paper that I was missing, then another one saying I'd been found, that I'd been hit by lightning and had amnesia. I simply didn't deal with all those messages for a while. One thing I'd learned as I grew old was that not everything was an emergency. But the calls kept coming, so I began to answer them, refused to speak with a reporter, and reassured my small circle of friends I was okay, just needing to be quiet for a while.

Then on Tuesday evening of the second week I was home, I got a call from Martha, a client I'd been massaging for many years, every other Wednesday at four. She was younger than I, still in her sixties, one of the few clients I kept working with because I loved her and she needed my help to ease her chronic pain.

"I read in the paper you'd been lost in the mountains," she said. "The second article said you'd been struck by lightning. How are you? We have an appointment tomorrow? Are you okay to work?"

"I'm fine. I'll see you at four as usual."

"Are you sure?"

"Yes."

"I'll be there then. I'm looking forward to it."

Now I'm in for it, I told myself after I hung up. She's not going to have trouble placing me, not walking into my studio.

The next afternoon at four, I heard the doorbell, and went downstairs to my studio. I had put on a shirt Martha would recognize because she'd often said she liked it. She was already there when I entered the waiting room, her back turned as she took off her shoes.

"Hi, Martha." My voice at least was the same.

She turned, smiling. "Hi." She stepped back. "Oh. I'm looking for Clara. We have a session scheduled for four."

"I'm Clara," I said.

She tilted her head to one side, then the other, searching my face, her own face expressing increasing bewilderment. "No, the Clara I'm looking for is an older woman, though you look something like her. Are you a relative?"

"Martha," I said firmly. "I'm the Clara you're looking for."

Her jaw dropped. She stared. "Clara? What happened? You look… Is it really you?"

"It's really me."

"But…"

"I know I'm changed. But it's just my looks. The rest of me is the same." Which wasn't quite true, but I needed to reassure her.

"What happened? What have you…? You look young! Like a thirty-something kid."

"Well, I'm not," I said in a firm old-woman voice. "I just turned eighty."

"That's right. You were going to the mountains to celebrate… then got lost. But how…?"

"I had an altering experience," I confessed. "But I can still give a massage. Come on in. How are you doing?"

My attempt to turn attention to her was only partly successful. I led her into the studio to sit in our accustomed places by my desk and took up my pen to take notes. She seemed eased by these familiar routines.

Still she stared. "You look beautiful. But you always were. I didn't think you were into dying your hair, though."

"I didn't exactly." I floundered, realizing the makeover story wouldn't fly with Martha; she knew me too well. "Look, Martha," I said. "It's very hard to explain, but I'm still me. Please trust me. Tell me how that left hip is doing."

She let it go for a time and told me about her various pains. We set to work easing her chronically tight neck and shoulders. I was only ten minutes into the session when I realized how seriously lack of energy had dulled my work in recent years. It had often been hard to get though a session. I was a good massage therapist and my basic competence had served my clients well, but I had forgotten what it was like to be creative, intuitive, inspired. With my newfound energy, all that came rushing back.

My fingers were strong, unhindered by arthritis, my vision clear. I soon found new angles to approach the troubled body of this friend I had worked with for so many years. When she stood up at the end of the session, she was easier and more balanced than I had ever seen her.

"I feel incredible," she told me.

She dressed, then turned and looked deeply into my face. "Clara, talk to me. What really happened? An 'altering experience,' I guess so! It seems more like a miracle from God."

I hesitated, shaking my head. "I don't know."

"What can it be then?" She reached out and touched my cheek. "You're clearly all new—and inspired! That was an incredible session. And you don't even look tired, the way you used to at the end of a session."

I felt briefly embarrassed that she had noticed that in the past. "I'm not," I admitted.

"Can't you tell me? I know so many people old and in pain. If they could access… It's so amazing. Everyone who sees you will want to know how you were changed, to have what you have."

"I know." I shrank away from her. "And I can't tell them. I've been hiding, afraid of just that."

"Why can't you?"

"Because… I can't explain it. It happened because I was dying. I stayed too long above tree line and was hit by lightning."

"They said that in the newspaper and that you had amnesia."

"I don't remember everything." I was lying; my memories were vivid, but the amnesia provided the perfect excuse. "It *was* a miracle. But… please don't ask anymore. Believe me, if I could give it to you, I would."

"You have," she said softly. "God must have a high purpose for you to renew you like this." She embraced me, started to go, then turned back. "Now you have more energy, would you consider taking a new client? I know someone who really needs help."

"I don't know." A struggle awoke inside me. No. I'm retired. I don't want new clients. But look what you just did for Martha. You're inspired again and have plenty of energy. How can you not serve when you have skill in your hands and there is need?

Martha watched me with her kind eyes. "She could really use your help."

"Yes. Well. Okay. Yes. Give her my number."

☙ ☙

The experience with Martha opened the door. I realized I couldn't hide out forever. I was lonely and needed my friends. That Martha had accepted my awkward explanations, decided it was a miracle, and not pressed further gave me courage.

The next day I picked up the phone and called my closest friend, Anne. Although she was twelve years younger than I, we had shared most of our adult lives. We had met in the late sixties, and supported each other through marriages, children, divorces, relationships and separations. We were also colleagues, both massage therapists, and often traded sessions. She'd called me several times since I returned, but I'd been afraid to have her see me, unsure whether I could tell her the whole story. She was fascinated with the paranormal, always trying out a new healer, a new psychic, and had a wide circle of friends who shared her interests. I feared she would be so excited by my story, it would be impossible for her not to leak it in some way. But I missed her and longed for her company.

"How about a walk?" I said when she picked up the phone.

"That would be great. Are you feeling well enough to walk? I've been worried about you, the lightning and all."

"I'm fine."

"Good. I'm excited to see you. I've got a client until four-thirty this afternoon. How about five o'clock? Where shall we go?"

"Five o'clock would work. I was thinking of the trail by the old ranch."

"Okay. I'll meet you there. Okay. All right. Okay. Bye." I chuckled. Anne always said okay a lot at the end of her phone calls.

She was already there when I drove into the parking lot at the trailhead, leaning against her car, tall, elegant in her slim jeans, the late afternoon sun glinting off silver streaks in her straight dark hair. I felt a rush of love when I saw her.

She recognized my car and ran to meet me as I parked, but stopped short when I got out.

"Anne." I opened my arms to hug her.

"What...? Wait." She held me away from her, her hands on my shoulders, staring. "Who are you?"

"I'm Clara."

"No—" Her eyes moved across my face, my throat, the curls sticking out from under my hat. "You can't be."

"I am."

"No way. Clara's an old woman; she's eighty. I know. I'm a close friend. And you are young—very young." She gripped my shoulders tighter. "Who are you anyway? Why are you telling me you're Clara? What are you doing with her car?" Her glance swept my hiking skirt and shirt, the blue hat I always wore. "Wearing her clothes." Her voice rose with an edge of panic. "Where is she?"

"I'm right here." I felt my lips tremble and pressed them together to hold back tears that threatened. I had thought surely Anne, of all my friends, would know me.

"Anne," I said, trying to the control the shaking in my voice. "I've been through an extraordinary experience. I know it's changed the way I look, but I'm still me."

Anne was shaking her head.

"Remember what I looked like when we first met? In 1969? When you were still married to Mike and I to Dan? In the meditation workshop at Esalen?"

She softened then. Frowning, she studied my face more closely. "An extraordinary experience?" That had connected for her. "But your eyes are different."

I realized with relief that she finally believed me. "I know. They changed them along with everything else."

"*They?*"

"Let's walk," I said. "Will you walk with me?"

"Yes. Yes, of course."

The path was wide and smooth, with plenty of room to walk side by side. We walked a while in silence, enfolded in the peace of tree and meadow. Anne kept turning her head to look at me. She dropped behind me for a moment, watching my gait. "You're walking really well. That limp you've had ever since your hip replacement is gone."

"I'd sort of forgotten about it," I said.

She caught up with me again, stopped me, standing in front of me. "Who are *they?* What extraordinary experience? What in the world happened to you?"

I wavered a moment, then decided. I had to tell her the truth. She was the one person in the world with whom I had always shared everything, and I couldn't bear for that to change. "I'll tell you," I said. "But you must promise, absolutely promise, to keep it a secret. You'll understand why."

"I promise." Her face was alive with curiosity.

"Okay." I took a deep breath. "I thought I was going to die after the lightning strike—"

Anne interrupted me with a fierce hug. "I'm glad you didn't. I've been so worried about you. After reading the paper I thought you'd be in the hospital. Then when you didn't want me to come over…"

"Let's sit down."

We climbed up the bank on the side of the trail and sat on the dry prairie grass. Before us wide meadows spread out to the reservoir, blue in the late afternoon sunlight.

I took Anne's hand and held it while I told her the story. She listened, her eyes wide with amazement, occasionally interrupting with exclamations. When I finished, she sighed with wonder.

"There really *are* intelligent beings on other planets. I've always thought there must be. Remember all the media reports about flying saucers a couple of decades ago? But you've actually been in their ship, they've touched you, communicated with you." She smoothed my cheek. "And healed you. You look gorgeous. What a blessing."

"Maybe."

"Maybe?"

"It's disorienting. I don't know who I am anymore, and I'm afraid to meet people. When I first came down from the mountain even Robin and Greg had trouble recognizing me."

"I can see why."

"And the mountain rescue team—" I told her about them and the woman in the hospital, hamming it up, and we laughed. Anne was always fun to laugh with.

When our laughter subsided, she said, "I understand what you mean about being disoriented. But it's only been two weeks. You'll get used to it."

"I don't know. I'm eighty, and I look and feel as if I'm thirty. Not so young as twenty. But inside I'm still eighty. I'm uncomfortable being so beautiful. The man at the driver's license place who took my picture was hitting on me."

"Did you go get a new driver's license?"

"I had to. You need a picture ID everywhere and my old one doesn't look like me anymore."

"Oh, my God. How'd you pull that off? They want your birth date and everything."

"Sheer luck." I told her about the zombie clerk and the guy with the mustache and we laughed some more.

Anne took her water bottle out of her pack and we both drank. "Are you ready to walk?" she asked.

As we continued along the trail, Anne said, "I love the idea of the *ulada*. Just think what our planet would be like if all of us were born with a special task to create harmony, and knew it and did it. I bet everyone on earth asks at some point what the purpose of their life is, and most of us don't know, or spend our life trying to figure it out. What do you think your *ulada* is?"

"At this point in my life, for better or for worse, I've done most of it. Bringing up the children is certainly part of it. My work—massage, teaching dance and yoga and meditation. Maybe what I've learned from all my relationships."

"I think my *ulada* is similar—kids, massage, relationships. But you—now that you're young again, maybe you haven't done most of it. Maybe you have a whole new *ulada*."

"That's a daunting thought. I still think of myself as old, that I'll die sometime in the next ten years. I've felt my *ulada* was almost complete.

When I thought I was dying I was upset, because I didn't feel quite finished. But I don't want another whole lifetime."

"Why not?"

"Because… It's hard to explain. I've had a long life already, full of joy and suffering, love and loss. I don't feel I can hold much more."

We walked on. It was so good to talk with her, to share my confusion, the wonder of my healed body, all my experiences since coming home, to laugh together. We stayed out until the last glow of sunset faded from the hills.

After my walk with Anne, I began to emerge, connecting one by one with my few close friends. It was a challenge each time, but I held to my story that I didn't remember what had happened. After a while they stopped asking, though I would often find them looking at me when they didn't think I saw, question and awe in their eyes. For a while a story circulated about a miraculous healer roaming the tundra to assist those in trouble; but soon the first snow fell closing the high country to all but the most intrepid, and the story, always improbable, faded away.

Martha's friend did call, and I began to work with her. As if some mysterious grapevine had sprung into action, I began receiving other calls, former clients wanting a tune-up, my new client referring her friends. Soon I was seeing three or four clients a day. My old skills came flooding back, enhanced now with the wisdom of my quiet years. I wondered if having Elirian eyes had given me some of their perception. It seemed I could see into a body in a way I'd had moments of in the past, but now more clearly and reliably.

It was exciting—I had always loved my work—but I often felt bewildered by my changed life, a life like the one I had enjoyed for many years, that now felt strange, misplaced somehow.

I missed the quiet days, easy mornings sleeping late, lying on my pillow watching the sun touch the leaves of the cottonwood, meditating as long as I wanted, practicing yoga with no time limit. Solitary walks, hours dreaming in my garden, reading, writing in my journal. Now everything was on a schedule again. I found myself hurrying and didn't like it.

Sometimes I sat in my garden between sessions. The season was moving on, though we had not had frost yet. One afternoon I cradled a spray of snapdragon in my hand. The flowers had passed. Round brown seedpods dropped tiny black seeds on my fingers when I touched them. Another snapdragon was still blooming, bright purple-pink flowers, the color of Kiria's iridescence. I spoke to the blooming plant. "It's time to be making seeds, don't you know that? Frost will come soon now." Then I thought that I was like that plant, foolishly blooming in the fall of my life when it was time to be withering and creating seeds for the next turn of season, whatever that might be.

෩ ෬

It was a month before I had the courage to go back to tango. Of all my social connections, I knew my tango friends would be the most avid to learn how I had changed and how they could access a similar transformation.

There was a paradox of intimacy and superficiality in the tango community. We danced a most intimate and sensuous dance, we greeted each other with hugs and kisses, yet we knew little of each other's lives outside tango. It was considered ill form to talk while dancing; the communication was all in the connection. I knew the men by the quality of their embrace, the way I fit in their arms, their favorite steps. The women would cluster and visit while waiting to be invited to dance, but our talk was most often about our clothes or shoes or the skills of the men we danced with. Sometimes the conversation would dip deeper, but we all understood that it would be dropped between one word and the next if one of us were asked to dance. Our intimacy was based mostly on the fact that we spent so much time together. Before

I had aged and stiffened, I danced two or three times a week. Others danced tango every night.

I had gone seldom during the last year, but now, with my vitality high, I was eager to dance again. My email was full of announcements of tango events. I decided on a Sunday night *milonga* at the Avalon Ballroom. (*Milonga* is the word used for a tango social dance and also the name of one of the tango rhythms.)

What to wear? My dance clothes were clingy, sparkly, low-cut. Slit skirts, lace, velvet and satin. I stood in front of my closet, sliding the hangers, and looked them over, torn between the fun of dressing up and my recent reticence for revealing my beauty. Finally I said, "Hey, it's tango," and pulled out a pale pink lace top, low cut, and a pink satin skirt.

They still fit, except that the skirt was a little loose around the waist. A quick tuck in the skirt was all that was needed. I gathered my curls into a soft knot, put on long earrings and a necklace of black pearls. In the bathroom I applied eyeliner, though my eyes hardly needed accenting, a glossy neutral lipstick, and a few drops of the rose-lavender perfume I always wore for tango.

As I dressed, I thought about how I had come to tango, going to a class on a whim, twelve years ago, how, from the first moment, I had loved it, the music, the elegance of the dance. My touch-hungry body drank in the nurturance of close embrace, and my sensuous nature reveled in the opportunity to express itself in a safe container. I delighted in the costume part, going all out to be as beautiful as I could. Of course, I was already old then, but that made it somehow safe.

Not so safe now, I thought as I surveyed myself in the mirror. I shied back from my reflection, then pulled myself together. You've been given a gift, I told myself. Enjoy it. Tango is the perfect place to let it shine.

The *milonga* was in full swing when I arrived. I scanned the floor for potential partners. There was Tim, who always danced with me, often two or three times in an evening; Steve, who was my first tango partner when we were both learning and now, in my opinion, the best dancer in the community; Roberto, a warm Mexican man with a delicious embrace; and five or six other favorites. It would be a good night.

Marco whirled by me with a lovely young woman in his arms who wasn't following very well. He was a good dancer and looked as if he'd be fun to dance with, but although we'd shared the dance floor for countless evenings, he'd never invited me.

I settled myself in a chair at the edge of the dance floor, waiting for the changing of partners at the end of the *tanda*, a sequence of three or four songs. Next to me was a woman I'd often chatted with. She turned to greet me, looked at me for a moment with a puzzled frown. "I don't think I've seen you here before. Are you visiting?" she asked kindly.

I decided not to hide. "No, Sally. It's been a while, but you know me. Clara."

"Clara! Oh, my God! I didn't recognize you." She turned in her chair to face me fully. Her eyes widened and her mouth fell open. After a stunned moment she asked, "Are you really Clara?"

I nodded.

"Oh my God," she said again. "You've done your hair... your face. How did they get your face...? You look fabulous. Way younger. Where'd you get that done?"

"I have to confess I don't know. I was hiking last summer and got hit by lightning. I've had amnesia since. I can't tell you where I've been."

"You don't remember?"

"No."

I was getting more skilled in my lies, but was still uncomfortable. Sally was inhaling to ask more when Tim appeared in front of me. I stood and stepped into his arms, resting my head into the familiar hollow of his cheek. Over his shoulder as we moved away, I saw Sally staring after me, her mouth hanging open again.

We had danced only a few steps when Tim stopped short in the middle of the line of dance and held me away from him. "Clara?"

"Yes."

"I didn't recognize you. I thought you were someone new. You look different. Way different, but I know how you dance."

"We're disrupting traffic." Dancers were swerving around us.

"Right." He took me back into his arms and we moved on around the floor. "You smell the same."

"I'm still me."

He opened up out of close embrace and set me spinning in a series of rapid turns, watching me. When he gathered me close again, he asked, "What have you done? You look younger, really pretty." He gave me a squeeze. "And you feel just as delicious as ever."

I was touched that he accepted me, but it was not surprising. He knew me. After all, we had danced two or three *tandas* a night, several nights a week, for years.

When he led me back to my seat, women clustered around me.

"Clara, we've missed you. Where have you been?"

"You look fabulous."

"Your hair, your face. It all looks so natural."

"Look at your skin! Didn't you use to have a lot of freckles?"

Their questions and comments came quick and fast, bewildering me. I couldn't tell if they were just humoring me, or if they really believed all my changes came from a makeover. Looking into their faces, I saw a mixture of disbelief—and hope. If I could be so changed, then maybe…

"Where did you get that done?"

"She can't remember," Sally said. "She was struck by lightning and has amnesia."

"Can't remember?"

"No."

"Oh, come on. How could you forget a place that made you look so great?"

"Don't hold out on us."

"Are you sure you're Clara? You do look like her. Maybe you're her granddaughter."

I began to feel desperate. "Steve's asking me to dance," I said, catching his eye across the room.

He came and swept me away into a waltz. "You're creating quite a stir," he whispered into my ear. "You look gorgeous. Every woman in the room is curious."

"I know. Thanks for rescuing me." We danced. Waltz was my favorite of the three tango rhythms and Steve was the best dancer of all. I hadn't realized how much my dancing had been dragged down by the low-grade chronic ache of my aging body. No longer. Light and fluid, I whirled, floated like milkweed down on the wind. Sheer bliss.

I had barely sat down after dancing with Steve when I saw Marco smiling at me from across the room. Oh, I thought, now he sees me. I felt a bit miffed, remembering all the times I'd tried to catch his eye over the years, and how he'd looked right through me. But I was curious to know his dancing, so I nodded and he came to me, beaming, his hand extended. He *was* fun to dance with, but all through the *tanda* I couldn't get over feeling put out that while I was old he'd never noticed that I was a good dancer. He was noticing now as I followed him faultlessly through a lively and intricate sequence.

"*Uno mas?*" he asked at the end of the *tanda*. One more?

"*No, gracias,*" I responded and turned away to go to the ladies' room.

As I made my way down the hall, I heard voices in the coat room. "I just can't believe she's Clara. There's no makeover that could change her that much."

I drew back. I should have gone on, but curiosity rooted me.

"Then who is she? She's wearing Clara's clothes. How many times have we seen that same pink outfit? And why in the world would a young woman say she was Clara, who, everyone knows, is old? It doesn't make sense."

"It certainly doesn't. Whoever she is, she's messing with us."

I peeked around the corner. Liz and Cynthia, women I'd been friendly with. Their backs were turned.

"It's pretty weird," Cynthia said, "but I think she really is Clara. I was watching her dance. She does the same ornaments Clara does—that little tap between steps and her unique way of doing a *boleo*. The guys think she's Clara."

"She can't be." Liz half turned and I ducked back. "How could any makeover get her face that smooth? She doesn't have that stretched facelift look. She used to have wrinkles in her cleavage and now she's all round and firm. And the skin on her chest and shoulders—how could they do that?"

"I don't know." Cynthia shrugged. "And she's not telling. But she must have spent a fortune to get all that done. I never thought she was that well off. She hardly ever had new clothes. Maybe she got an inheritance or something. Imagine being so vain, at her age, to redo herself so completely."

That stung. I'm not vain, I protested inwardly, but was stopped by shame that I'd cared so much about being pretty all my life.

"Well, it's working for her," Liz said, turning her back again. "Whoever she is, she's the center of attention for sure. Marco walked right by me to ask her to dance."

There was jealousy in her voice. I slipped quickly by the open door and into the ladies' room, and hid myself in a stall. My heart burned. I didn't want to make them jealous. I didn't even really want to dance with Marco. I may have been too concerned about how I looked all my life, but I never would have done a massive makeover. It was a gift, I wanted to tell them. But I couldn't.

I sat in the stall feeling a pang of loss. I had always been well-loved in the tango community, warmly greeted, supported, especially in the beginning as I learned the dance. An old woman is no threat, I thought sadly. I'm still not. Maybe they'll realize that after they get used to me.

It took a while for the discomfort to settle. Then I came out, smoothed my hair in front of the mirror, and made my way back to the dance floor, not wanting that bit of overheard gossip to spoil my evening.

The rest of the night went better. The men seemed to accept me. As the evening went on, some of the women I had been close to came, one by one, to talk with me. I could see them searching my face, glancing down at my full, young cleavage, noticed how they subtly guided the conversation to see if I knew what Clara should know. When the conversation ended, I felt at least tentative acceptance.

I had plenty of partners and lots of energy to keep dancing. After a while I relaxed. They could accept me or not. I was just happy to be dancing again, joyous to dance without pain.

I stayed until the dance ended, a thing I'd never done before.

"I never saw you last this late," Tim said as I helped him rearrange the chairs. "Looks like you got some kind of healing, too."

"I did," I said. "And I've had a great time tonight." I gave him a hug. "Thanks for all the dances."

☙ ❧

The first frost came with a heavy wet snow at the end of October. Most of the trees were still flaunting multicolored leaves. The weight of the snow bent them, broke many branches. I went out into the garden with my long walking stick and shook the limbs of the young maple that were dangerously bowed under the white weight.

"Let go your leaves," I told the tree as I bumped the branches as high as I could reach with my stick. "Don't you realize it's almost winter and it's going to snow? Let them go." Snow fell on my head in wet clumps.

Fortunately the maple lost only a few small branches before the sun came out and melted away its burden. Other trees were not so lucky. The street was littered with huge broken limbs. Most of those trees quickly shed their leaves, but not the maple. The next week another snow fell. "Can't you get the message?" I asked the tree as I stood under it again, tapping its branches, showered with snow. "Winter's coming. Drop your leaves. You're all out of sync with the season."

As I was brushing myself off on the porch, I looked back at the tree. Who are you to talk? it seemed to say.

Once I started dancing again, my life became even fuller. I worked all day and danced in the evenings. Although I had danced tango for many years and was already accomplished, I started taking classes again, refining my skills and mastering new techniques, ones my grumpy knees wouldn't have tolerated before. I loved it all, but there was a discordant restlessness in me. Finally I decided I was doing too much. I turned away clients and limited my practice to three days a week. Still I was busy. There was the garden to put to bed, leaves to rake, and always the many chores necessary to keep my house and business going.

As often as I could get away, I ran to the foothills, climbed the ridges until I was breathless, and sat gazing out over the plains. All kinds of shoulds arose. Now you have all this energy, this new life, an inner voice admonished me, you should be serving more. You shouldn't turn away clients. You should get involved again in the political chaos sweeping the country. What right have you to rest and read and dream as you used to, now that you are strong?

Under the shoulds flowed a deep tide of yearning for the quietness and depth of my former life. An ebbtide, running in conflict to the strong flood tide that swept me.

Your ulada is almost complete, the Elirians had sung as we parted. Was it? Then why did they give me this strength of youth? I wondered if they understood aging. Perhaps not. They spoke of just sinking into their planet when their *ulada* was complete, arising again when called by a new *ulada*. Maybe Elirians didn't age, and those who had rescued me didn't realize what they were doing when they transformed me.

One day in November as I was shopping, I passed a kite shop on the mall. A kite! I hadn't flown a kite since Robin was a boy. Impulsively I went into the shop and bought one shaped like a dragon. Katie and Colin, Robin's children, especially enjoyed dragon play. Even before I was renewed, we used to pretend to be dragons together, enacting their dramatic fantasies. Colin used to curl up in my lap and pretend to be a dragon egg, just hatching. I loved that.

The following Sunday I took the kite and went to visit Robin and his family. They had adjusted to my change in previous visits. Robin had told Alice the whole story. She marveled, kept my secret, and clearly didn't know what to make of a mother-in-law who looked younger than she. The children accepted my transformation with little fuss. Katie, who was eleven, said she liked my white hair better, but it was okay that it was brown now. She and Colin were glad that I could run and romp with them as I hadn't been able to before.

They loved the kite. We took it out to the park near their home. I remember that afternoon vividly. It was one of those warm sunny days that can show up in Colorado even in November. We ran along the side of the creek on the brown grass. The wind was just right and the kite went high. We shouted and laughed, our three spirits soaring as one with the kite.

Soon we were into the long dark nights of winter and the holidays were approaching. Winter Solstice was the most powerful of them for me, that longest night, the still point of the turning seasons. I loved bringing in the greens and lighting the candles to call back the sun. After Solstice I had always closed my practice until the New Year, honoring the impulse to go inward until the sun grew stronger.

More than ever this year, I felt the disharmony between that impulse and all the hullabaloo of Christmas. But there was no help for it. Lisa and her husband, Phil, and their sixteen-year-old daughter, Jocelyn, were coming from Brazil, and there would be a big family gathering, presents, lots of Christmas cooking, big turkey dinner, the works. And I, as mother of the family, was on. In previous years I had been gradually shifting some of the preparation to Alice, who liked to cook, but this year, in my strength, I had no excuse. Greg and his family would not be with us, but there would be plenty of action with both Robin's and Lisa's families here together.

So I hung Christmas lights on the porch, decorated the house with greens and candles, went shopping for presents, and bought a big Christmas tree. By now I was used to having everything be physically easy, but every so often I remembered what it had been like to do those things the year before. How long it had taken, how awkward and perilous it had been climbing the ladder to hang the lights, how I had bought only a small tree because a bigger one was too hard to set up, how I had shopped from catalogues.

Finally the day came when Lisa and her family would arrive. On the phone, I had warned Lisa that I looked different since the mountain trip, that maybe she wouldn't recognize me.

"Mother, I'd know you anywhere."

But she didn't. I met them at the airport bus as I always did. Lisa walked right by me looking for me beyond me.

Jocelyn recognized me. "Wow, Grandma, you look great." She grabbed her mother's sleeve. "Mom, she's right here."

Lisa spun around and stared.

"You walked right by me," I said. "Your own mother."

"Mother?" She put her hand to her mouth, her eyes huge. "What happened to you?"

"I said you might not recognize me." I held out my arms to her.

"I do now." She hugged me then and I held her close, Lisa, beloved daughter so seldom with me.

Phil was busy gathering up their bags. "Where's Clara?" he asked.

Jocelyn was having fun with the situation. "She's right here," she said laughing. "She's had a makeover. Doesn't she look great?"

Phil gave me a long look. "Whoa! She sure does. Hi, Clara." He gave me a hug, stared at me again, frowning, then turned back to the luggage.

As soon as we reached the house, Lisa called Robin. They had been bonded ever since the moment Lisa first held her newborn brother in her arms. Half an hour later, Robin and Alice and the children arrived. Jocelyn loved her younger cousins. She, like them, had no lack of dramatic fantasies to enact, and soon the three of them were tearing through the house with piercing screams. The adults were gathered around the dining room table, laughing, talking loudly.

I was putting on the teakettle when Colin came zooming through the kitchen in mad flight from monster Jocelyn. I caught him and spun him around, released him as Jocelyn came after him. I loved it.

And I could remember how in previous years it had almost been too much when all the family gathered, how I would retreat to my rocking chair and let the younger ones handle the children, make the tea.

The children took their screaming drama downstairs into the studio. Carrying the tea tray, I joined Lisa and Phil, Alice and Robin around the dining room table. I was quiet, listening as talk and news flew back and forth. Lisa was watching me with her keen blue eyes, wise from many years of working as a trauma therapist. I could feel her taking in every detail and knew she wasn't fooled by the makeover idea.

In a lull in conversation, Robin said, "Tell Lisa, Mama. She's going nuts trying to figure you out."

"Yes, please, Mother. What happened to you?"

I looked around the table. "This is not a story for the children. You and Phil must keep it an absolute secret. You'll understand why."

"We can keep a secret, Mother."

"And you may find it hard to believe."

Lisa shook her head. "It couldn't be harder to believe than the way you look, the way you are."

I thought of the Elirians every day, but, as I told my story, I was swept again with awe and stumbled for words as I tried to express their perfect love. Lisa, who had shared my spirit as a child so deeply she had to flee from me, never took her eyes off me. I looked into her face as I spoke and knew that she understood all I couldn't find words for.

Phil nodded his head. "Amazing. Very interesting creatures. But it's not so unbelievable, Clara. There's been talk of flying saucers for years. I bet there's lots of people who would like to connect with them as you did. I wouldn't mind being rejuvenated myself."

All through the familiar rituals of Christmas—the stockings, the special rolls for Christmas breakfast, the presents, the big turkey dinner, the pumpkin pie—I felt Lisa watching me.

Finally, the day after Christmas, when Robin and Alice took all three children to the zoo and Phil went off to visit some friends, Lisa and I curled up on the couch for a quiet talk.

"How is it, Mother?" she asked me. "What's it really like to be young again?"

"It's confusing," I confessed. "I thought I'd get used to it, but I haven't yet. I love having my body strong again, being able to dance and hike, do everything I want and not hurt. But it feels as if there's a responsibility that comes with it." I rubbed my brow.

"When I was old, I could just be lazy, take everything slow. People didn't expect much of me. But I felt as if I were doing something important, not in an outward way—inside. I don't know how to explain it. Maybe preparing for death, for the next cycle, whatever it will be. And now I don't have time for that. I'm caught up in the life of a young woman. But I'm not a young woman. I'm eighty."

She listened and more poured out. "I don't know how long I will live now. I've felt for years I didn't fit in this world anymore, it's gotten so impersonal and cyber-oriented. I was glad I'd be leaving it soon. And now—I might outlive you children. That's a terrible thought."

Lisa took my hand. "If you could, would you go back to how you were?"

I started. A shiver ran through me. That was a question I hadn't asked myself. I was shocked at the relief I felt just hearing it. But I couldn't answer it. I bent my face into my hands and began to cry. Lisa sat quietly beside me.

"I understand," she said. "You're incongruent. You have the spirit of an old woman and the body of a young one. That must be hard."

I nodded, shaken by a fresh round of weeping.

"But here I am," I sobbed. "Here I am, and everyone says how great I look and how wonderful that I have so much energy, and my massage is better than it ever was, and I can do all these challenging yoga postures, and hike all day, and dance all night if I want to. I should be grateful, and I *am* grateful not to ache and be tired all the time. I love that part." I spread my hands, an impatient gesture. "Anyhow, here I am. This is how it is."

A few days later Lisa and Phil and Jocelyn left to spend the New Year with Phil's mother. I took them to the station and we stood together in line for the bus. Lisa clung to me as we said good-bye. "Take care of yourself, Mother." The line began to move. Phil and Jocelyn hugged me. Lisa hugged me again, and they climbed on. They waved to me from the window, the bus pulled out, and they were gone. It might be a year or more before I would see them again.

The house felt as empty as if a huge vacuum cleaner had roared through and sucked all the life out of it. I set about returning my studio from guest room to work place. As I carried a bundle of linens and pillows up the stairs, a single word rose in my mind.

Incongruent.

Chapter 6

Choice

After I put the laundry in, I fled the empty house. It was beginning to snow lightly, fine flakes drifting down. I walked quickly, my staff in my hand, my cloak wrapped tightly around me.

I had been so busy the last few days that I'd had little time to process my talk with Lisa. Now as it flowed back to me, I was haunted by her question. Would I? Would I want to go back as I was, a congruent old woman?

I felt my strong, easy stride, my vibrant health, and remembered the constant low-grade pain, background for sharper pain, the unsteady heart, aching knees, fatigue. No. I didn't want to go back to that. But…

I circled the lake, gray reflecting the gray sky, snow melting into its surface. Wind moved across the open water, blowing snow into my face, sharp and cold against my cheeks. On the far side of the lake I took the path up the ridge. I climbed as fast as I could, my legs powerful, my heart robust, but I couldn't outrun the question. At the highest point I sat down, settled my back against a lone leaning pine, tightened my hood around my face, and stared out into swirling snow. Mid-winter dusk was already descending.

I wish I could speak with the Elirians, I thought. I wonder if it's true they don't understand aging. I wonder how they're doing, if they're finding other people to study, what they're learning. I hope they're safe.

I bent my head down on my drawn-up knees. A thread of song wound through my memory, their voices singing to me as we parted. *We are with you always. You can call on us anytime and we will answer.*

Oh! I leaped to my feet. Before I even intended, I called. *Kiria, Lillilia, Tirini, Rosiri, Merilea, can you hear me?*

Music flooded my heart, all their voices singing together. *We hear you. We are near. We are returning a child to Earth. Then we will come to you. We see your light on the hillside.*

I will wait here for you. I sank down again, lost in wonder that they really had heard my call.

Night folded around me and snow settled on my hood and shoulders, but I was not cold; the warmth of their voices lingered in my heart and spread through me. I tilted my head back against the tree trunk and looked up. I don't know how long I waited, aquiver with anticipation.

Then, all at once, among the swirling snowflakes, gleaming silver in the night, their ship appeared and hovered above me. The door slid open. I glimpsed the warm light within, and Kiria floated out. I stood, reaching my hands up toward her. She caught them with two of hers, drew me up to her and wrapped her other three arms around me. Cradling me close to her heart as she had on the night I was dying, she carried me into the ship. The door slid closed and the ship rose up. The other four gathered around and passed me from one to the other as if I were a newborn child. Each one held me close to her heart. Their voices wove, singing, *Welcome, Clara.*

I breathed in the ineffable fragrance of the rainbow air circling around us and felt I would burst with joy to be with them again. As we settled in a circle on the soft, warm floor, Lillilia on one side of me, Tirini on the other, holding my hands, I looked into their deep, luminous eyes. They were smiling.

How are you? I asked, remembering to still my voice and ask with thought. *How does your work go? Have you found many people to study?*

Kiria sang. *There are so many of you, like seeds broken from a seedpod, scattered over all the Earth. We in our ship study this continent you call North America. We have brought up many to study and heal. You told us *truly that you are alike in the parts of your bodies and your organs, but you are all so different in other ways. It is wondrous how many of you there are, each singing a tiny, unique fraction of Earth's song. So complex you each are, so very complex that song.*

The others joined in. *We found a male who almost died going fast in the snow on a mountain on… skis, he called them. He hit a tree.*

Their songs poured through me.

We have found children. Some are dying because they do not have enough to eat. They cannot live on light. We heal them, but then must put them back and fear for them.

We brought up a female with her baby dying in her arms and healed them both and learned how a female feeds her child from her breast. As you told us.

We have rescued some from crashes when your cars run into each other.

It is harder to reach those in the cities. Our ship is shielded, but we are not, and there are so many people day and night.

Oh, be careful! I broke in, terrified by an image of some ruffian seizing one of them and carrying her away, fur flying.

We are. We have found some on rooftops, in parks, deserted streets. Everyone is different. People in cities have a different song than those in the mountains.

Or the desert, or the farmlands.

Some cannot hear our voices, cannot communicate with us, do not believe we are real, even though we heal them.

There is so much sadness. Rosiri's song dipped to a minor key. *They don't listen to the love in their hearts. Some do not even seem to know it is there.*

And fear, Merilea sang in her rich, deep voice. *We have not experienced fear before. Its song is dark and acid. It withers.*

It is not their essence, Lillilia sang. *But they have forgotten their essence. Except for a few, like you.*

They were silent. I saw in their eyes something I had not seen on my first visit. They had tasted the sorrow of Earth, and they grieved.

Kiria touched me with her seven-fingered hand. *You called us. There is trouble in your heart?*

Yes, I answered. *Not terrible trouble, but I am confused, an old woman in a young body. Incongruent.*

Incongruent? They sang the word back and forth, tuning in to me, seeking its meaning.

Do you understand aging? I asked. *On Eliria do you get old, do your bodies wear out?*

No, Rosiri answered. Her song held a puzzled note. *We sink back into our planet.*

They speak of pain, Tirini added, her gold-flecked eyes troubled. *We feel their pain, but we of Eliria do not have pain of our own. We did not know of pain until we came here.*

What a blessed life you have! I exclaimed. How terrible Earth must seem to them. I thought of all the pain of incarnate existence— hunger, exhaustion, cold, high fevers, spasmed muscles, broken bones, headaches, heartaches. All the fears—losing your mother, snakes under the bed, being different from the others, not having enough money, being abandoned, being helpless, dying.

Do you die? I asked. *When your ulada is complete and you sink back into your planet, do you die?*

The council told us about dying and death on Earth, so we know of it. Lillilia's pale pink fur fluttered. *We knew you were dying when we found you, but we do not die.*

We sink into Eliria, they all sang together. *We sink into her heart and rest until we are called again.*

And when you are called again, I asked, *are you the same? The same iridescence, the same name?*

Yes, we must be, Kiria answered. *We each hold a part of Eliria's song.*

I sat silent. Then they didn't know. They didn't understand what they had done for me.

Lillilia still held my hand. *Tell us more. Speak to us of aging. We only begin to understand.*

When we are born, I explained, *we are all new, though our bodies need to grow and develop. Then we are grown, in our prime we call it. Most of us mate and have children. Then our bodies begin to wear out. We get sick, our organs don't work as well, our joints get stiff and hurt. That's what we call aging. Finally something vital fails and we die. It's like the seasons of our Earth—the newness of spring, the fullness of summer, the withering of fall, the death of winter.*

They were watching me closely, their luminous eyes puzzled and intent. *So when you found me,* I told them, *I was old.*

We remember, Tirini sang. *Your body did not express your essence. Only the light within you did.*

When you changed my body to express my essence, you made me young again. But inside I am still old. You said my ulada was almost complete, but I won't die unless I get sick or hurt until I grow old again. It could be many years. That is the incongruence—my young body and my ulada almost complete.

We sat in silence again. Outside the big windows I could see that the snow had stopped and stars shone between the scattering clouds.

We have much to learn. Lillilia's high, sweet song was muted. *Speak to us of dying. What happens when you die?*

We don't know.

Their songs wove in puzzlement and concern. *You don't know? Do you sink into your Earth?*

We can't sink in as you do. If we left a body lying on the earth—it sometimes happens when a person dies alone and is not found—then it would deteriorate and finally sink in. But there are so many of us and the body smells as it deteriorates, so we burn the body and scatter the ashes, or dig a hole and bury it. We have places we call graveyards. We mark the places where our people are buried with big stones carved with the person's name, to remember them, because we don't come back the way you do. When a person dies it is the end of that body, that name. That we know.

A burst of song rippled through me, the Elirians exclaiming to one another.

What we don't know is what happens to the spirit of that person, I went on. *Some say it dies with the body. Others say the spirit lives on. There are many stories.* In spite of myself I felt them receiving images of blank blackness, angels on clouds, wheels of incarnation, tunnels of light. *Some say it will be this way. Others say no, it will be that way. And many become frightened when they hear a story different from their own, because if that story is true, then maybe theirs isn't. They may become so afraid they kill the ones whose story is different from theirs.*

You kill over a story? Merilea asked, her dark eyes wide with shock.

Her incredulity touched a pit of despair within me.

Yes, I answered. *Because we are afraid. Because it is unknown. Much of the violence on Earth is because we fear death. We fight over things that we hope will protect us from death, but in the end nothing does. We walk on the brink of the unknown and try to hide from it, deny it. But inside we all know we will die, and most of us are afraid. Some aren't. Some trust in their story and die peacefully. Some are so tired of sorrow and struggle they are glad to die and end it. And some seek to end it, to kill themselves, because they feel life is too hard, too painful.*

My throat thickened as I remembered a day when I had been so crushed by loneliness and despair that I had almost thrown myself into a rushing mountain stream, seeking a quick, cold death.

The Elirians caught my image. *Ah,* they sang.

It's all right. I didn't, I told them. *As you see.*

I looked out the window, swallowing back the tears that clogged my throat even though that day had been thirty years ago. The clouds were gone, the sky pinpricked with the cold clarity of winter stars. I turned back to the warmth and love in the eyes of my companions.

Sometimes, I told them, *we humans think that because we are going to die anyway it doesn't matter what we do. That nothing matters.*

They responded with a burst of song that rose, passed among them, and became a polyphony.

It matters.
When you hold the light,
When you are kind,
When you laugh and are happy,
When you create harmony among you,
The web eases.
The whole universe shifts.

The lines of words and melody interwove, repeating, until coming at last into a unison finale: *It matters.*

The sweetness and power of their song loosed the tears I had been holding back. Many hands touched me, soothing me.

Are you afraid to die? Rosiri asked me.

Yes. No. Sometimes. I drew in my breath and wiped the tears from my face. *But I fear also to live too long, to see my children die before me, to be out of harmony with the seasons of my life.*

A question was rising in me, pressing on me, a question far more fearful than the one that had pursued me up the ridge. I struggled with it, not wanting to face it, much less express it. Then I realized that the Elirians had known it for some time, perhaps from the moment I first called them.

Could you… my thought stammered to them, *would you… if I asked… Could you put me back as you found me?*

They were silent, their loving, luminous eyes resting on me. Their fur fluttered.

You were in such pain, Kiria sang.

Yes. I shivered with the memory. *I'm not asking you to, only asking if you could.*

We could. Rosiri touched me gently with her seven-fingered hand. *We would have to fold time.*

We could, Tirini sang softly, *but only when we are here circling your Earth.*

I shivered with fear, remembering the terrible night of paralysis, death descending. *Could you put me back, but keep me from dying just then?*

Again song wove among them. *Yes,* Kiria answered, *we could stay with you and keep you warm until your people came for you.*

We were silent then. They gathered close around me, their soft fur enfolding me, their hearts beating against me, their arms around me. So many arms to hold me.

Is that why you called us? Lillilia asked. *To ask us that question?*

Yes. I nestled my face against her silken pink fur. *Yes. But I didn't know when I called you; I only knew I was confused.*

It is possible, Kiria sang, *but we sense that you don't want us to change you now, maybe not ever. You are glad of the strength and health of your body?*

Oh, yes. I lifted my face from Lillilia's fur. *Please do not think me ungrateful. I love being strong, not hurting, being able to dance and hike and work again, my heart beating steadily. You have given me a great gift.*

Their eyes were smiling. Lillilia stroked my hair with a gentle hand. *We, too, are grateful. You have taught us more than any other we have found.* It was Kiria's song in my heart. *The light within you is a gift, the same whether you are young or old.*

How long will you be here, circling Earth, studying us?

Our ulada has called us here for one of Earth's years, Tirini answered. *The thread of the web we traveled on connects to your mountain. We will return there one year from the time we found you and from there we will leave Earth.*

I would like to see you again before you depart, learn how your mission went. Just be with you. I couldn't bear to think of them leaving.

We would like to be with you again, too, Lillilia sang. *Can you come to us on your mountain, one year from the day we found you?*

Yes. Easily.

Their voices blended. *Then we'll meet you there, hold you next to our hearts, and bid you farewell.*

Will you stay with us tonight? Kiria sang. *We would welcome your presence. We are so glad to see you again.*

Yes. My heart spread wings. *I never want to leave you, though I know we must take separate paths.*

Not until morning, they sang together.

I slept in their arms, enfolded in their shining silken fur until the first red of sunrise brightened the meeting of plains and sky. Tirini brought the ship almost to the ground. I embraced them, touching my heart to each of their hearts. The door slid open. I jumped out onto the snowy hillside. As I watched their ship ascend and speed above the plains into the rising sun, their song still sang in my heart.

Slowly I descended the ridge. The lake below was rimmed with snow, white against blue.

"They could," I whispered to myself, "but only until they leave the Earth. Only until my next birthday."

Chapter 7

Zachary

For many years it had been my habit on New Year's Eve to curl up in my rocking chair by the wood stove and read over my journal for the past year. But this year, feeling my vitality, I thought, why not… ?

There was always a big tango dance in Denver on New Year's Eve. I could carpool with Tim and Sally. Before the Elirians had touched me, I had given up on dances in Denver, not feeling confident enough in my night driving skills to go alone, and never wanting to stay as late as those I might ride with. But now—

I called Tim. Yes, he and Sally were going and he'd be happy to give me a ride.

I was excited. It would be a big dance. When the day came, I washed my hair, shaved my legs, and searched through my closet. I chose flowing pants of silver satin (that I had made long ago to cover my knee braces), a sparkly, tight-fitting silver top, and long, blue lapis earrings with a matching necklace. When I was dressed, standing in front of the bathroom mirror to put the final touches on my makeup, I admired my reflection. I did love being beautiful. Especially for tango.

The Turnverein Ballroom in Denver was a fine example of early twentieth century elegance, with its high ceiling, tall, arched windows, and crystal chandeliers. The dance floor was filling rapidly when we arrived. I began the evening with Tim, and danced steadily for several hours with one partner after another.

When at last I had a break, I sat wrapped in my blue shawl, watching, drinking in the music, noting with interest who was there and who was dancing with whom. A young man, someone I hadn't seen before, danced by. He was quite handsome, with dark curly hair, a small curly mustache, striking blue eyes, and a trim athletic build. He danced well, the movements of his feet clean and precise.

When we women want to know if a man is a good dancer we check out his feet, but even more important we observe the expression on his partner's face. This man's partner looked absolutely blissful, eyes closed, a half smile on her lips. Mmm, I thought. I'll try and catch his eye at the end of this *tanda*.

The proper way for a man to invite a woman to dance in tango world is to make eye contact across the room. If she assents with a nod or smile, only then does he cross the room to stand before her and hold out his hand. That glance is called the *cabecceo*, and the custom evolved to protect the man's fragile ego, so he would never have to face the humiliation of being seen asking a woman to dance and refused. It didn't always work so well for the women. Several times, before I learned better, I stood when a man approached me, thinking he had his eye on me, only to find he was inviting the woman next to me. Embarrassing.

At the end of each *tanda*, the men escort their partners to their seats and then look around for their next partner. I kept my eye on the man with the curly dark hair. He was scanning the room. When he met my gaze, he looked startled, stared a moment, then tilted his head slightly, giving me a clear *cabecceo*. I nodded and watched him approach. There was something about his eyes.

I rose to meet him, slipped off my shawl, placed my right hand in his left, and stepped into the curve of his arm. After a few steps I moved closer, draping my left arm lightly around his shoulders. He gathered me in and I rested my brow against his cheek. His embrace was luscious and he was indeed a good dancer, his lead subtle and sure, guiding me into delightfully unusual patterns. I let myself go into tango trance.

About halfway around the room, he whispered in my ear, "You have Elirian eyes."

I stumbled. He caught me with his arm, lifted me, covered for me. We continued dancing. I tilted my head back to look at him. That's what it was about his eyes! "You do, too," I breathed.

"We'll talk later," he said softly, "Dance now. You're terrific."

We danced. At the end of the *tanda*, he did not take me to my seat, but asked, "*Uno mas?*"

"*Con gusto*," I answered, and we danced again, our bodies one, living the music. I had never had such a skillful partner. At the end of the third *tanda* I felt tears of bliss spilling over when I looked up at him.

"Do you always cry when you dance tango?" he asked as he kissed a tear off my cheek.

"Never before."

"Come." He took my hand and led me to a table off to the side of the ballroom. "Can I get you something to drink?"

"Yes, thank you. But no alcohol. I can't drink and dance."

He smiled, his amazing blue eyes crinkling at the corners. "They have sparkling cider."

"Perfect."

He left me, weaving between the dancers crowded around the refreshment table. I watched him, noting how gracefully he moved. He was soon back with two glasses of sparkling cider and a plate of cheese and crackers. He sat down opposite me at the small table, reached out and took my hand.

"My name is Zachary."

"I'm Clara."

We looked into each other's Elirian eyes.

"How did you meet them?" he asked.

"I got caught in the high country by a thunderstorm, was struck by lightning and paralyzed, soaked by the rain, dying of cold in the night. They came and carried me to their ship and healed me. And you?"

"I was skiing. I always go off the groomed slopes because there are so many people. I hit a tree. Would have been done for. The same thing.

They came for me and fixed me all up, then set me back down by the tree that should have killed me. My skis were there, totally shattered. I had a long hike out in the deep snow, but I was fine. It was like… like they made me better than I was before."

So he was the one they had spoken of, on skis, hitting a tree.

"They did that for me, too, made me way better than I was before." I didn't want to tell him I was eighty, not yet, lost as I was in the magic of the evening. "I was off the trail, too. I know what you mean about too many people."

We were silent again. His hand was warm around mine.

"That was the wildest, most awesome experience." His eyes went vague with wonder. "You know"—he looked at me intently again— "I had just about decided it was a dream, that somehow I had gotten lucky, even though my skis were toast. That it couldn't be real, until tonight when I saw you, your eyes. It brought it all back."

"It wasn't a dream. They're real. I met them again just a few days ago and spent the night in their ship."

"No kidding. Were you in trouble again?"

"No, not like before. I just needed to talk with them. I called them and they came, and we talked a long time about aging and dying on Earth. They don't age or die; they wanted to understand. Did they tell you they had come to study us?"

He rubbed his brow with his free hand. "Yeah, now that you mention it, they did. They were real interested in male and female. Asked me a lot about what it was like to be male."

"What did you tell them?"

"That it was cool. That I liked it. I do, especially tonight dancing with you."

We laughed, not because there was anything funny really, but because we were falling in love. That kind of laughter.

"You remember everything about when you were with them?" he asked.

"Vividly."

"Wow. It sure slipped away from me. 'Till I saw you. Did you say you called them?"

"Yes, they told me when they set me back down on the mountain that I could call them anytime. So I did."

They're real, huh?"

"Definitely."

"You talked about aging and dying?"

"Yes."

"Deep."

The music for the next *tanda* began. Zachary lifted his head. "It's a *milonga*. Let's go." Still holding my hand, he led me out onto the floor and into the dance.

Milonga is the liveliest and most playful of the tango rhythms, and Zachary was the most exciting *milonga* partner I'd ever had. He held me close against him. Our feet flew, as he led me into unexpected combinations, sudden pauses, dashes around the floor, until I laughed with delight. By the end of the first song, we were both laughing, that same falling-in-love laughter.

We danced together the rest of the night. When midnight approached, the music stopped and champagne was passed. We all toasted the New Year, 2012, and healing the world through tango. I thought of the Elirians singing *When you laugh and are happy, it matters.* At midnight, someone rang a loud bell and we all cheered, and Zachary kissed me, a deep kiss on my mouth, such a kiss as I had not felt for more than a decade, maybe ever. Passion swept through me. I had forgotten those feelings, that intensity. *Oh, my God!* I thought and wrapped my arms around Zachary and returned the kiss.

We danced again, time lost in tango trance. As we paused between *tandas*, Tim tapped me on the shoulder. "We're heading home now."

"Oh." I looked up at Zachary. "I need to go. My ride is leaving." I gave him a hug and turned toward Tim.

"Wait, Clara." Zachary caught my hand. "When will I see you again?"

"I'll be at the Avalon on Sunday." I hugged him one more time. "Thank you for the most delicious tango night ever." Then I slipped out of his arms and fled. Separating from him felt like tearing Velcro apart.

"That guy sure monopolized you," Tim complained as he helped me into the car. "I only got one *tanda* with my favorite partner."

He and Sally sat up front. I sat in the back in a daze as we spun through the night city. I was moist between the legs and my eighty-year-old consciousness was topsy-turvy.

"Did you tell him how old you are?" Tim asked as he swung onto I-25.

"No!" Sally exclaimed, indignant. "She shouldn't. She looks fabulous and young. She doesn't need to tell him how old she is."

"I didn't," I confessed. "Not yet."

❧ ❧

It was 2:30 when I let myself in my back door. I was tired, but had such a buzz overlaying the fatigue that I was dubious about the possibility of sleep. I took a warm bath, drank a cup of hot milk, and lay down. Tango music throbbed through my body. I kept seeing Zachary's blue eyes with the slight Elirian tilt at the corners, reliving his kiss and the feel of his body becoming one with mine as we danced. Liquid fire ran in my blood. I tossed from side to side. Finally I threw off the covers and got up.

I wrapped a blanket around myself, sat down on the pillow in front of my altar, and lit a candle.

All right, Clara Norwood, I admonished myself. What do you think you're doing?

The candle flickered. I tried to quiet my breath. Never mind, I told myself as I breathed studiously in and out. Never mind that he has just the kind of looks you most love, dark curly hair and blue eyes like your father. Never mind that he has such a luscious, elegant body, and not too tall so you fit perfectly in his arms. Never mind that he is a divine dancer and danced with you all night. He could be your grandson.

Back to the breath. Slow. In. Out. Cool at the nostrils as you breathe in, warm as you breathe out.

"Deep," he says. You'd better believe he's not troubling his curly pate about aging and dying. He's still on the upswing. Thinks he's immortal. Skiing into trees.

Back to the breath.

You know perfectly well how tango creates a romantic illusion. There we all are, dressed up in our best, dancing this sensuous, seductive dance to beautiful music. What does that have to do with life? Nothing.

Breathe.

You also know perfectly well it is considered poor form, even though the dance is seductive, to let yourself get turned on.

I didn't until he kissed me.

But then you kissed him back. Fool. Remember who you are.

Who am I?

Breathe.

Memories poured over me. All the years after Jon left that I'd searched for a new partner—desperately, that was the trouble. The nights I woke in anguish, longing for touch, for belonging with someone, for a life companion. All the tries and failures. The several years of fruitless on-line dating services. Finally, at age seventy-five, letting it go, accepting my singleness.

Fool, I told myself. Do not let one handsome young man, one kiss, upset that fragile peace.

Breathe. In. Out. Gradually I quieted.

My head jerking forward woke me. I opened my eyes and saw out my east window bare tree branches, black against the red of sunrise.

It was a week until the Sunday night dance at the Avalon, so I had plenty of time to think about my next meeting with Zachary.

If he came.

Oh, the insanity of romance, the uncertainty, the anticipation. Will he be there? Will he dance with me again? What if he becomes infatuated with a different partner? What shall I wear? My inner old woman shook her head at my fluster.

Careful, she cautioned. Remember Dan, how romantic he was at first. Then how he just walked out one day to live with a woman fifteen years younger than you, with bigger breasts and longer hair. Leaving you, the worn-out wife, to bring up the children alone.

I did remember. The anguish of his betrayal still seared me whenever it surfaced. I pushed it aside. It's different now, I told my inner old woman. I know what I'm doing. She didn't believe me.

On Sunday night Zachary was there. His face lit up when he saw me enter the ballroom. He hurried toward me without even the caution of a *cabecceo*. With even less caution I ran to meet him. He embraced me in the middle of the floor while the music of a waltz filled the hall and dancers swirled around us.

"Clara, I'm so glad you came. I couldn't believe I let you go the other night without a phone number, any way I could reach you. I don't even know your last name."

"It's Norwood," I told him. "I don't know yours either."

"Conner. Let's dance."

Going into his embrace was like coming home, already so dear and familiar. We danced the whole evening together. Once I saw Tim frowning at us and knew I shouldn't ignore an old friend, but the magic of dancing with Zachary overrode loyalty.

Partway through the evening we sat together at one of the tables, getting acquainted in the way one does with words. He was a software engineer with IBM, had just transferred from Seattle. I focused our conversation on him, not feeling ready yet to reveal myself. It wasn't hard. He liked to talk about himself. When he got around to asking what I did, I told him I was a massage therapist.

He'd had massage and loved it. "I had this kinky back problem. When I was sixteen I took a pretty bad fall doing competitive ski jumping. The massage helped a lot. But you know… I just realized it still always bugged me until those furry aliens came along and fixed me up. I knew I felt better, but didn't connect it until just now. I guess they must be real."

"You live dangerously," I noted. "Ski jumping."

"Yes." His eyes sparkled. His smile curved up under his curly mustache and my heart flipped, remembering the brush of that mustache when he kissed me. "And dancing with you is one of the more dangerous things I've done."

Little do you know how dangerous, I thought. But I said nothing. Not yet.

A waltz *tanda* came on and we danced again, melting into each other until the last song of the night. He walked with me to the coatroom. "I'm not going to let you get away this time without a phone number."

I searched in my dance bag for a card. It was an old one, but my number hadn't changed. He took the card and put it in his wallet. "Will you have dinner with me? I want to get to know you better."

"I'd love to."

"I'll call you."

He walked me to my car, took me into his arms, and kissed me long and deep, until my knees went weak.

I lectured myself all the way home as I tried to calm my racing hormones. You can't keep this up, I told myself. It's insane. You have to tell him he's kissing a woman old enough to be his grandma. As I turned into the garage, I resolved to tell him over dinner.

Two evenings later we met in the elegant dining room of the St Julian Hotel. I asked the host for a corner table, requesting the quietest possible place so the background noise of the restaurant wouldn't overwhelm my fading hearing. Only after we were seated did I realize I didn't need to do that anymore.

Zachary looked especially handsome in a blue silk shirt that enhanced his vivid blue eyes. He ordered wine, and we studied our menus. I held mine out at arm's length.

"What are you doing?" he asked.

Embarrassed, I put it back on the table. I could see it perfectly.

"Would you like an appetizer?" he asked.

I looked up at him and forgot about the menu, drawn in by his eyes. "I wonder if they give the shape of their eyes to everyone they touch."

"What? Who?"

"The Elirians. We recognized each other because of our eyes."

"Oh, right. But I was checking you out before I saw your eyes. You have a great bod and you were dazzling when Bob led you through all those turns."

"I was checking you out, too."

He chuckled and lifted his wine glass. "To us. Tango partners supreme." His face grew serious. "And much more, I hope." We touched glasses with a light musical clink, and each took a sip, looking into each other's eyes.

I was shaking inside. Now. I told myself. Now. Don't let this go on any longer. "Zachary, there's something I need to tell you."

He took another sip of wine and put down his glass. His cell phone rang. He had it handy, clipped onto his belt. "Excuse me a minute. Hey there, Meg… Yeah… Cool… I'm fine." A long pause. "Sure, send it to me. I'd love to see it." The conversation went on and on. I turned my attention to my menu, but couldn't focus, nervous and increasingly irritated.

"Okay," Zachary said. "Hey, listen, I'm out to dinner with this gorgeous woman… Yeah, I will. Good to talk to you. Night, honey."

He clicked off his phone and slipped it back onto his belt. "My sister. She's sending me a picture of her kid with Santa Claus. She's got the cutest little boy. You started to tell me something?"

"Yes." I swallowed. "I'm not quite as I seem—"

His phone beeped. He pulled it out again. "Wait a minute." He opened it. "Great. Here's the picture. Look at that. What a sweetie." He held his phone out to me across the table. The picture on the small screen showed a little boy, about three, sitting on the knee of a young-looking Santa Claus, whose belly pillow had slipped a bit to one side.

"He's cute," I said politely. "Looks sort of like you."

"My nephew. He's the first grandkid in the family, even though my sister's younger than I am. We're all so proud of him. Chris is his name." He turned the screen back to look at it again, sighed, closed the phone, and put it away. "I want to have kids someday. How about you?"

It was an opening.

"I don't know quite how to tell you this, but I'm not as I seem—"

"Don't tell me." I had his attention now. "You're lesbian."

"No. I have to tell you that—"

"You're married?"

"No. What you need to know is… the Elirians found me on my eightieth birthday."

"What? Eighteenth?"

"No, eightieth. I'm really an old woman, Zachary. The Elirians gave me a young body when they saved my life, but I'm really eighty years old."

"No way!" He laughed. "Clara, you're teasing me. What an idea! Don't look so serious."

I was sweating, my stomach clenched. "I'm not teasing. I'm an old woman. I already have three kids. The oldest two are fifty-five and fifty-six. I have five grandchildren, and the oldest of them is already twenty."

"Clara, what are you talking about?" His brow was furrowed.

"I'm telling you who I am. I thought you should know before we get any more involved."

"What a wild idea. You couldn't be eighty, you're so luscious."

"I am. Eighty, I mean. One reason I'm so sure the Elirians are real, not a dream, is because they completely transformed my life. They didn't know. They didn't understand aging. So when they found me, an old woman with all kinds of failings even before I was hit by lightning, they just healed everything, like they did your back, everything, including my white hair and wrinkles and unsteady heart."

I stopped, holding my breath. I could feel tears coming into my eyes. He stared at me. "I don't believe it."

"Please. It's true. I'm old enough to be your grandma."

"No way." He shook his head. "No way. They couldn't do that."

"They healed your back. They brought you back to life when you should have died. They've done that for lots of other people. They told me about it. They're miraculous healers from another planet, so different from ours we can't have any concept of what they can do."

A waitress appeared beside our table. "Are you ready to order?"

"Not yet, thank you," Zachary said.

Even in my tumult, I noticed how courteously he spoke to her. She moved away.

Zachary turned back to me. He reached across the table and brushed a tear off my cheek. "Clara, don't cry. It's okay. I don't understand yet, but we'll get it straight. Maybe the lightning…"

I pressed my lips together so as not to cry anymore. I was undone by the way he touched my cheek to brush away my tear, the way he sought to comfort me. I should have known from dancing with him that he would be sensitive and caring. Why else would I have surrendered so completely to his embrace?

"Look," he said. "Let's order. I'm starved and you probably are, too. We can talk more about this when our blood sugar is restored."

I nodded and focused again on my menu, but I couldn't see anything, my eyes blurred with tears. We were silent, he perusing the menu, I struggling to control myself. After a bit, he said, "I eat here often. Their curried shrimp is quite good. Would you like to try that?"

I looked up gratefully and sniffed back my tears. "That sounds great."

While he beckoned to the waitress and placed our order, I found a tissue in my pocket and blew my nose. He took another sip of wine. "This is a very nice wine. Try it."

I hadn't touched mine since we clinked glasses. I took a sip. It was smooth and slightly sweet, warm in my throat.

"Do you go to tango festivals?" he asked.

"Only the ones in Denver. I hear they have a good one in Seattle once a year."

"They do. I also like to get to the ones in Portland and Tucson and San Diego."

"That's a lot of festivals."

"What can I say?" He smiled, his mustache curling. "I live to tango."

I took another sip of wine, seeking to compose myself. "How long have you been dancing?"

"Ten years." He went on to tell me how he began, who his favorite teachers were. I had studied with some of them when they came as guests to our Denver festivals. We compared notes on their teaching styles.

Then we spoke of our families of origin. I said nothing more about my children or grandchildren.

Zachary buttered bread for me and I ate, sipped more wine, and got a little tipsy. Our dinner came.

I asked him if he had a spiritual path.

"Not really. I've just been too busy with life. I'm not opposed to spirituality or anything. I guess nature is my temple. When I'm out in the mountains or by the ocean, that's when I feel most connected to… God, something beyond myself. How about you?"

"Nature is sacred for me, too. But I've tried a lot of things—Christianity, yoga, Sufism, shamanism. Most recently I've been influenced by Buddhism, but they all flow together into one path for me." I didn't enumerate all the years I'd spent with each tributary to my path.

He looked at me searchingly, frowning again. "That's a lot of exploration." He took another sip of wine. "Tell me how you got into massage."

We ate and talked. I felt as if I were holding down a volcano inside of me. At the same time I was enjoying our conversation, delighting in his elegance and grace.

At one point his phone rang again. He excused himself, and talked to someone, apparently from work. Much of the conversation on his end was a jumble of letters and formulas that made no sense to me. It could have been a foreign language, except for the occasional English word. While he talked, I incubated a plan.

Dessert came, chocolate mousse.

"You said you have kids?" he asked.

"Yes. Three. A daughter and two sons."

"You've been married?"

"Twice, but I've been single for almost thirty years now."

"That's about how old I figured you were. Thirty."

"Add fifty and you'll be right on."

"Clara, there's no way I can believe that story."

"I know. When you take me home, how about coming in for some tea? I'd like to show you some pictures."

❧ ❧

He looked around my living room as I hung up his coat. "You've got a sweet little place here. Cozy."

"It's home. Come on in the kitchen and tell me what kind of tea you'd like."

He picked out his tea and a green mug from the ones hanging on the wall above the counter. As we waited for the water to boil, he stood behind me and wrapped his arms around me. I leaned my head back against his shoulder and we blended together as we had when we danced.

"Ah, Clara," he murmured. He kissed my hair, my cheeks, my neck, sending electricity streaking through me. The teakettle whistled.

I drew myself out of his arms. We took our tea to the dining room table and I pulled a pile of photo albums out of the cupboard under the bookshelves.

For the next hour I showed him pictures. Me as a child with my bicycle, my stuffed panda, a kerchief tied over my hair and under my chin as we did in the forties. My high school graduation picture—fifties hair style. Wedding pictures of me and Dan. The portrait taken of me at age twenty-two when I started teaching elementary school. He stopped my hand from turning the page and looked closely at the portrait, then at me.

"You look almost the same, but you're more beautiful now. I don't quite get what it is."

"At that time in my life I was uncomfortable with myself. That's what you're seeing. Years of spiritual practice have changed that. There are some gifts to aging."

"Getting more comfortable with yourself. I could use that."

I showed him pictures of me holding baby Lisa.

"You look kind of tense," he commented.

"I was. I loved her so much I wanted to be a perfect mother. And perfect is not a word you can apply to parenting."

Pictures of Lisa and Greg growing up. Pictures of me and Jon and our wedding in the forest, all of us dressed in beautiful, flowing, hippie-style clothes. Pictures of me holding newborn Robin, my hair already showing its first streaks of gray. Pictures of my children's weddings. Pictures of my grandchildren.

I took him to my computer to show him more recent pictures, ones I'd used for on-line dating in my late sixties and early seventies, my hair still curly, but white, my face creased in wrinkles, my smile the same. Last I showed him a family portrait taken at my eightieth birthday family reunion last July—before my birthday, but the only time I could get everyone together. They were all there, Lisa and Phil and Jocelyn, Greg and his wife and children, Robin and Alice, Katie and Colin, and I at the center, my wrinkled face beaming, my hair unruly as usual.

He looked a long time at that picture, then turned away from the computer. On my desk was a picture of me and Robin, sitting on the couch together, taken last summer before my transformation.

Zachary touched it. "You're wearing the same blouse you have on tonight."

"Yes. One good thing was that I didn't change size much when they healed me, so my clothes still fit."

He leaned his elbow on the desk and dropped his head into his hand. I saw that final detail had clinched it for him.

"I get it." His voice was choked. "It's totally weird, but I get it."

I got up from the computer and went to kneel by his chair, looking up into his face. I laid my hand on his knee. "I'm sorry," I said. "I should have told you sooner, but I was enchanted. I never danced with anyone who matched me so perfectly, invited me to dance all I knew of tango, and taught me more. Maybe we can still dance together. I hope so. But we shouldn't fall in love or anything like that."

He lifted his head and looked long into my eyes, touched my cheek, my hair. "Too late," he said.

He got up. "I have to go. I need to think about all this. I'll call. I promise."

We walked in silence to the front door. I helped him on with his coat. He took me in his arms and held me tight. Then he left, his feet swift on the porch steps.

I gathered up the albums and put them away. Now you've done it, I told myself. He'll never call. He shouldn't. But I couldn't have done anything else. Exhausted by emotion, I went to bed and slept.

Two hours later I woke, every inch of my skin crying out with touch-longing. All the desires I had painstakingly folded away for the last five years came crashing back like an ocean storm breeching the levees.

Zachary was right. It was too late.

Chapter 8

Sweet and Bitter

For the next three days, I jumped whenever the phone rang, told myself he wouldn't call, maybe he would, he shouldn't, asked myself what I would do if he did. On and on.

Inner old woman laughed at me. Remember Jon? she began.

Hush, I told her. The memory of Jon was still a knife under the heart. I had loved him without reserve. We had told each other we were soul mates. Then, when Robin was only ten, Jon became restless, unilaterally decided we should have an open marriage, and neglected me for one young woman after another. When I finally couldn't bear it anymore and insisted on monogamy, he was gone in a month and we never heard from him again. Robin still carried the pain of that abandonment, and I struggled with it for years, unbelieving.

Inner old woman persisted. About this Zachary. Let it go, she advised me. Just let it go. It won't work. Easier to let it go sooner than later. I knew she was right.

But my body was young and full of desire. Never had I felt more incongruent.

On Friday afternoon, at 3:30, when the phone rang it was Zachary. "Let's take a walk," he said without preamble.

"Okay."

"I'll be right over."

Before I had time to do more than run a comb through my hair, he was at the front door. He came in and hugged me tight. "Let's go."

I searched his face. He was holding in emotion, but I couldn't tell what kind. I put on my boots and cloak and followed him out the door.

It was cold at the lake, the sun already low over the hills, the fields hushed under their blanket of snow. We walked without speaking, but our hands found each other. Even through our gloves, I felt the warmth and comfort of his touch. We circled the lake and headed up the ridge. Without planning to, I found I was leading him to the place I often sat to muse, the place where the Elirians had come to me only two weeks before. I wondered where they were now. They had spoken of going north. I imagined them rescuing an Eskimo from sea ice or the jaws of a polar bear.

There was some bare earth scattered with pine needles on the south side of the lone pine. We sat cross-legged facing each other. He held both my hands in his warm clasp, and began to speak, his words tumbling over each other.

"I've been thinking about you nonstop for the last three days. It's the weirdest… I never thought I could believe such a thing, but you convinced me with your pictures. You're right. They're so different from us anything's possible. Also I'm realizing my back is super. I was just taking it for granted, not noticing, but it doesn't hurt any more at all. The docs said, after that fall I had ski jumping, that I'd probably always have some pain, and maybe need surgery later. I know now I won't, unless I do something stupid." He grinned and shrugged. "Like skiing into a tree."

He stopped speaking. He was looking into my eyes, his eyes both soft and intense. I was quiet, waiting, but my heart pounded and ached almost the way it had before Kiria laid her hand on it.

"Here's what I think," Zachary went on. "I think it's destiny or something like that, that we were both found by the Elirians, that we both dance tango and recognized each other's Elirian eyes, and that you are young again so we can be together. It's too much to be just chance. And I've never met anyone who fits me like you do. You said that, too.

So I want to go on with you. I want to see you lots, dance with you, share life with you. Maybe we can go to Buenos Aires together. What do you think?"

"I... I don't know." I felt as flustered as a teenager. I closed my eyes so as not to be distracted by his. Maybe he's right, I thought. Maybe this is the opportunity I used to say I wanted before I died, another chance at a relationship, now that I am wiser and could maybe make it work. Only I had imagined an older man, about my age, retired. I remembered a night, only last summer, when I looked in the mirror as I pinned up my straggly white hair before my bath and said to myself, "That face will never be the face of anyone's beloved, the face that makes a man light up when he sees it." I'd persuaded myself I had let go of such desires, but in that moment the thought hit me like a cold blow and I lay in my bath and grieved. Now—I could be someone's beloved. Oh, to be loved like that! To be "the one" for someone. And someone so sensitive and fine as the man sitting opposite me holding my hands.

I opened my eyes again. His face was anxious and tender. Red flags waved in the back of my mind, but I saw only the love in his eyes. "Maybe we should check it out," I said.

"Yes!" He pulled me to him, rolled me over into the soft pine needles, and kissed me.

⁂

I fixed him dinner that evening in my little house.

"Sweet," he said. "Look at you in that long apron. You're so old-fashioned."

"I guess I am, now days. Long ago, all us wives stayed home and kept house and wore aprons. Back when I was young—"

"You're young now."

"The first time I was young. Back in the forties all the girls were required to take sewing in seventh grade and cooking in the eighth grade, home economics they called it. Of course I've learned a lot more since then, keeping house and raising children over the years. So I made this apron, and I can fix you dinner."

"I love it. I guess they don't do that home economics thing anymore. I know a lot of women who can't cook worth a darn."

I served up our plates with steamed rice, chicken thighs sautéed in coconut oil, lemon juice, and herbs from my garden, a big helping of green salad. He sniffed appreciatively. "That looks yummy."

"Have you ever been in a long-term relationship?" I asked as we started to eat.

"Yeah. Once. A girl named Suzy. We went together for about five years. She runs a dance studio in Seattle. You know, ballet and tap and acrobatic for kids. Ballroom for junior high and up. Adult classes, too. I used to help her teach tango. She was just starting up when we were dating and at first it was okay. Then she got so busy she didn't have any time to hang out with me. It got to be a strain. It was like she was married to her studio. So I started dating some other women and she got mad and it ended."

Another warning signal flared in the back of my brain, but I brushed it aside. I loved having company for dinner, and was still vibrating from his kisses and the warm length of his body against mine as we lay under the pine tree.

Still I asked, "Since then?"

He shrugged. "Some short-term girlfriends, nothing serious."

"Did they all dance tango?"

"Of course." He grinned at me. "That's a non-negotiable requirement for any woman I date."

"You really are a tango junkie."

"What can I say? It's tango night at the Mercury Cafe tonight. Shall we go?"

We went and danced until the ballroom closed at 2:00 a.m. When he walked me to my door, he said, "Let me stay with you."

"Not yet."

"Not yet? Come on."

"No. We've only known each other for a little over a week."

"A week and five days."

I couldn't help smiling. "A week and five days, yes. But that's not really very long. If this is going to last, we have time. And if it isn't—well, then it's better not to."

"I want you, Clara."

"I want you, too. But not yet."

He sighed, kissed me deeply, and left me standing on my doorstep wondering how I could have said not yet.

⇆ ⇇

For the next two weeks we saw each other every night for dinner and dancing. During the weekdays when he was at work, I saw my clients, took long walks, planned dinners in a way I never did for myself alone. I marveled at his energy, that he could dance until late at night, get up in time to be at work at eight o'clock, work all day, and be ready to dance again when evening came. I also marveled at my own energy, that I could keep up with him, though I did not start work as early as he did and still gave myself the luxury of an afternoon nap. Each night he asked to stay, and still I steeled myself to tell him not yet.

In my saner moments I had reservations and seriously considered at least some of the red flags. Our pace was different. On our weekend walks, he had a goal in mind and became impatient if I wanted to stop and watch the magpies or admire the way the ice changed on the lake. He always had his cell phone on him and frequently interrupted our conversations to talk with one of his colleagues or text friends and family in Seattle. That annoyed me. When I started to speak to him of my children and grandchildren, he became uncomfortable and changed the subject. In many ways he was quite self-absorbed, as young men often are. At times he seemed to want me to mother him. I knew that was a bad idea. The biggest red flag was that he wanted to be married and have children, and I could not imagine taking on that long commitment again.

I called Anne and we walked and talked together. "Look," she said, "maybe it won't last, but you're really having fun with him now. Why not enjoy it?"

"Should I sleep with him?"

"Do you want to?"

"God, yes. But—"

"You won't get pregnant, will you?"

"No. I didn't get that part back."

"Is he clean?"

"I'd have to ask him that."

"If he's clean, why not?" She sighed. "I wouldn't mind a gorgeous young man hungering after my body."

I told Robin I had a boyfriend, a tango dancer, a beautiful young man. In no time word spread through my family. Greg called.

"Tell me about this guy." He had the energy of an old-fashioned father checking out his daughter's suitor. Never mind that I was his mother. "How old is he?"

"Thirty-four."

"What kind of car does he drive?"

"I don't know. It's blue."

"No, Mom, what make?"

"Greg, I don't notice those things. It's a nice car."

"What kind of shoes does he wear?"

I started laughing. "I don't notice that either, except for his dance shoes. He has elegant dance shoes. He probably has a good income, if that's what you're getting at."

"Doing what?"

"He's a software engineer at IBM."

"Hmm."

"I'm just dating him, dancing tango with him. I'm not going to marry him."

"Maybe you should consider that. Sounds as if he's solid, not like some of those flaky hippie guys you used to date. You've got a long life ahead of you. It might be nice to have a husband. I know you've been lonely."

I shuddered. I didn't like to think about that long life. "Don't rush it. I've only known him a few weeks."

Alice called. "We'd like you and Zachary to come over Sunday for dinner. The kids have been missing you."

"I've been missing them, too. I'm sorry I haven't come to visit recently. New love is very absorbing."

Alice laughed. "We're so happy you have someone. Of course Robin wants to check him out. And then Greg wants to know what Robin thinks."

"I've already talked with Greg. He had a lot of questions."

"I bet he did. How about it? Will Sunday work?"

"I think so. I'll check with Zachary." It felt strange to have to check with someone else after all the years of making my own decisions.

Zachary could come, though I sensed a reluctance in him. "I think you'll enjoy the children," I told him. "And you and Robin have a lot in common. He's just finishing his Ph.D. in computer science."

We had a pleasant afternoon and evening at Robin's home. Katie and Colin were glad to see me and gave me their usual warm and rowdy welcome. Zachary related well with the children, complimented Alice on her cooking, and talked a long time with Robin. But under his poise and graciousness, I could feel his discomfort.

On the way home I asked, "How was that for you?"

"Okay," he answered. "You have a beautiful family. The kids are amazing. Your son is very intelligent, and Alice is a great cook. But…" He trailed off.

"But what?"

He hesitated, then burst out, "It's just so weird to hear the kids call you grandma, and Robin—he's older than I am—calling you mama."

"It kind of puts it in your face that I'm really not as young as I seem."

"Yeah." He drove a while in silence. "It's okay," he said finally. "You're you and you're beautiful. You're great with those kids, the way you make them laugh. And you're the most fabulous tango partner ever."

I reached over to touch him. "You are, too."

Our dancing became more and more like making love. He would stroke my back, sandwich my feet, step boldly between my legs, brushing my inner thighs. All quite acceptable tango moves, but now loaded with invitation. I would respond by caressing the back of his neck, nestling my head against his cheek, burning with unacceptable fire that I knew he could feel.

At last I surrendered. On a Sunday evening after a *milonga* that ended at ten, I invited him into my home, into my bedroom.

He was as sensitive and skillful a lover as he was as a tango dancer. For years I had thought that never again would I be touched like that, lie skin to skin, feel my breasts cupped, my nipples kissed, experience the insistent pressure of being entered, the merging, the light exploding. I lay in his arms washed in bliss.

Once we'd opened the door, we couldn't get enough of each other. We slept together every night and made love before sleeping and again when we woke. It was like springtime in my body, all my cells pulsing with new life, the best sex I'd ever had. The inhibitions that had haunted my earlier relationships melted away. As for the red flags, I banished them.

Even so, finally I wanted some space. "I need a night off," I told him as I kissed him goodbye one morning.

"Why? Is something wrong?"

"No. I just want to sleep alone tonight. I've been so absorbed in you, I've forgotten myself."

"Okay." He looked disappointed. "I guess I could clean up my apartment. I've just been dumping stuff when I go through. Hey. You want to spend night after next at my place? We can bless it with our passion." His mustache curled with his smile, his blue eyes crinkled at the corners. "But be prepared. I'm going to love you all night long, to make up for missing tonight."

❧ ☙

I leaned back against the closed door, listening to Zachary's car pull out of the driveway. Two days and a night of solitude. Oh, I was ready. My young body was able to keep up with Zachary, but my old spirit sorely needed a slower pace.

I had clients but already felt the day to be more spacious, knowing I had the night to myself. I finished my last client at four, made myself a cup of tea, and sat down in my rocking chair with a novel Lisa had given me for Christmas. I had just gotten started on it before I met Zachary, and hadn't gotten back to it since. It was an absorbing tale and I got lost in it, leaving behind all the drama of my own story. The February afternoon lengthened into dusk. When I reached up to switch on the light, I realized I was hungry.

There were leftovers crowding the refrigerator from all the dinners I had prepared for Zachary. I pulled out a few, heated them up, and took my book to the table to continue reading while I ate.

A quiet evening. Around eleven o'clock, I finished the novel and sat a while, thinking over the story and how it had touched me.

Then a long hot bath. Zachary and I always showered together, which was fun, but I had missed lying in the bathtub with fragrant bath salts, relaxing until I dozed.

I had a double bed, the same size I'd shared with both my husbands in the days before larger beds were fashionable. After Jon moved out,

I had grown used to having it to myself. Sharing it with Zachary was sweet but crowded. Now I stretched out on my back, arms and legs spread wide.

Around two a.m. I woke. Luxury to turn on the light. I picked up the novel and reread a few favorite scenes, then slept again. In the morning, I got up late and moved slowly into my day with meditation and yoga. Blessed solitude.

After a quiet day, two clients, and a long walk at my own wandering pace, I was looking forward to seeing Zachary again.

Zachary's apartment was a two bedroom on the second floor of a big complex at the intersection of two main streets. It was only a little more than a mile from my house, but I hadn't been there before. I was curious to see how he lived.

We met that evening at the tango class we took together on Wednesdays and I followed him home. He came to my car window as I drove into the parking lot. "I'll go ahead and turn the lights on." I gathered my purse and overnight bag and followed him up a flight of metal stairs on the outside of the building.

When he opened the door to let me in, he had his phone in his hand. "Come on in. I'm just checking my messages." He kissed me, took my coat, and turned his attention back to his phone.

I sat down on his couch. His living room was simply but elegantly furnished. There was a glass-topped coffee table in front of the couch, two matching lamps with stained glass shades on tables at either end, a leather recliner, a television, and a whole wall taken up with a stereo and shelves of CDs. Sliding glass doors, draped now, opened onto a balcony I had noticed as I came in. A counter separated the living room from the kitchenette.

Zachary looked up from his phone. "I just need to return one call. Go ahead and look around. I got it all cleaned up for you."

I stood up and wandered into the kitchenette, peeked into the cupboards. Only the bare essentials, but what was there was high quality. Everything was clean and orderly.

Zachary was still standing in the entryway, talking computerese on his phone. I could feel my irritation rising. When he finally closed the phone, I asked, "Who in the world are you talking business with at 10:30 at night?"

"Oh, that's Alex. He's such a geek, he never sleeps." Zachary put his phone back in his belt. "Come on, let me show you the rest of my place."

He had his office set up in one of the bedrooms, a large computer monitor on a big cluttered oak desk. The other bedroom was filled with a king-size bed.

It looked huge to me, for one person. "A king-size bed!" I exclaimed. "It takes up the whole room. You can get lost in one of those."

"Lots of room to play. I won't let you get lost." He stood behind me, his hands cupping my breasts. I leaned back against him, softening.

His phone rang.

"Don't answer it," I pleaded.

He pulled it out and looked at it. "It's Meg. I need to take it." He sat down on the bed. "What's up?... Oh, no."

I walked back into the living room, my interrupted passion becoming anger. I paced. I could be home, I thought, going to bed. I sat down on the couch, picked a *Newsweek* up off the coffee table and thumbed through it. Nothing I wanted to read. I slammed it back down, walked to the balcony doors, opened the drapes, and stepped out. The air was sharp and cold, the stars dimmed by the lights on the streets and in the buildings all around.

"Hey, it's freezing." Zachary was finally off the phone. "Get in here." He closed the doors and put his arms around me again.

"What was all that about?" I asked.

"Poor Meg. Chris is sick and she's worried."

"Doesn't she have a husband to share her worry with?"

"He's a jerk. Sound asleep. He doesn't understand her like I do. I got her calmed down." He smoothed my back, kissed my neck. I sighed and rested my head on his shoulder.

His phone rang again. He pulled it out and looked at it. "Alex. Probably still having trouble with that program."

I snatched the phone out of his hand. "No! I've had it with that phone interrupting us." It kept ringing. "I've half a mind to pitch it off the balcony and watch in glee while it smashes into a jillion smithereens in the parking lot." I took a step toward the balcony, the phone still ringing in my hand.

"Clara!" He caught my wrist and retrieved his phone. He looked truly shocked. "Do you know what that would do to me? I've got everything on there. I'd be destroyed."

"Everything on there but me."

The phone stopped ringing. He backed away from me, clipping it onto his belt.

"Turn it off." I was furious. "All the way off. No rings, no vibrates, no moans, no beeps. Off! Or I'm going home."

"Calm down." He took his phone off his belt, punched a few beeping buttons, and closed it. "It's off. I guess I can help Alex in the morning."

"I guess you can."

"Clara, what's wrong? What's going on?"

"I told you. I don't like having our conversation interrupted and then sitting around waiting and waiting, as if I had nothing better to do, while you talk and talk to someone else. The way I was brought up, that's just plain rude."

He sighed and drew me down to sit beside him on the couch. "It's a different world now. Everyone does that. It's important to stay connected."

"Connected to whom? Everyone but the person you're with?"

"Don't, Clara. You don't understand."

I sighed. I was suddenly weary. "I guess I don't," I said. "Are you okay with leaving your phone off for tonight?"

"Yeah, I'm okay."

He put his arm around me, but I didn't melt. We made love, but I didn't come. After he fell asleep, I slid over to the other side of his huge bed and curled up with my back to him, pressing a pillow against my belly.

We worked through our spat over the cell phone and made some agreements. He would check his messages at the beginning of our time together, handle anything urgent, then turn his phone off. Also we agreed to sleep separately one night a week. I knew I needed an occasional break from our all-consuming relationship, and he admitted he'd gotten behind on his work and could use that night to catch up.

He didn't give up on trying to persuade me of the necessity of virtual connection. One night after dinner, he showed me all the wonders of his smart phone, how he could take pictures, text, connect to the Internet, talk with his two hundred plus friends on Facebook. "You should join Facebook. I can set you up."

"No," I said. "I don't need two hundred friends, just a few good ones that I can talk to face-to-face, see their expressions, hear their voices, touch them. I don't want to communicate on a silver screen. Imagine what we'd be missing if our relationship were only on Facebook."

"Of course. But Clara, look at this. I have my whole calendar here with reminders, like this one to call my mom on her birthday. And look at this. I can just enter the address wherever I am and it will show me all the restaurants within a mile of my location." He touched his screen rapidly and held it out to show me. "There's all kinds of apps I can put on here."

"Apps?"

"Yeah, apps. You know."

"No, I don't."

"Apps. Short for applications. All different kinds of programs. See here." He took his phone back and touched the little screen again. "Here's a note-taking one, where I can draw data from all kinds of sources—Wikipedia, YouTube, texts and emails people send me, and it automatically organizes it all for me." He showed it to me. I couldn't make any sense of what I saw.

"You can even watch movies on it."

"Kind of a small screen."

"And you can text. It's very efficient. With texting you can surf the web, play video games, and talk to as many people as you want all at once."

I was outraged. "How can you pay attention to all of that? I don't want you playing video games when you're talking to me."

He sighed. "Clara, you need to get with this. It's how everyone's connecting. And it's going to get more so. How are you going to manage for the rest of your life if you don't learn this stuff?"

"I don't know. Let's not talk about it anymore." I bit my lip. The thought of a long life stretching ahead of me full of ever more complex smart phones and people that depended on them was overwhelming.

"Hey." He touched my cheek in that tender way he had. "It'll be all right. You're smart. You can learn. It's not that hard. I'll teach you. It's not as hard as tango."

I didn't want to learn. In spite of some obvious conveniences, it felt all wrong to me. Wrong to depend on a smart phone to remember your mother's birthday, wrong to substitute Facebook for real connections. Just wrong, taking us farther and farther out of meaningful contact with each other and the natural world. But I didn't say that. What was the use? I got up and started clearing the table.

Zachary tapped his screen a few times. "Speaking of tango. It's seven o'clock. Time for *practica* at the Pearl Street Studio. Shall we go?"

Around the middle of February, Zachary made a four-day trip to Seattle to handle some business and visit his family.

While he was gone, I decided to catch up with my journal. It had been my habit to write in it three or four times a week, recording the events of my days, my thoughts and feelings. But since Zachary had come into my life, I'd been too absorbed in him to think much of myself or take time to write. My last entry was only a brief account of Zachary's and my visit with Robin's family.

So much had happened since. We had become lovers, fought over the cell phone, danced and danced, spent most of our nights and mornings and all of our weekends together. I realized as I wrote how deeply I had fallen in love with him, how much I had lost myself.

"Danger," I wrote. "This is all out of balance. This can never be more than a passing affair. It's not responsible for me to go on. I am not a young woman, not thirty, no matter how my body looks and feels.

"But I love him. I've never had such dancing, such ecstatic sex. And I'm not lonely anymore. His face lights up when he sees me. I'm 'the one' for him. That's so precious.

"Then how will it end? There will be pain. Is it worth it? Does it have to end? Oh, I don't know. I don't know."

Suddenly irritated, I pushed my journal aside. I can't think about it anymore. I don't know what to do. Let it be.

It was evening. I got up and went dancing, danced with all the partners who had been my favorites before Zachary.

"Where's lover boy?" Tim asked.

"On a business trip."

"Did you ever tell him how old you are?"

"Yes. I had a hard time convincing him, but he finally believed me. He's not very comfortable with it but seems to have accepted it for now."

"He should. You're a catch. And dancing better than ever." We circled the floor. "What really happened to you?" he asked. "Everyone's wondering. It can't be just a makeover. I don't see any white roots in your hair. And you never used to have as much energy as you do now. It seems like you really are as young as you look."

"It's true. I've had a miraculous healing. But I can't talk about it. Let's just dance."

He let it go and the *tanda* ended. I enjoyed the evening and the variety of my different partners, but none fit me as well or danced as beautifully as Zachary. I missed him and didn't stay late.

He was home again by mid-week, and I was glad to see him. One night alone once a week was fine, but after three nights I longed for the warmth of his body, the sound of his voice, the way he teased me and made me laugh, his companionship.

I had dinner ready when he came to my house from work. We ate together, went dancing, made love, and slept in each other's arms. But something was different; he was remote. Telling myself it was only because he was tired from his trip, I brushed aside the anxiety I felt. In the morning he seemed himself again.

Saturdays we always celebrated the weekend by sleeping late and taking lots of time to make love. The Saturday after his trip, as we lay together in post-sex bliss, he stroked my belly. "Clara, is there something you want to tell me?"

I turned my head lazily to look into his eyes. "There's always lots of things I want to tell you, but nothing special right now except—you're so yummy." I rolled over to kiss him, sensed a question. "What is it?"

"Well, I was wondering. We've been together for two months now, and you haven't had a period. I know you asked me about STDs and all, but you've never asked me to wear a condom. So I was wondering if maybe you wanted, if maybe you were…"

I sat straight up on the bed. "Pregnant?"

"Yeah." He smiled, his blue eyes crinkling at the corners in the way I found so enchanting. "I'd love it if you were."

I was flabbergasted, speechless. The implications of his words battered me from every direction. "I… Zachary!... I wouldn't," I stammered, then finally managed to get out, "I'm not."

"Oh, too bad." He reached up his arms for me.

I pushed him away. "Are you out of your mind? We've known each other for two months, *only* two months, and you're thinking I'd just… maybe just happen to get pregnant?" I gestured wildly. "Don't you realize that having a kid is a very big deal, a serious, huge long-lasting commitment?" I closed my eyes and shook my head, blowing out my breath, then opened my eyes and glared at him. "If you want to have kids, there's a right way to do it. First you spend at least a year getting to know each other, maybe living together, to see if you can get along. Kids need their parents to get along. Then you marry. Then you wait at least another year to settle into your marriage, because believe me, once the kids come, it puts a big strain on your marriage. Then you *talk it over* before you start trying to make a baby."

He bounced up to sit opposite me. "Calm down. That's very old-fashioned. Most people don't do it that way now."

"No, they don't. And there are a lot of unwanted children in the world. I can't believe you would think I'd just let it happen, without being married, without discussing it first."

He looked puzzled. "Then how come you didn't ask me to wear a condom?"

"There are other kinds of birth control."

"I know. But you haven't had your period. I was just hoping." His face was tender with hope.

I softened. "Look, I probably should have told you. But we're just getting started; it seemed premature. I didn't ask you to wear a condom because I'm sterile."

"Sterile!" His brow wrinkled.

"I'm not bleeding because I went through menopause twenty-six years ago."

"But you're young again now."

"They didn't give me that part back."

"Oh." He touched my cheek. "Maybe you could call them, the aliens, and ask them to make you fertile again. They probably could. I'm so gone on you, I want to marry you, spend the rest of my life with you, grow old with you. I want you to be the mother of my kids."

"But I don't want more children."

"You don't? Why not?"

"Because, like I said, it's a huge long-term commitment. I've done it. I've even done it twice. Lisa and Greg were grown when I started all over again with Robin. I wouldn't have missed it for anything, but I don't want to do it again."

"I don't get it. You'd be a terrific mom. I saw how you were with Katie and Colin. And you have all that experience."

I shivered. I reached over the side of the bed, picked up my discarded nightgown, and slipped it over my head. "You don't have a clue. It's a long haul. There's diapers and shots and having your sleep interrupted for years, figure three years for each kid. There's school and homework and lessons and driving them everywhere. Then high school and them learning to drive and all the trouble they can get into. Then college and weddings and grandchildren. And it doesn't end there. I'll be a mom until I die."

"I guess it is a lot of work."

"Tons. Twenty-four seven. But that's not the half of it. There is no love so deep as what you have for your child. At first they're so little and vulnerable. They cry with belly aches and get sick and you can't take their pain away. Then they get bigger and fall off things and injure themselves, and get their feelings hurt and struggle with life and have disappointments—and you suffer it all with them as if it were your own suffering."

"They're also cute and adorable and amazing, like my nephew Chris."

"Which only makes you love them more. I don't think I could bear the intensity of that love again. I already have it for Lisa and Greg and Robin and their children. My heart is full. And I don't even know if I'll be around much longer."

"Why not?" Zachary caught my hands. "You're not sick or anything, are you?"

I froze, as shocked as Zachary by what I had said. Since meeting him I had buried the possibility the Elirians had given me, but clearly it was still percolating under the surface. "No, no. I'm not sick. I'm okay." I took a deep breath. "Look, Zachary, we shouldn't be talking about marriage and children. We're just beginning our relationship and we've spent most of our time together dancing tango, an unrealistically romantic activity in which you have undisputed lead. You need to know that's not how it would be if we made a home and raised a family together."

He chuckled. "I've had a hint of that."

"And," I went on, "there's also the fact that I am forty-six years older than you, two generations older, brought up in a world you can barely imagine. You know my young body, but I don't think you can ever know my old spirit."

He smoothed back my love-tousled hair. "I know your spirit. I see how gentle and loving you are, how playful and fun, the way your family adores you, how wise you are. Why do you think I love you so much?" He gathered me into his arms and rolled me to lie down on the bed with him.

"I just need to take it slowly," I whispered against the sweet skin of his shoulder. "I'm still trying to figure out who I am. It's been such a big change for me."

"It's okay. It's okay." He stroked my back, kissed my hair. "We can take all the time you need. We're young still."

The days lengthened. I planted seeds in trays on my south window sills—tomatoes, marigolds, basil, snapdragons and lobelias. Some days it was warm enough to putter in the garden, cutting back dead stems, clearing out leaves. The first crocuses opened golden in the sheltered garden at the top of the studio steps. Spring was coming. I knew it could snow again more than once, but there was a smell in the air, a different hue in the sky, and happiness bubbled up in me. I began planning to open up a big vegetable garden in the back yard where I'd had one years before. As I grew older I had decided a big garden was too much for my aging body and had sodded most of it over, leaving only a narrow strip next to the house. But now with my renewed strength I looked forward to opening it again, to eating from it all summer long, and freezing some vegetables for winter.

Every so often Zachary would ask me if I had thought about calling the Elirians. I thought about it a great deal. Some days I almost convinced myself I should ask for my fertility back, marry Zachary, and raise a family with him. I was pretty sure he would eventually move on if I couldn't have children, and I couldn't bear the thought of losing him. Also Greg's point was well taken that it might be good to have companionship in the long life stretching before me. But I didn't call the Elirians. Every time I thought of it my stomach would clench. I didn't know what I really wanted to ask them.

When I meditated, deep conflict arose but I found no resolution. So, as the spring unfolded, I let the days and weeks pass, drifting in the sweet, passionate life I shared with Zachary.

"I have a vacation coming up," he said one evening. "Shall we go to Buenos Aires?"

He had been several times. I had always wanted to visit that birthplace and heart of Argentine tango, but had been too timid to go alone. "I'd love to! When is your vacation?"

"The last week in April. I'll get the tickets and arrange everything. It's all on me." He whirled me away from the sink where I was preparing vegetables for dinner and spun me around the kitchen. "We'll have a fabulous time."

I was excited. I set up a private lesson with the teacher who had been my mentor for the first years of my tango life, sorted through my dance clothes, and called Anne to see if she would take care of my seedlings while I was away.

Zachary invited me to his apartment for dinner the following week. "I'll cook for a change." When I arrived, he was on the phone, tense and frowning. He nodded to me and took the phone into the bedroom. As he swung the door to, I heard him say, "Suzy, I can't talk any more right now. I'll call you tomorrow, I promise, and—" The door closed.

I stood in the hall with my coat in my hand. Suzy? Wasn't that the name of his former girlfriend, the one with the dance studio?

He came out a little later, rumpling his hair.

"Is something wrong?" I asked.

"No. No, nothing serious." He smoothed his face. "Hi." He smiled and kissed me, held me close for a long moment. His heart was beating faster than usual and I felt him trembling slightly.

"Are you sure nothing's wrong?"

"I've had a lot on my mind at work. Let's go out for dinner. I was going to cook but I got home late."

We went to the same restaurant where we'd had our first date. He was clearly troubled, but also clearly didn't want to talk about it. As we finished dinner he said, "Let's not dance tonight. I just want to go home and hold you in my arms. Horizontal tango." He made love to me that night with more than usual intensity and held me tight even when we slept.

It was snowing the next morning when I got home, a wet spring snow. Fortunately the trees had not leafed out yet. As I shoveled the walk and the studio steps in preparation for my first client, I was uneasy.

Suzy. What's going on with her that he's so upset? And why wasn't he straight with me, pretending it was about work?

I found out the following weekend. It was Saturday night, late, after an evening of tango in Denver. We were sipping hot cocoa at the counter in his kitchenette and I was babbling away about how excited I was to go to Buenos Aires. We were due to depart in only two weeks.

He put his hand over mine. "Clara, I've got some bad news."

"What?"

"We're going to have to postpone our trip. Something's come up at home and I need to take that week to go back there and handle it."

I felt a sharp pang of disappointment and under that a rush of anxiety. "Oh, are your parents okay? Is anyone sick?"

"No. My parents are fine." He bumped his cocoa cup with an abrupt movement of his hand, and cocoa spilled on the counter.

"I'll get it." I got up, fetched a sponge from the sink, and mopped up the cocoa.

"What is it then?" I asked. "It must be something serious for you to give up going to Buenos Aries."

"We'll go. I've already talked to the airlines. Our tickets are good for a year."

"But what's happening in Seattle?"

He turned his face away. "Just some family stuff. I'll handle it, and when I get back we'll make new plans to go to B.A. Okay?"

I looked at the half of his face I could see and felt my throat tighten. "Does it have anything to do with Suzy?"

He spun around. "Suzy! What are you talking about?"

"Isn't she the one who used to be your girlfriend? I heard you speak her name when you were talking on the phone the other night. Before you went into the bedroom. And then you were upset, though you told me it was about work."

He turned his face away again, drumming his fingers on the counter, and didn't answer.

I laid my hand over his agitated fingers. "Zachary, look at me, please. What's going on? You've never been evasive like this with me before. Please be straight with me."

"Okay. Okay." He turned back to face me. His eyes were dark, his jaw clenched. "Remember when I went back last February to do some work in the Seattle office?"

"Yes."

"Well, I went dancing one night and Suzy was there. So we danced together and afterward we went up to her place. It wasn't serious, just casual… for old time's sake. Only now… She called me that night when you came over. She's pregnant."

I stood up slowly, gripping the counter. A cold wind blew through me. In that moment, all the betrayals of my long life lined up behind this new betrayal, creating a howling abyss at the core of my being. My stomach twisted into an icy knot. I wanted to double over and retch, but I held myself straight. "You had sex with her? And then came back three days later, only three days later, and told me you wanted to marry me? How could you?… Did you tell her about me?"

"No."

"No. I guess not." I spun away from the counter into the bedroom. My overnight bag sat on the bed. I grabbed my few personal belongings from the nightstand, my slippers from under the bed. Zachary was behind me. He caught my wrist.

"Clara, it wasn't anything."

I twisted my hand free and whirled into the bathroom, swept up my toothbrush, hairbrush, cosmetics, and stuffed them into my bag.

"What are you doing?"

"I'm going home."

"Wait, we need to talk."

"I can't." I could hardly breathe. I rushed to the hallway, pulled my coat out of the closet. I lost my balance as I pulled on a boot. Zachary caught me.

"Don't go. It didn't mean anything. You're the one I love."

"Great way to show it." I stamped my second boot on. "Didn't mean anything. Just know it meant something to me. Like I can never trust you again."

I yanked the door open and ran out, down the metal stairs to the parking lot. Only then did I remember that Zachary had picked me up that night and my car was in the garage at home. I stood still a moment, lost. Zachary opened the door above and called, "Wait, Clara. I'll give you a ride."

I couldn't bear the thought of sitting beside him. I ducked behind a row of parked cars and took off at a run across the parking lot.

It must have been two a.m. or later. The streets were deserted. It's not far, I told myself, only a little more than a mile, not as far as around the lake. I crossed the big intersection with the light and started running down the dark residential streets, my bag bumping against my thighs. "Not again, not again," I sobbed as I ran.

Before long I became aware of a car behind me, its lights shining on me, moving slowly. I stopped and waited for it to pass. The car stopped. Fear choked me. I began running again, and the car followed, slowly, not passing, pinning me with its lights. I glanced back as I ran, trying to see what kind of vehicle it was, but the lights blinded me. Newspaper stories of late-night assaults flashed through my mind. Desperate, I dashed off the street onto a nearby lawn and dropped down behind a hedge. The car stopped again. I could hear the motor running, the sound of the car door opening. I crouched lower behind the hedge, frozen. Then I heard Zachary's voice. "Clara, it's me."

I stood up shaking and sobbing and came out from behind the hedge. "What the hell are you doing?" I yelled at him. "You scared the shit out of me."

"Didn't you know it was me?"

"How could I know? All I could see was headlights."

"I couldn't have you walking home alone late at night. It isn't safe. Come on."

He held out his hand. I didn't take it. He opened the passenger door. I got in and sat hunched over my bag.

"You're crying."

"No shit."

He drove me home and walked me to the door. My hand was shaking too badly to handle the key. He took it from me and unlocked the door.

"Please, Clara. We need to talk."

"I can't. I can't now. Later."

I slipped inside, shut the door, and leaned back against it.

❧ ❧

It was almost morning before I got to bed. I was cold, cold. Even wrapped in my down comforter I couldn't get warm. I longed for Zachary's arms around me, his warmth next to me, and knew it would never happen again. I cried, horrible wrenching sobs.

Dawn came. I saw its first light touch the swelling buds on the cottonwood tree. Dragging the comforter, I crept to my altar, settled on my pillow, and lit my candle.

For the first hour I raged. Perfidious men! How could I have been such a fool as to open up again? Didn't I know better? How many times have I come to this bitterness? Is the ecstasy worth it? I know perfectly well the more charismatic and enchanting they are the more likely to be philanderers. Where would he be when I couldn't go dancing with him because I was home walking up and down with a colicky baby? To think I even considered having children with him. What kind of perfect idiot was I to imagine even for a moment it could work between an eighty-year-old woman and a dashing young man. Never mind that I look young. I'm still an old woman. There were red flags flying everywhere, and I paid no attention. I knew something had happened when he came back from Seattle. I *knew*. I could feel it. And I just brushed it away. Denial. Denial. I thought I was "the one" for him. Ha!

I wept again, bitter sobs tearing through me.

Finally they ceased. In the quiet after the storm, relief welled up. It's over, I realized. Over. I don't have to try to act young when I'm not. I don't have to learn to use a smart phone, or even consider the possibility of marrying and having children again. I don't have to hold the tension. I can just be my old woman self.

I climbed back into my bed and slept. When I woke it was early afternoon, a sweet April day. I dressed and took my brunch out onto the patio. The deep inner cold that had tormented me all night began to melt away in the warmth of the sun. The flickers were calling back and forth to each other, their mating song, a quintessential spring sound. When I finished eating I stretched out on the grass under the maple tree, gazing up through its budding branches at the April blue of the sky.

It's not quite over, I thought with a sigh. I need to make closure with Zachary. I still had a headache and felt raw inside from the hours of crying, but my strength was returning. Best to get it over with. I got up, gathered the dishes, and went inside.

He answered the phone on the first ring. "Clara, I was hoping you'd call. I'm so sorry. Can we please talk?"

"I'm ready now. Come on over."

As I hung up the phone, anger surged through me. Self-absorbed, undisciplined jerk. He didn't even bother to use birth control.

He reached out to hug me when I opened the door, but I held him away. Grief rose up. I wrapped it in ice.

He touched my cheek. "You look kinda rough. As if you've been crying."

I pushed his hand away. "Sit down. We need to talk."

He sat down on the couch and patted the place beside him. I shook my head, pulled up a chair, and sat facing him.

"We'll keep this brief—" I started to say.

"Wait," he interrupted. "Everything's okay. We can work this out. Just give me a chance to explain."

"Explain!" I burst out. "What's there to explain? You were unfaithful, plain and simple."

"No. You don't understand. It didn't mean anything."

"Didn't mean anything? How can you say that?"

"Clara, listen."

I couldn't listen. "I trusted you," I blurted. "I thought you loved me."

"I do love you." Zachary sat up straight and pounded the couch where he had invited me to sit. "Quit being so old-fashioned. People don't make such a big deal out of sex anymore."

"Well, I do. I bet Suzy does, too. Especially now that she's pregnant. How come you didn't tell her about me if it's no big deal?"

Zachary was clenching his jaw, but I couldn't stop. Bitterness rose in me like bile. "Is it no big deal that we've been lovers for the last four months?"

"That's different. I want to marry you. I'm serious about you."

"So serious it's no big deal to screw around as soon as I'm out of your sight? You couldn't keep your pants zipped for four days for the woman you're serious about?"

Zachary bounced off the couch and stood over me. "You're hanging on to all these old-fashioned ideas. Why don't you act your age?"

"What? I *am* acting my age. Old-fashioned, old-fashioned, you keep saying. Don't you remember?" I stood up, too, not wanting him towering over me. "I'm an old woman."

He grabbed my shoulders. "No you're not. You're a young woman. Get with your biological age. Join the twenty-first century. You're going to be here for a while."

Cold ran through me from head to toe as his words sank in. I stood stunned. "Let go of me," I said finally.

He let go. My knees were shaking. I felt behind me for the chair and sat down. He was right. I needed to act my age. I hadn't meant to lose my temper. I only needed to tell him it was over. Just that. "Please sit down," I said. "I'm sorry I lost my temper."

He sat back down on the couch. The charge between us evaporated for the moment. He looked weary.

"It hurts," I said more quietly, "what you did. It hurts a lot. But this whole affair has been insane from the beginning. The young woman you're looking at is not me. It's a cloak over who I really am, an illusion."

Zachary leaned forward. "It doesn't feel like an illusion in bed." He smiled, laying on the charm, the corners of his eyes crinkling, his mustache curling up.

I pulled back from him. "Don't. Listen, I have just one thing I need to say to you. It's over between us. This is the end of our relationship."

Zachary looked as if I'd punched him in the stomach. "No way. I won't accept that. I'll go and handle things with Suzy, then I'll be back and—"

"She wants the baby, doesn't she."

He stiffened. "Yes, but I'm going to talk to her. I'll tell her about you, that we're serious."

"That'll make her day. You're planning to push her to have an abortion?"

"Well—"

"An abortion's a terrible thing for a woman. Don't ask it of her for my sake." I realized my sympathies were with Suzy. What a raw deal he was trying to lay on her. Is this how he treated women? Would I have been next?

"Don't worry about Suzy," he said. "I told you I'd handle it. Trust me."

"*Trust* you?"

Zachary paled. "Damn it, Clara."

I tried to quiet my voice, get back to the point. "It's over, Zachary. You're not going to change my mind. I mean it. I can't marry you. Certainly not now. We're coming from totally different worlds about everything except tango. You having sex with Suzy and telling me it doesn't mean anything makes that crystal clear. So it's over. Don't consider me in your plans."

He shook his head. "I can't believe you're saying that after all we've shared."

"After all we've shared, I can't believe you had sex with Suzy."

"Stop!" Zachary pounded his fist in his hand. "It was just once. I won't do it again."

"I've heard that before."

"Let it go. Can't you let it go? Just this once?"

"No."

"How can a woman who dances like you do," he said through his teeth, "follows at the touch of a feather, be—so—damn—stubborn?"

"Life is not tango." A wave of loss flooded me with the memory of dancing with him. "You should marry Suzy," I said. "That's the honorable thing to do when you get a woman pregnant. You wanted kids? Well, you've got one on the way."

"The honorable thing to do. Now you really sound like an old woman."

"Because I am." I stood, walked to the door, and opened it. "It's time for you to go. I've nothing more to say."

"I've got more to say."

"I don't want to hear it. Please go. Don't make it any harder than it is."

He followed me, took hold of my shoulders. "Clara, don't send me away. We can overcome this. If Suzy wants to keep the baby, I make enough money I can support her and the kid and still be with you."

I put my hand in the center of his chest, not sure if I were pushing him away or touching his heart one last time. "Go. Please go. Now."

"All *right*. I'm going." He spun and left. I closed the door and leaned my brow against it, hearing his feet pound down the porch steps, the sound of his car starting up, driving away, the tires screeching. I turned and walked through the silent house to my bedroom, lay still on the bed, staring out the window. I ached with relief, but tears blurred my eyes. "It's over," I whispered to the quiet room. "Now what?" When the tears cleared, I noticed that during the day the buds on the cottonwood had unfolded into new green-gold leaves.

Chapter 9

The Way Home

That night I dreamed I was running down a long, dark tunnel deep in the earth toward a far-away light that I was desperate to reach. The tunnel opened into a forest of ancient evergreens. I had been there before. The tall black-robed figure of Death seemed to wait for me near the path, but when I ran toward him, reaching out my arms, he turned away and disappeared among the trees. The light receded, hopelessly far away. I stumbled as I tried to run faster, and fell. The light vanished.

I woke in pre-dawn dark, weeping.

In the morning I canceled my clients, telling them I was sick, which was true if you count heartsick. I puttered around the empty house, lonely, lost. Outside in my garden, spring was bursting. Inside my body it was bitter winter.

I sat down and cried some more. I loved loving and being loved. Why did it always end in pain? For some people I knew it was otherwise. I had friends who had been married since their youth and now, in their seventies and eighties, were still devoted to each other. I had never imagined any other future for myself when I was an innocent young bride of eighteen. But that was not the way my life had unfolded.

Finally I gave myself a shake. "Enough," I said aloud to myself. "Go out in the garden. That always makes you feel better."

It was a soft, warm afternoon, the sun in and out between clouds, trees budding, birds calling among the treetops, squirrels running along the fence. I decided to open up the big vegetable garden I had been dreaming of. I knew it would be hard work cutting through the sod, but maybe that was just what I needed, to work so hard I would be exhausted and sleep when night came. Images of the dream I'd had the night before flickered through my mind, and fear rose. "Don't go there," I said to myself. "It was only a dream."

I went to the garage and got the shovel and edger. In the back yard I paced out the shape of the garden. I wanted to recreate the circular garden I'd had before with a spiral path of flagstones leading to an altar at the center.

For a while I was absorbed in marking the boundaries of the garden with the edger. But when I picked up the shovel and set it in the groove I'd made, I froze. Wait.

If I open this garden I'm making a commitment. To stay. To keep the body that can care for it. I took my foot off the shovel and surveyed the wide expanse of garden I had outlined. Like the long expanse of life that lay before me.

My thoughts stormed. I can't bear the conflict anymore. Big garden, little garden, young woman, old woman. I don't know who I am, why I'm here. I don't want to go on and on. It's been too long already. Too much pain.

The shovel fell with a soft thud on the lawn. I looked again at the outline of the big garden, threw my hands out in a wild gesture, and dropped beside the shovel, face down in the grass.

I have to decide. They said they could change me back. But only until they leave Earth. Do I want them to?

Yes! Just let me be myself again.

I lay a long time, thoughts and images racing through me—memories of my long life, children and grandchildren, recent memories of being old/young, Zachary on his cell phone, the dying face of a friend taken by cancer only a year ago, newspaper headlines of a world gone berserk, fears, longings, all tumbled together.

The smell of crushed grass filled my nostrils. The sun warmed me. If they change me back, I thought, I will die soon. My old heart isn't going to last much longer.

Oh, I love my strong body. I love the beautiful Earth.

Maybe I could go on. I could continue doing massage, teach dance again, and yoga. Memories of the all the classes I had taught, all the different classrooms, faces of all my clients and students over the last sixty years poured over me in a blur. No. I don't want to do it anymore. I'm done, burned out. Then what would I do? How would I fill my days?

From the walkway outside the high fence that sheltered my garden I heard the voice of a mother calling her child. "Come on, Lori, we're going this way."

And the child's voice, young, plaintive. "I don't want to go that way. I want to go home." Her words slid into my heart like a narrow knife, exquisitely sharp.

The dream came back to me again—Death turning away. No way home?

I lay still, barely breathing. Wind stirred the treetops. A cloud moved over the sun and I shivered.

Slowly I sat up, rubbing the imprint of grass from my cheek, and crossed my legs to meditate. It would be hard to hurt again, to be slowed by aching knees, unsteady heart, and faltering energy. But I had been okay before. I had accepted it. After all, I had climbed all the way to my special place. I was still able to give a massage, do my yoga postures. My life had been good. And I had been myself, whole, not torn apart by conflicting identities.

I sat a long time as the decision clarified. I will. I will ask them to change me back when I meet them on the mountain. They said they could. I let out a long sigh. Peace poured into me, a quality of peace I had not felt since I first saw myself in the mirror the day I came down from the mountain.

I got up slowly, pushing myself off the ground with my hands as if I were already an old woman. Twilight had come and the air was growing cooler. I walked around the groove I had made in the grass, smudging it with my bare foot.

There are times in a woman's life when what she needs most is a woman friend. The following morning was one of those times. I picked up the phone and called Anne.

"Can you come over?"

"I can't. I've got a client in just a few minutes, and then a full day. What's up?"

"I broke up with Zachary."

"No! I thought you guys were doing great, going to Buenos Aires in two weeks."

"Not anymore."

"Oh, Clara. I'm so sorry. Listen, my evening's free. Come over for dinner. I've got some salmon."

"Thanks. I'd love to. I'll bring salad."

"Are you okay?"

"Mostly. I just need to talk. What time shall I come?"

"I'll be done by six. Oops, there's the doorbell. I've got to run. Love you. Okay, all right, okay. Bye."

"Bye." I hung up the phone, smiling at her characteristic closure.

I spent the morning working in my little garden. I spread compost, dug it in, then sat breaking up lumps in the soil with my hands, comforted by the connection to earth and the warmth of spring sun on my back. When the soil was smooth and fine, I planted greens—lettuce, spinach, Swiss chard, kale.

In the afternoon I wrote in my journal. I filled pages, seeking to integrate the lessons of the last months and glean some wisdom from the affair with Zachary. I wrote more, sorting all the thoughts and feelings that had come to me as I lay on the grass the day before, committing to ink and paper the decision I had made. As I wrote, I felt again the peace of it, the relief that I would soon be myself again, even if it meant dealing with the pain of my old body.

Anne had a little house in the old part of town. Her calico cat Camille was sitting on the vine-covered front porch, tail wrapped around her front paws, when I arrived. She got up to greet me with a meow and a leg-rubbing caress.

Anne hurried to the door to hug me. "I've got a nice organic wine. Let's start with that. I'm dying to hear what happened."

We settled on her couch with wine. Camille came to nestle between us, purring sporadically.

"Now tell me," Anne said. "I can't believe you broke up with Zachary. It seemed like it was going so well."

I gave her a brief account of the ending with Zachary.

"Men!" Anne exclaimed. "They think they are God's gift to women and it's their *ulada* to spread the joy around." She'd had her own fill of unfaithful husbands and lovers. "How're you doing? You seem calmer than I'd expect."

"I've done a lot of crying. It hurt. But now I'm mostly relieved. It never could have worked long-term. One part of me enjoyed the ride for sure, but there was always another part—I call her my inner old woman—who knew from the beginning it would have to end, that we were on diverging tracks, and all we really had in common was sex and tango. Ephemeral pleasures.

"But there's something else I want to talk to you about, something much more important than Zachary. I made a big decision yesterday."

Anne refilled our wine glasses and nodded to me to go on.

I bit my lower lip, suddenly tense, fearing that if I could not persuade Anne of the rightness of my decision, I might dissuade myself. I took a breath.

"It came up because I started to open a big garden like the one I used to have. You remember?"

"Yes. With the flagstones and beds in a spiral and the medicine wheel made of flowers at the center. It was beautiful."

"Well, when I started to lay it out, I realized I'd need a strong young body to take care of it"—I started speaking faster—"and that I didn't want to be an old woman in a young body anymore. So I decided not to open the big garden and to ask the Elirians to change me back to how I was when they found me."

Anne's eyes widened. "But you were dying."

"They said they could change me back and keep me from dying, keep me warm—it was cold I was dying of—until people found me."

"I thought you were dying from lightning." Anne put down her wine glass and leaned over to touch my thigh. "Did you already ask them?"

"Not exactly. I only asked them if they could. When I connected with them just after Christmas, before I met Zachary."

"Maybe you shouldn't be making a decision like that so soon after breaking up with him. There's more to life than a relationship to a man."

"Of course. But my decision isn't because of Zachary, except that the failure of our relationship only clarified how out of sync I am."

"Clara, this is huge. You're so beautiful, so alive. You have everything."

"Yes." I couldn't keep the irony out of my voice. "I know, the wisdom of age and the strength of youth. And a split personality. It feels awful."

"I didn't know you felt that way. You seemed so happy, especially when you were with Zachary."

"That was actually when I felt most torn."

"But you were failing before. You had so much pain, and your heart—I was worried about you. If you go back to how you were you might not live much longer." Anne picked up her wine and sipped. There were tears in her eyes. One slid down her cheek, leaving a faint salty track behind.

"I know," I said, "but I don't want to go on and on. I don't fit in the world anymore. And I wasn't that decrepit. I did make it up to my special place."

"Okay." Anne turned to face me. "I'm getting contradictory messages. You don't want to go on and on, but you want the Elirians to keep you alive after they change you back."

"Because I haven't completed my *ulada*."

"Couldn't you complete your *ulada* in your young body?"

"And then go on and on?"

Anne gestured briefly.

"I thought of keeping my young body until my *ulada* was complete and then—but I couldn't. An old body near death I might hasten along, but not this perfect young body."

"No. That wouldn't be right."

"Besides, even though I don't know what I still have to do, I'm clear I have to do it as an old woman. Which makes this young body even more of a problem."

Anne was silent. I reached over to take her hand. "Listen. I lay on the lawn for hours yesterday afternoon, going over it all. I need you to hear me."

"I'm listening."

"Remember when gas stations were service stations? You'd drive up and a friendly man would come out. It was always a man; gender roles were still set in those days. He would greet you, check your tires and oil, and wash your windows while the tank filled. We'd chat about the weather, or whatever, connect. Remember that?"

"Yes. Sometimes they'd even sweep out the floor of your car."

"Now I swipe my credit card, pump my own gas, and leave without a word to anyone. Remember when you walked on a trail and people greeted you, sometimes stopped to exchange a few words, even if you didn't know them? Now the people you meet have plugs in their ears, listening to who-knows-what or busily talking on their cell phones. Eyes don't even meet."

I watched Anne's face. Her lips were pressed together, holding back protest. "Remember when going to the library was a time to chat with the librarian about the books you had just read and get help in finding the next ones? Remember the card catalogue? I know computers are probably more efficient, but I miss the card catalogue. You could touch it. Most days now I walk into the library, find the book I want, check myself out electronically, and leave without speaking to anyone. Everything electronic."

"Clara, that's how the world is now."

"I know. My point exactly. I hate it being so impersonal. Someone used to answer the phone when you called a business. Now it's press this, press that, and often you never get to speak to a real person."

Anne poured us more wine. I took a sip. "Everything electronic," I repeated. "Zachary with his whole life on his cell phone, people thinking they have 'friends' on Facebook. I can't function in the electronic world. I don't belong. I don't know how."

"You could learn."

"I don't want to."

We sipped our wine. Anne frowned.

My voice caught when I spoke again. "But the worst thing is, if I lived on and on I'd be lonely. I've been lonely enough in this life, always the odd one on the outer edge of the social spiral. You know. But I've had a few friends and my children and brief times of respite when I became involved in a new love affair. Always too brief. Then the loneliness returning."

I took another sip of wine. "My friends. As I am now, all my friends are forty or more years older than I... Remember Shirley?"

"Of course. It was shocking how fast she went."

"I sat in hospice with her the last three days, watching her struggle, holding her hand when she breathed her last breath. Who will be next? Sage? Amanda? You?" My fingers tightened around her hand. "I don't think I could bear life without my friend Anne."

Anne moved closer and put her arm around me, upsetting Camille, who jumped up and stalked off.

"My children," I said. "I don't want to sit in a hospice room and watch my children die."

We sat together in silence. I could hear the clock ticking in the kitchen. Evening light came through the window, touching the silver in Anne's hair, the laugh lines around her eyes. I leaned my head against her brow.

"That's how it would be," I said after a while, "everyone I loved dying, one by one, until the only people left were today's young people, absorbed in their electronics, who could never understand me. I can't stand another lifetime of loneliness."

Anne tightened her arm around me. "I get it. Oh, Clara. Your beautiful young body. It's a lot to give up. And a lot to take on, being old again." She shifted to look into my face. "You're really going to do it? You're sure they can change you back?"

"They said they could."

"When?"

"We arranged to meet again at my special place a year from when they first found me—that will be my next birthday—to say goodbye before they leave Earth. I'm going to ask them then."

"What if it was the lightning you were dying of? What if you die after they leave? It's all very well for you to talk. What about me? How do you think I'll feel if you get changed back and then just die?"

"Anne, I'm going to die. And so are you. It's the only thing we can be sure of. One or the other of us will go first."

Like rising flood waters, sorrow filled the room. Death loomed, both friend and foe. His shadow fell between us.

I tried to lighten up. "Maybe you could get that psychic friend you've been telling me about, the one who communicates with people on the other side—what was her name? Morna? Who would name a child that?"

"No one did. She chose it."

"Even worse. Maybe after I die you could get her to put you in touch with me, and I'll tell you all about it. Maybe when you die you'll find me, and we'll dance together again."

"Maybe." Anne brushed away a tear.

It had grown dark. She kissed my cheek, then reached past me to switch on a lamp. "I'm famished. Let's fix dinner."

"I think I'm tipsy."

She picked up the wine bottle and held it up to the light. "I think I am, too. No wonder. We almost finished this bottle." She stood. "I'll start the salmon."

I got up unsteadily. We were clumsy as we prepared our meal. We collided in the middle of the kitchen, I with a bundle of asparagus heading toward the sink, Anne with salmon on a plate heading toward the stove. I lurched and the asparagus flew out of my hands to land in a jumble like pick-up sticks, fortunately on the counter. The salmon was not so lucky. It slid off the plate and landed on the floor. Anne barely had time to retrieve it before Camille pounced. We started laughing. There were more bungles. We laughed harder with each mishap until we were in tears.

When we finally sat down to eat, the salmon was beyond crispy, the asparagus limp, and the salad wilted, but we were too hungry to care. We bowed our heads and gave thanks for life and ate. Camille relished the salmon skin we scraped into her dish when we were through.

⚘ ⚘

Zachary called eight times. I counted them. I checked my caller ID, did not answer, and erased his messages without listening to them. Finally he gave up. Then the week came when we had planned to go to Buenos Aires, and I imagined him returning to Seattle. I wondered what he would do about Suzy.

Tim called a few weeks later. "Lover boy's gone," he reported. "You can come back now."

"He's gone?"

"Yeah. He got transferred back to Seattle. Said he had family stuff to deal with. Sally and I and Roberto are heading down to Denver tonight. You want to ride with us?"

"I can't tonight. Thanks for thinking of me. Have a great dance."

Even after I knew I wouldn't meet Zachary, I didn't go back to tango. There is an expression in tango world, the tango moment. A tango moment is a *tanda* that is perfect and luscious, everything we long for the dance to be. It is said that when you have a tango moment, you should go home so as not to diminish it by following it with a lesser dance. I had had a four-month tango moment with Zachary, and could not bear the thought of dancing with any other.

Not dancing left a hole in my life, but there was plenty to fill it. Four months, I told myself, before I lose my strong body. Remembering the fatigue of being old, the awkwardness of painful knees, I resolved to put my house and garden in perfect order so they would be easier for me to care for when I returned.

I went through every cupboard, closet, and bureau drawer in my house, clearing out things that I knew I would never use again. As I worked I kept up a steady stream of chatter to myself—"You certainly don't need that anymore… Maybe I should keep these… You haven't worn that in years"—to focus my mind and shut out thoughts of Zachary. I cleaned out the basement and the garage. Big piles for Goodwill. I filled the recycle bin with the contents of my files, keeping only essential documents. I took boxes of books to the used bookstore.

Spring is always a busy time in the garden, but that year I worked harder than ever. I planted the small vegetable garden on the south side of the house with peas, tomatoes, pole beans, zucchini, and greens to feed myself for the summer. I worked over all my flowerbeds, putting in perennials that would be easy to care for. Flowers had become even more important to me than vegetables in recent years. Especially roses. Food for the soul. Beauty.

I went back and forth about whether to tell my children about my decision, and finally decided not to. I knew they would try to dissuade me, and that would make it hard for me to stand firm. I could spend time with Robin and Greg over the summer, and Lisa—she was so far away. I would call her often. I will see them all again after it's over, I assured myself. The Elirians said they would not let me die.

I continued my massage practice, but did not take new clients. I had decided to close my practice on Summer Solstice and spend my remaining months of strength in the mountains.

Sometimes I woke in the night gripped by fear. Was I insane to let go of a healthy body and return to the pain, the fatigue, the racing heart? I didn't know what damage the lightning had done before the Elirians healed me. I remembered the black headache, the paralysis, Herb saying there had been blood on the rock. What if I lived the rest of my life twisted and crippled, unable to care for myself? What if, after all, I died when the Elirians left? I knew I must die eventually, that indeed I was making this choice in order not to live on and on, but I wasn't ready. Something was still incomplete. When the fear was worst, I told myself I could always change my mind. But I knew I wouldn't.

Then with morning light, morning meditation, clarity would return, and I would rise from my pillow and plunge into the next task.

⁂

I thought of Zachary more than I wanted to. Sometimes I raged at him, all the words I hadn't said, all the hurt. Other times I grieved and ached with longing. Still other times, these extremes dissolved into quiet caring for him. I hoped he had married Suzy. After all, they'd gone together for five years and found each other so attractive they'd had sex the first time they met again. They both danced tango and wanted kids. It would probably work. Having a child might settle him down.

Then I would rage anew. Maybe it will be better, I told myself, when I'm old again. I was peaceful then. Maybe this tumult is just because of my young body.

One afternoon when I was in rage mode, I left the house seeking to calm myself with a walk. As I passed through the back entry, I saw a bottle of bubble soap I kept handy for when the children came to visit, and impulsively stuck it in my pocket. I'd always enjoyed blowing bubbles, loving the way they caught the sun in rainbows, floated on the wind, and then just burst. Gone.

The spring afternoon was cool and sunny. I walked swiftly through the quiet neighborhood and came to the lake. There I slowed my pace, drinking in the light on the water, the new leaves unfolding, the song of a meadowlark.

As I came to the far side of the lake and started up the path into the foothills, I felt the jar of bubble soap in my pocket. I pulled it out and sat down on the hillside overlooking the lake. Maybe, I thought, some bubbles would lighten my mood. Under me, the new grass was soft and green, growing up between last year's dead stalks.

Then I had an idea. A bubble for each lover I've had in my life. Let them drift away, burst, and be gone.

Taking the wand out of the jar, I opened my memories and began. A bubble for the young boy to whom I surrendered my virginity at age fifteen. It didn't go far before it burst in thin air. A bubble for Dan. His caught an updraft, shone briefly with a rainbow, then drifted downhill and broke against a young willow. A bubble for Jon. His came out, not singly, but in a cluster of bubbles. For him and all his mistresses, I thought. Four more for the men with whom I futilely sought love and permanence after Jon left. I spoke each one's name as I sent a bubble out into the soft spring air. None of them lasted long.

"Let them go," I whispered.

Last of all, a bubble for Zachary. It floated high, a rainbow bright in its curved surface, then descended, caught on a dry stem of last year's grass, and burst.

"Let him go. Let them all go," I murmured, my throat thick.

I sat a while, gazing over the lake below me, watching the ripples moving in the sunlight.

There was more to let go. It was not coincidence that the other half of all those relationships was the same person—me. Let go my unskillful ways of relating. I began blowing bubbles again. Let go clinging too tightly. Let go fearing and pushing away the very intimacy I longed for. Let go trying too hard to please until I was all bent out of shape and resentful. Let go complaining. Let go making poor choices of lovers out of desperation. Let go hanging onto relationships long after it was clear they would never fly.

All the futile ways. Let them go.

For a moment I wavered on the brink of tears. Then I picked up the wand and blew three more bursts of bubbles. As they drifted around me, I let out a long sigh, and lay down on my back on the sweet earth, arms and legs spread wide.

～ ～

On the day of Solstice, I took my first high country hike. Anne went with me. But we got only as far as Sapphire Lake before we were stopped by snow. Two days later I went alone carrying snowshoes and climbed Whale Ridge, a long, rounded mountain that humped up south of Silver Lake and rose to over 12,000 feet. The snow was deep on the forest path, but at the top the ground was blown clear. I hiked to the highest point I could reach and opened my heart to the immensity, mountains upon mountains spreading away into the distance. I will drink this in, I promised myself. I will fill myself with this glory so if I never come to these high places again after this summer, I will still be full.

Several times I hiked with friends, but soon knew I needed to walk alone. Conversation distracted me from being present with the gifts of every turn in the path, from stopping to lose myself in the heart of a tiny alpine flower or in the distant purple peaks. When Robin knew I was hiking alone, he asked me to call him before I left in the morning and when I got home in the evening. "Just in case, Mama. I know you're strong and careful. I also know you go off the trail a lot and if anything happened…"

"Thanks, Robin. I'll be okay. I'm very careful. But I'll call you."

All through the summer, three or four times a week, I walked in the mountains, through fields of brilliant flowers, along rushing streams, beside tumbling waterfalls, across scree marked only by cairns. Often I took off my boots and, barefoot, left the trail to find the solitude I so deeply craved. I scrambled through bogs, dipped in icy streams and lakes, stood again and again on the continental divide, buffeted by wind, exulting. I walked on days of cold rain, the colors more vivid under the gray sky, the rocks shining with wetness, each leaf and pine needle dripping jewels of water. I wandered the long loops of trails in Rocky Mountain National Park. I grew lean and strong and brown. I walked farther and higher than I ever had before.

When Robin and his family invited me to go camping with them, it was good to play with the children and sleep out with them under the stars, teaching them the constellations, but I was impatient with the pace of the family walks. I wanted to go higher and faster, then remembered how only last summer they had slowed to accommodate me. And that they would again.

At the end of July I drove down to Santa Fe and took a three-day backpacking trip with Greg to the high places he loved. We were both strong and acclimated to altitude and challenged each other, climbing steep slopes at 12,000 feet and above, walking miles each day. Ravens circled above us. The first night we camped in a dell nestled between rocky outcroppings. It was cold, but the moon was nearing its full and we slept out in its splendor. The second night we camped by a lake that reflected the white jewel of the moon as we sat by the water's edge and talked deeply of the life we had shared, of the parts of our lives that we hadn't shared, of love and death and God. We returned more deeply bonded than ever, all past hurts from his turbulent adolescent years healed at last.

Then it was August. Only four more weeks. I started going to the high country every day, coming home only long enough to tend the garden, pay the bills, and go to the grocery store.

One day I lingered so long by the tarns above Blue Lake that twilight caught me unaware. The moon was waning, rising late, and I realized it would be unsafe to walk down in the dark. I found a sheltered spot, a hollow between two boulders, curled up in my gray cloak, and slept, woke cold and cramped, and rose at sunrise to dip in the icy tarn.

When I got home that afternoon, there was a message from Robin on my phone.

"Mama, are you okay? I just realized you didn't call last night. Please call. I'm worried."

I called and explained.

Robin was not mollified. "Don't do that again. If I hadn't been so distracted last night trying to get the bugs out of my program… I didn't realize. You could have died up there and I'd never forgive myself. I won't forget again. So you come home at night and call."

I felt both touched and constrained by his caring, but knowing what was coming, I was grateful.

On the last day before my birthday I hiked all the way to the point of Whale Ridge where I could look down on Sapphire Lake far below. No one was there. I lay on my back watching clouds fly on the wind, and prayed to my elusive God that however I emerged from the lightning strike, I might have the strength to complete my *ulada* in integrity before I was called through the dark door of death to unimaginable home.

Chapter 10

Birthday

On the morning of my birthday, I woke before dawn. I turned on my side, seeking to sleep again, but it was no use. The immensity of the day loomed over me.

Finally I got up, shivering with trepidation and anticipation. I looked in the bathroom mirror as I combed my thick gold-brown curls, washed my beautiful face. "Goodbye, young beauty," I whispered to my reflection. "Thank you for the gifts you have given me, for the lessons you have taught me."

My hands shook as I prepared tea and packed my lunch. They still shook on the steering wheel as I drove up the canyon. I felt as I had before my hip surgery, terrified of the pain yet eager to get through it so I could begin to heal. Only now—I sought an un-healing of my body in the hope I could be whole again.

The strangeness of this thought made everything feel unreal, even the familiar curves of the canyon, the winding road that led to the trailhead.

The air was chill, the morning just opening when I reached the parking lot. There were only two cars there. A third car rolled up as I was putting on my boots, and three young men climbed out. They greeted me as they wriggled into their big backpacks. I was startled to see their interest, their appreciative smiles. In my mind I was already an old woman. They lingered, chatting with me. I bent my head and fiddled with my pack until finally they wished me a good hike and set off down the trail.

What shall I do with my keys? My hand holding them trembled. I won't be able to drive down. What will happen with my car? Not knowing what else to do, I put my keys in their usual pocket of my pack. Then I was ready, my pack settled over my gray cloak, the straps tightened, my sunhat tucked in my belt, my staff in my hand.

Once I started walking, fear dissipated. It had rained the night before. The moist, pungent smell of the forest, the glisten of early morning sunlight on wet pine needles, the softness of damp earth under my feet absorbed my senses. I settled into the long, easy stride that had carried me many miles a day throughout the summer.

As I walked the wide path beside Silver Lake I came to the place where I'd noticed the dead tree that reminded me of Death the year before. It was still standing, black amid the green of the living trees.

"Not yet," I whispered to it. "Please not yet." Fear shivered through me again and I walked more quickly. I passed through the gateway between the big ponderosas, followed the path along the river valley, past the little track that led to the foot of the waterfall and up the last steep ascent to Sapphire Lake. There was no one there. I looked at my watch. It was only eight o'clock. I had walked all the way in less than forty-five minutes. I recalled how I had come up the year before, slowly, taking two hours, stopping often to rest, to look, to remember.

Grief swept through me. How could I have come so fast? I didn't look at everything. I may never walk this trail again.

I spun around. Weeping, I ran back down, jumping over the rocky place, hurtling down the steep place, running, running, along the side of the river valley, through the ponderosa gate into the forest. A few people coming up the trail greeted me, but I did not answer, tears streaking my face. I ran until I saw the parking lot through the trees. There I stopped, breathless, and turned around. The trail up lay before me.

I rubbed the tears off my cheeks and took a drink from my water bottle. Slowly I began to walk. Look at everything, I told myself. Feel the path under your feet, smell the forest, breathe the air. Touch the pine needles and feel the raindrop that falls off cold on your fingers. Sniff the butterscotch aroma of the ponderosa trunk. Pick off a bubble of sap and rub it under your nose. Pause to listen to the sound of the rivulet crossing the path. Look through the trees at the reflections in the lake. Bend and touch the tiny elephant-head flowers by the side of the path. Don't overlook the flaming paintbrush. Sit down on the bridge, take off your boots and put your feet in the stream, feel the cold caress of its swirl. Stand a long time in the ponderosa gate and look up at the peaks as if you had never seen them before. Wonder at the tiny worlds of moss and flowers in the crevices of the rocks. Trace the lichen with your fingertip. Do not pass by the path to the waterfall. Stand and breathe the air off its tumbling tumult, see how the flowers in its midst bend and sway with its movement. Feel the strength of your legs as you ascend the steep place, your balance as you clamber over the rocks.

So I came again to Sapphire Lake. I sat in the sloping meadow where I always rested, tilting my head back to drink in the peaks. Light shifted on the surface of the water, deep blues and greens merging as in the eyes of the Elirians. Soon I will be with them again, I thought, hear the music of their voices, feel their silken fur, the beating of their hearts as they hold me close. Just one more time, and then they will be gone. The thought of them brought me to my feet and I began striding up the trail.

No. Slowly. Look deeply. You may never see these lichen-covered cliffs again, the swift shimmer of the stream as it rushes around rocks, the dark green of pines against the blue, blue sky. Slowly, then, I went on until I came at last, barefoot across the high valley, up beside the waterfall that divided around purple-pink flowers, to my special place.

The sun shone down on the bright green grass by the water's edge and into the deep pool, sparkling on ripples where the current swept around its curve. In the quieter part of the water, blue sky and white clouds were reflected, their images blending through the clear water with the gray-brown shapes of the rounded rocks on the bottom. The boulder rose above me, vivid with multi-colored lichen.

I sighed deeply, slipped off my pack, dropped my staff and boots, and sank to my knees, resting my brow in the softness of tundra grass. Sacred place. I lifted my head, sat back on my heels. After today will this be only a memory for me? Am I all amiss to love so passionately an earthly place so high I may never reach it again? To love so passionately anything but God?

I got up and walked around, looking, touching, my senses highly attuned as they had been all the way up the mountain. I climbed up the side of the boulder, past the fateful place where I had fallen a year ago, to the krum tree. The greater part of it lay brown and withered, the long, black scar on its trunk, its dead branches crushed to the rock by the last winter's snow. But near the ground there was a short piece of trunk unburned. New green branches had grown out from it. Wonder flooded me. The tree was not dead after all. I curled my hand around the stub of trunk where it emerged from the rock it had split long ago at its beginning.

"You will live," I said to it, "and I will live—a little longer. You will probably outlive me."

I sat running my fingers through the soft new needles and felt the burden of living on and on slip off me. Only a little longer, a year or two maybe to complete my *ulada*, and then—

A fleeting image came, the black robed figure, turned toward me now, holding his cloak open. Awe shook me. My hand tightened around the trunk.

For a moment the warmth of the sun dimmed. I looked up. The sky was blue with scattered white clouds, and the one that had briefly covered the sun was already moving past. Probably no storms today. Yet I shivered.

I climbed down the side of the boulder, shed my clothes, and squatted on the rocks at the water's edge. "Wash away fear," I whispered to the deep, clear pool. I plunged and came up gasping, tossed water over my head and watched it fall down sparkling around me. Let go fear.

But back out on the grass, I still trembled. I opened my pack and pulled out my bathing cloth, a new one Anne had given me, and dried myself.

Standing in the soft grass by the water's edge, I began to move, stretching freely at first, then allowing yoga postures to flow through me. Feel it. Treasure it. I will never do yoga like this again. Sun salute, slowly, deeply breathing. I must let it all go, and receive whatever is given back after the lightning, gratefully, as a new gift. Cobra and bow. Perhaps I will do yoga again, even if it isn't like this. Wheel. Hips pressed up to the sky, fingertips touching my heels. Forward bend sitting. Perhaps I will even dance tango, walk in the mountains again. I just don't know. Shoulder stand, plow, curl down slowly, one vertebra at a time. Breathe. Trust.

Gradually I calmed and the inner shiver faded away. When I finished my yoga I sat again at the edge of the pool. An intention for the coming year.

May I trust. May I accept my body however it emerges from the coming change and live what life is left to me with gratitude. May I find my path to complete my *ulada* and then go gently, go gently.

It was a good intention. I slipped into the water again, dropped down to the bottom, then scrambled out and wrapped myself in my cloth. This time the intensity of that icy baptism was exquisite, cleansing. I dressed and snuggled into the warmth of my gray cloak.

A light wind came up. I pulled the hood up over my wet hair and rummaged in my pack for lunch. Bread and cheese, an apple, a thermos of peppermint tea. Leaning back against the boulder, I ate, sipped tea, and mused. My hands holding the apple were smooth. Soon they will be gnarly, I thought, wrinkled as all of me will be. It's all right. It's good. I will finally be myself again. But not as I was before. I am forever changed by knowing the Elirians, by all the events of the last year.

I know I will not long to be young.

So strange. The Elirians healed me to express my essence. If that is so, why am I so uncomfortable in this body? Maybe because an essence belongs on the eternal plane, and I am here in time, walking the earthly path between birth and death.

The sun angled lower in the sky. When will they come? I wondered. My hands trembled again as I packed up my thermos and lunch box. "Walk," I told myself, "walk while you can."

I set off up the valley, following the stream towards its source, weaving between bogs and tarns, walking over smooth, rounded rocks, warm under my bare feet from the long, sunny day. I walked all the way to the rock where the Elirians had set me down a year ago and sat looking up into the sky, searching. The sun had dropped behind the western peaks and the clouds were radiant with pink.

Then I remembered they said they would meet me where they found me. I jumped up. I had come a long way, wandering slowly, looking, touching, sensing. It was growing late. Anxious tension rose in me. Maybe they were already there. Though surely I would have seen their ship descending. Unless I was looking into a tarn or bending to smell a tiny alpine flower. I ran fast, lightly, leaping from rock to rock. Remember this. I will not run like this again. I was breathless when I returned to my special place. They were not there.

I fussed with my possessions, tucking away my sun hat, checking to be sure my socks were in my boots. Should I put my boots on? No, they were off when the lightning struck. Can I bear the pain when it comes?

All at once a new dread arose, terror deeper than the fear I had been fending off all day.

What if they don't come?

I crouched down, wrapping my arms around my knees, head bent. For a long time I could barely breathe. At last I lifted my head.

The silver disc floated high above the northern peaks, glinting pink with the last glow of sunset, then quickly descended until it hovered over a grassy spot on the other side of the stream. The silver door slid open and they floated out, singing my name.

⁜

We sat together on the soft floor of the space ship, rainbow light circling around us. They had welcomed me, holding me against their hearts, warming me with their touch and their love. All fear was gone. I felt only the joy of being with them again.

Tell me of your mission.

It has been good. Merilea's deep voice resonated within me. *We have learned what we need to know and much more.*

We have come to admire you humans, Tirini continued, her gold-flecked eyes shining. *We were wary of you because of the discordance we felt across the galaxies. It is true. There is much hate and violence, much hurt on your planet. But you are also brave to live as you do on the cusp of death, to bear pain and still laugh and love and go on. Your art, your dances, your music, your poetry and stories are beautiful. Many, like you, hold a strong light.*

It is a puzzle to us, Kiria picked up the song, *how you who have such gifts have gone so far astray. You damage your planet, your mother. We have looked into her essence. She is a powerful, deep being, but she cannot bear what you do to her much longer. She quivers inside, seeking to regain her balance. There will be more violent and frequent volcanoes, tidal waves, earthquakes, floods and droughts. Her poles are shifting and the oceans are rising. There have been such changes on Earth before, but never when there were so many people. Many will die, and there will be much fear.*

I felt my heart contract. Lillilia touched me. *The balance can still be restored. There are many among you who care for Earth and all her creatures. There is the possibility of a whole new culture emerging. We will advise the council to send many emissaries soon, to help guide your people through the times ahead.*

I don't understand. My thought reached out to them. *How can you return to the council light-years away and send emissaries back in time to help us? You said last summer you could be back in no time. How do you do it?*

We fold time. Rosiri's blue-tinted fur undulated in soft waves as she took the edge of my skirt and folded it. Holding it folded with one of her hands, she touched the two edges of the fold with two other hands. *This edge here is the exact time and place as this one. We return to the same time and place as if we had not been away. Yet all this*—she opened the fold—*that we have experienced here still happened and we remember it.*

I struggled to comprehend. My bewilderment must have been comic, because their song rippled with laughter.

Ah, Clara, Kiria's voice floated out of their medley, *time is not as you humans see it, not a line. Possibly more like a circle, or a spiral, flexible, mutable, but actually not real at all. There is only now.*

As for the emissaries, Tirini sang in her bell-like voice, *we can go to the council in an instant and they can send emissaries back in an instant, but once they come here they become weighted by Earth and must accomplish their mission in Earth time. So you may not know they are here immediately. But they will come. Do not fear.*

We sat silent together. Outside the big windows, twilight had become night. Stars were rising out of the valley, shining over the peaks.

Before you go, I began. I struggled to find images for my request, but they already knew.

Ah, they sang.

Lillilia's high, sweet song flowed out of their symphony. *You want us to change you back, as you were when we first found you.*

Yes.

Ah, they sang again, *we are sad for the pain you must feel, but we understand now about aging and the need for congruence.*

Can you change me back but not let me die? I don't feel that my ulada is complete… only I don't know what I still must do.

They watched me with their wise, loving eyes as I struggled with my confusion.

Maybe I shouldn't ask it, since there are difficult times coming and I am young and strong… My younger friends wanted me to get involved again, to go into the streets to protest, go to meetings. I bent my head in shame at my refusal. *But it didn't feel right. Even though my body was young, my spirit felt tired.*

It was not right. That is not your ulada now. Kiria's song was clear. *You have lived a long life and touched many with your light. You do not need to begin again and protest in the streets.*

Then what must I do?

Write your story, they sang together.

Write my story?

Yes, Tirini sang. *Write of what you have learned being old, being young, then choosing to be old again and why. Write about the seasons of life as you described them to us and about congruence. If those who read your story come to better understand their uladas and to have less fear of death, then violence will diminish.*

Write about us, Kiria continued, *and what we have taught you about the council. If your people understand those they call aliens are wise and benevolent, not cruel and violent as they imagine, then finally we may be able to communicate with them, and the web will shift.*

Is it part of my ulada, to write my story?

We believe it is, Rosiri sang. *We believe it was not chance we found you. We don't understand why, but of all the humans we have touched, you are the only one who remembers us, the only one who knows who we are and why we came. For all the others, we are only a dream. Like Zachary, they think they were just lucky they didn't get hurt in an accident, or that they had a miraculous remission of their illness. Zachary remembered only because of you, and he will soon forget.*

I went still inside. *It is a big ulada then. Important, since no one else remembers.*

They gazed at me with their wondrous eyes. *Yes,* they sang together.

Then I will, I will write my story. Tears welled up. *Though there are no words in our language adequate to express the wonder of you.*

I pressed my hands against my chest. *I think I will need to include what happens when I return to my old body. How will I know when the story ends?*

Kiria touched my heart. *When your ulada is complete.*

There is one more piece besides the story. Merilea's dark eyes smiled. *You will find it.*

We were silent again. I looked out the window at the dark sky. To the east I saw the stars coming close to the configuration they had been in when I first opened my eyes after the lightning strike. Fear rippled through me again. The Elirians felt it and gathered close around me.

It is true, Kiria sang. *The time draws near.*

How will you change me?

There is only one way we can, Kiria answered. *We are healers; we don't know how to reverse the process. We must fold time as Rosiri explained to you. Then you will be as you were when we found you. You have asked us not to let you die, so we will stay with you and keep you warm until your people come for you.*

Perhaps, Lillilia sang, *we can ease the effects of the lightning a little. It is hard for us to think of you in pain again.*

I trembled in their arms. Gentle hands stroked me. Their voices blended. *We will be with you. We will comfort you and ease your pain. Do not be afraid. Your people will come for you and you will live to complete your ulada.*

And you? I asked.

When we know you are safe, they sang together, *we will go to the council. When we have told them all we know, we will go home to Eliria. Our ulada complete, we will sink into her and be renewed until we are called to rise again.*

I felt the love and longing in their voices as they sang of their home.

And, Rosiri sang alone in her odd, haunting voice, *the song of Eliria will be forever changed because of what we have known here.*

When you have returned to Eliria, will I still be able to hear your voices?

Rosiri's response was sad. *No, it is too far. But our love will be with you always.*

It is almost time, Tirini sang.

I stood up, my heart pounding. *Shall I go to the rock?*

No need. Kiria drew me down again. *Stay with us. When time folds you will be there.*

I looked into their wise, deep eyes. *I love you. I will never forget you.*

They shifted me to the center of the circle and gathered close around me. Each one placed a hand on my heart as they linked their other hands in an intricate pattern that enclosed me. They all leaned toward the center of the circle where I sat. Softly at first, they hummed. The hum increased in intensity, a hum like no sound I had ever heard before. My skin prickled. The hum entered my body, piercing every cell until I felt charged with light, almost beyond bearing. Still it rose, higher and higher, stronger and stronger. Then stopped. The sudden silence crackled with power.

Pain crashed through my body with such intensity that I couldn't breathe, could barely exist. I was splayed out on the rock, prone, my head turned to one side, exactly as I had been before. I saw the stars over the valley exactly as they had been before. Something sharp pressed into my cheek and I could not move to push it away. My heart raced and pounded. Bitter cold penetrated me. Mindless terror possessed me.

Ah! Their song of compassion floated down into me. I felt Kiria's hand on my back over my heart. My heart slowed and steadied. *We are here with you,* they sang. *Do not be afraid. We will care for you.* Many hands rested on me, over all my body, sending warmth into me. One hand lifted my head, brushed away the sharp thing, and slipped something soft under my cheek. Their warm bodies clustered close around me.

I wept, all rational thought swept away by the stark terror of finding myself paralyzed on the rock again, and the blessed relief of their presence. They sang and stroked me. Little by little I was able to think, to remember why I was there, what I had chosen. As terror receded, the pain became less and I was able to send my thought to them.

Thank you. Thank you. I am doing better now. Even though I knew it was coming, it was a shock. Thank you, Kiria, for holding my heart. It scares me so when it races.

I felt Kiria's warm fur on my face as she bent over me. *I will give you a gift,* she sang softly, *a steady heart until your ulada is complete.*

We must not change too much, Merilea cautioned. *Part of her ulada is integrating this experience.*

Just the heart, Kiria answered.

And ease the head blow, Lillilia added. I felt her hand on my brow, penetrating the black pain with light.

Merilea sang again. *We will sing you to sleep so that you may rest until morning. We are here with you, our love around you.*

They sang. The beauty of their song, the depth of its resonance, swept away all awareness of pain. I became lost in it, as I had been the first time I heard it—music of the spheres, the stars dancing their circles in the vast depths of the universe.

I woke to dawn light and the sound of Robin's voice. "I remember this waterfall. It's close now. There's a deep pool."

"Pray she's not in it." Greg's voice.

A flurry of movement around me, the Elirians' song within me. *We must go now. Our love is with you always.* The spaceship swung into my view as I lay, still paralyzed with my head turned to one side. The silver door was open and Tirini hovered there.

Farewell, Clara.

Farewell, farewell, they all sang as they floated up and away from me into the open door. I felt the sharp chill of early morning as their warmth left me. The door slid closed at the same moment that my sons appeared on the rise above the waterfall. The silver sphere hung above their heads, then moved upward. The Elirians' sweet song of love and farewell sang within me at the same moment that my ears heard Robin cry, "Mama!"

Chapter 11

Rescue

My sons knelt beside me. "Mama, are you okay?" Robin's eyes, close to mine, were frightened.

I struggled to speak. Several tries, and a croak emerged. I tried again and managed, "Not okay, but alive." I smiled, suddenly delighted that I was alive.

"She's smiling. That's good." Greg touched my back. "What happened, Mom?"

"Lightning."

"Lightning! When?"

That stopped me. My mind spun. When indeed? "Last year."

They turned toward each other, then back to me.

"Mom, that doesn't make any sense. When did you get hit by lightning?" Greg bent to look into my face.

I couldn't answer. It was too hard to speak. I closed my eyes and drifted into pain.

"Call the rescue team." Robin's voice was urgent.

"Right. She's not walking out, that's for sure." Greg stood up and moved a few steps away. I opened my eyes. I could see his feet, caught scattered words—"We found her... No... bad shape, lightning... GPS..." and a jumble of numbers.

Robin stayed kneeling beside me. "Mama, it's going to be all right. There's a rescue team just down the valley. We'll get you out of here and taken care of."

There was a small white flower by his hand. Behind his head the rising sun touched the tops of the peaks. Greg came back and knelt by me. "Can you move?"

"Can't move."

"Whoa!" Greg came closer and knelt on the white flower. "There's blood. Looks like you cut your head." He touched my head and I gasped in pain. "Oh, sorry, Mom. God, you're soaked. Are you cold?"

"Cold."

Robin took off his jacket and laid it over me. From down the valley I heard a loud "Halloo." Greg jumped up. I saw his feet move away. "Up here!" he called.

I tried to speak, just to say Robin's name but it was too much effort. Pain crescendoed, and I slipped away.

What followed was a jumble of scattered perceptions. Many men's voices. "Hit that krum tree square on." I was lifted. "Careful of her neck." Somehow turned over, still stiff and immobile. In the sky, high above the peaks, I saw the tiny silver disc. Even as I glimpsed it, it winked out and was gone. I let out a cry of loss. Robin bent over me. I looked into his eyes, weeping. "They're gone."

"It's okay, Mama. They're right here taking care of you."

Blankets were laid over me. Straps were tightened around me.

Men's voices. "She's soaking wet."

"It's a wonder she survived. It was below freezing up here last night."

"Hypothermic."

"She seems to be paralyzed."

Greg's voice. "What's this?" My eyes opened. He was standing where I could see him, shaking out a silver cloth, iridescent in the dawn light.

I jerked into consciousness. The silver blanket. The blanket they had made for me from their fur when they first found me. That's what they had slipped under my cheek in the night. I would have reached for it if I could.

I summoned all my strength. It must not get lost in all the confusion. "Greg!"

"I'm here, Mom."

I wasn't on the ground anymore. There were men all around me. I could see their belts and the bottoms of their jackets.

"It's precious, the blanket. Keep it safe."

"Okay, Mom. How'd you get it under your face when you couldn't move?"

"They put it there."

"They?"

"The Elirians."

"Someone was here with you last night?"

I had spent my strength. "Keep it safe," was all I could manage.

A man's voice said, "Ready?"

I slipped away again, wove in and out of consciousness, aware of being carried, brief glimpses of cliffs, peaks, trees tilting over me. The ambulance, swaying as it wound down the canyon road. I opened my eyes. Matt sat beside me. "Hi, Matt," I whispered.

He looked surprised. "Hi there," he answered smiling. "How did you know my name?"

"From before. My sons?"

"They're taking your car down. They'll meet us at the hospital."

In the hospital, hands lifting me, peeling off my wet clothing, wrapping me in heated blankets. Tapes on my brow. Antiseptic smell. Wires. A needle in my wrist.

A woman's voice, "Rest now. You're going to be all right."

The remainder of the day was a confused blur. I was handled, moved about. There was an X-ray room. Voices of strangers intertwined with Robin's voice, Greg's voice. I was aware that one or the other was always with me, touching me, comforting me. The hospital room. Monitors hovering around me, an IV bag hanging over me. Pain, aching heaviness in my limbs, the black headache. Darkness again.

In the night I woke from a frightful dream, flinging myself about, crying, "I can't move! I can't move!"

Lisa was beside me. "It's all right, Mother. You can move. The paralysis has passed."

I lay still. Felt my left arm flung over my head. Lisa. I must be dreaming.

"Let's bring your arm down here. We don't want the IV to come out." She moved my arm to my side, then massaged it gently with her wise, strong hands.

I opened my eyes to the hospital room, to her face bending over me, her brown curls falling forward. "Lisa? Is it really you?"

"It really is."

"How did you get here?"

"On the first plane I could catch when Greg called me."

"So fast."

"I was already in the states, remember? Teaching in California. I called you to wish you happy birthday and told you, night before last."

I remembered then, but that had been over a year ago. My mind swirled in confusion.

"Oh," I said. "I can move?"

"You've been moving all around."

I signaled my legs and they straightened under the sheet. They ached, almost unbearably, but they moved. Immense relief. I sighed and closed my eyes again. Lisa came around to the other side of the bed and began massaging my right arm. I drifted away.

⤟ ⤠

Clear daylight came through the window when I woke. I lay still, feeling tired, but at rest, the pain eased.

Someone was talking, an unfamiliar voice, a woman. Quietly I turned my head. Lisa and Greg and Robin were all there, standing near the door of the room with a woman I didn't know. She was speaking.

"We've checked her over thoroughly. Fortunately there are no burns. Although she's had a concussion and survived a lightning strike, there's only slight disturbance in her brain waves. X-rays of her spine show no injury. She's come out of the paralysis. Her heart is surprisingly steady considering all she's been through and her history of arrhythmia. We started last night bringing down the sedatives, so when she wakes we can get a better sense of how she is. She may have some amnesia and persisting headaches for a while. But all in all, it looks as if she'll make a good recovery. Not too many eighty-year-olds roam around above tree line. She's a strong woman."

"She is," Greg said. "Thank you, Dr. Martin. That's all really good news."

"I'll stop in later and see how she's doing." Dr. Martin shook hands with each of them and went out.

"Hi," I said.

They came and gathered around my bed. Greg beamed down at me. "Hey, Mom."

Lisa bent and kissed my brow. "Good morning, Mother."

Robin took my hand.

"How long have you been awake?" Greg asked.

"Long enough to hear the doctor's report."

"You were just lying there quietly listening?" Lisa teased.

I smiled, happiness flooding me at the rare event of having them all there together. "I figured I had as much interest as anyone. They've had me on sedatives?"

"Yes," Lisa answered, "but they're cutting back now."

"Tell them to stop entirely," I ordered. "I hate being befuddled."

"You were in a lot of pain, Mama," Robin said. "They wanted you to rest."

"Okay, I've rested. I don't want any more of that stuff."

Greg chuckled. "She's getting feisty again."

"How are you feeling?" Lisa asked.

I went inside to explore. "Everything aches, but not too badly." I stretched a little. "I am so grateful I can move again."

They stayed with me through the day, brought me food from Whole Foods across the street to replace the paltry hospital fare. I drowsed off and on and woke to find them still there—such a comfort.

In the afternoon, the nurse got me up to sit in a big easy chair. With her support, I found that my legs could carry me the few steps between the bed and the chair, but the short excursion exhausted me.

I will be better, I promised myself inwardly as I sank into the chair. It's just the result of the lightning. Being old again doesn't mean I will be this bad until I die.

My children pulled up chairs to sit around me. Greg leaned forward and touched my knee. "Tell us what happened the day before yesterday. The whole story. We know you were struck by lightning, thank God not directly. That krum tree on top of the boulder took the direct hit."

"But that wasn't day before yesterday. The krum tree is growing back. That was a year ago. Day before yesterday there were no storms. I dipped in the stream and walked all the way up to its source. It's so beautiful up there. Then the Elirians came at dusk. I sat with them in their ship and they told me all they had learned in their year here. Then when it was time, they changed me back."

My three children stared at me.

"Mother, I think you're confused," Lisa said. "It was only the day before yesterday the lightning struck you. On your birthday."

"On my birthday a year ago," I insisted.

They looked at each other, then back at me.

"What are you talking about—the ship, they changed you back. Who?" Greg asked.

"You know. The Elirians. I told you the whole story a year ago. When you found me at the trailhead. How they healed everything in my body and made me young again. You barely knew me at first, remember?

You didn't recognize me at all, Lisa, when you came at Christmas." I searched their faces.

"You don't remember?" I felt a sinking in the pit of my stomach as I looked at their blank faces. "I was young for a whole year, younger than you. Strong. We went backpacking only a month ago, Greg, just you and I. You took me way high. It was glorious."

Greg's eyes were wide and shocked.

A shiver passed through me. "You don't remember?"

I turned to Robin. "You remember. We went camping with your family. You and I swam way upstream and floated back down. And you met Zachary. Remember meeting Zachary?"

"Mama, I don't think you could have swum upstream with me last summer. I don't know who Zachary is."

I started to tremble. "Lisa, you remember. Remember last Christmas when we talked and you said I was incongruent? That was really the turning point, but it took me months to realize I needed to ask them to change me back. Because I met Zachary and…" I trailed off. Lisa clearly didn't remember either.

She came and sat on the side of my chair and put her arm around me. "It's okay, Mother. It sounds as if there's more of a story than we thought, that we're not remembering things it's important that we know. Why don't you tell us the whole story. Begin with climbing the mountain on your birthday."

"My eightieth birthday, or my eighty-first?"

They looked at each other again. "Your eightieth," Lisa said.

Something tickled the back of my mind, but my head ached and I couldn't grasp it.

"Tell us." Robin came to my other side and took my hand. Greg sat facing me, a worried frown creasing his brow.

I told them, beginning with my eightieth birthday. I told them about the walk up, how hard and slow it had been, the lightning, the dying, the rescue. The Elirians, their radiant fur, their song, the wonder of their ship, their healing touch. "They are beings of perfect love," I told my children. "You cannot be with them without being changed forever."

"What happened then?" Greg asked.

I continued, telling how I had discovered I was young when I took off my clothes to dip, how I had come down from the mountain and found Greg and Robin looking for me, how I had looked in the mirror and discovered myself to be beautiful with Elirian eyes, all the adventures of the year that followed, the whole affair with Zachary, the point of choice with the garden, the amazing summer in the mountains. They listened with rapt attention, sometimes exclaiming, often exchanging glances with each other.

"I didn't tell any of you when I decided to change back because I was afraid you would try to dissuade me. I knew you were glad not to worry about my aging difficulties. But I couldn't go on that way. I don't belong in this world anymore. I don't fit. I couldn't bear to go on living another whole lifetime, watching you die before me. I was all out of sync with myself. So day before yesterday, on my eighty-first birthday, I went back up to my special place and they met me and folded…"

Then I understood.

"What year is it?" I asked.

My three children were silent, staring at me, then looking at each other.

"Two thousand eleven," Greg answered.

"They folded time," I whispered. "They put me back in the exact time and place in which they first found me. It was the only way they could change me back. I should have realized. Rosiri explained it to me, how they fold time. That's how they travel across the universe in no time at all. *They folded time.* Then they stayed with me and kept me warm so I wouldn't die. And Kiria gave me a steady heart. And they put the blanket they made out of their fur under my cheek. Greg! You saw the blanket, the silver blanket. Where is it?"

Greg's mouth was open. He closed it carefully. "I put it in your pack. Robin brought your pack and boots down."

"My staff?"

"I brought that, too," Robin answered. "All your stuff is in your house."

"What's the silver blanket?" Lisa asked.

"They made it for me out of their fur, singing while they wove it. Because I was so cold after they took off my wet clothes. At first they thought my clothes were fur. That first night when they found me. You must believe me now. You held it, Greg."

"It was unusual," Greg said slowly.

"They were still there when you came. Their ship was right above your heads and they were singing goodbye to me. When the men turned me over I saw their ship up high above the peaks. Then I saw it blink out. They're gone."

I slumped down in the chair, suddenly exhausted, and began to weep. My head pounded.

"Mother?" Lisa bent over me.

"I'm tired."

"We need to get her back in bed," Robin said. "Should we call the nurse?"

"No." Greg was emphatic. "She'd just come and bother her, checking everything. We can get her back. Come on, Mom."

The three of them helped me stand and supported me back to my bed. Once settled, I fell heavily asleep.

It was dark outside the window, a light on in the room when I woke again. Greg and Lisa and Robin were still there, Greg ensconced in the big chair, Lisa sitting cross-legged at his feet, and Robin in a chair opposite them. They had trays on their laps and there was a smell of food in the room. Another tray was on the table by my bed.

Robin sighed and set his tray on the floor by his chair. "I just don't know what to make of her story."

"She got struck by lightning," Greg said. "And had a mind-altering vision. That's clear. But there's stuff I can't figure out. Like how she survived the night, soaked and splatted out on the rock like she was, paralyzed, with temperatures below freezing."

"And that blanket," Robin put in. "I want to have another look at that. I don't know how she got it under her cheek."

"She must have been carrying it when she fell," Greg said.

"But it looked like she had her pack in one hand and her boots in the other. They were lying on either side of her. And the blanket was folded up like a pillow."

"I don't know." Greg shook his head. "It's clear she totally believes her story, that it really happened. But it couldn't have. It's too fantastic. Maybe just her believing those creatures were with her during the night was what kept her alive."

"Her eyes are different," Lisa said. "Bigger and deeper colored and tilted at the corners like she said."

"Maybe they just look bigger," Greg said, "because she's so pale and her hair is kinda lank, not fluffy around her face like it usually is."

Lank, I thought. Ugh. Do I really still have Elirian eyes? How could that be?

I stirred in the bed. "Hey."

Lisa jumped up. "Mother, you're awake. How are you?"

They gathered around me. I investigated. My body still ached all over. The headache was becoming part of me. "Okay," I said. "Maybe I'm hungry."

They helped me sit up and visited with me while I ate, then kissed me good night and left.

Lisa stopped by early in the morning to say goodbye. Already she had shifted into her on-the-go mode.

"You're looking better, Mother." She set a bundle on my bed. "I brought your bathrobe and toilet articles and the books that were on your bedside table. I hate to leave you, but there're only three more days to my class and I don't know what my assistant's been doing in my absence."

"Thank you so much for coming," was all I could say. I didn't want her to hear the sorrow I felt at having her flit away again.

"You're going to be fine," she said briskly. "The doctor says that if you can get up and move around today, you may be able to go home tomorrow. Greg will stay and take care of you your first few days home, and after that Robin will look in on you."

She bent and kissed me. "I love you, Mother dear. Goodbye." Then she was gone. Brief, beautiful butterfly in my life.

A crisp young nurse came in and helped me get up.

"Would you like to take a shower?"

"Yes. Thank you," I said gratefully. I hadn't been wet all over since my last dip in the stream. It was only two days ago, but it felt like a millennium. The nurse brought me a walker and accompanied me to the bathroom. After my shower, I assured her I could get back to bed okay, and she left.

The mirror was clouded with steam. I used my towel to wipe it off and looked in.

Through the streaks of moisture that still blurred the reflection, an old woman looked out. Relief flooded me. "There you are," I said softly.

My white hair, still wet, clung thinly to my head. The wrinkles were back, the moles, the long cords standing out in the front of my throat, the cheeks sagging around the jaw line, the sun-damage freckles all over my chest and shoulders. An added attraction—a bluish lump on my right temple, partly covered with a white bandage.

In the midst of it all, my eyes were still Elirian eyes, large in my pale face, deep blue-green-gray, slightly tilted at the corners. I looked into their depths and felt Elirian love enfold me. They marked me, I thought in wonder, in spite of the fold in time. Every time I see my reflection I will remember them.

My breasts hung. The mirror didn't show me the rest, but I could feel with my hands the soft sag of my belly, the long indentation of the scar on my hip.

I looked back at my face and sighed, a long, deep sigh of welcome and recognition. Then I picked up my comb and began to coax my wet hair into what I hoped would be wispy curls when it dried.

Toward mid-morning a physical therapist came and led me through some exercises to awaken my arms and legs. It helped. They still ached, but not so badly, and it was good to get them moving again. When we finished, she suggested I take a walk down the corridor using the walker for balance. That sounded exciting. I put my green silk bathrobe on over the hospital gown and ventured out.

Halfway down the hall I met a man coming toward me, bent over, leaning heavily on his walker. We nodded and smiled at each other as we passed, sharing a moment of walker camaraderie. I went on around several turns in the corridor. On my way back to my room, I saw him again, sitting in one of a row of chairs opposite the nurses' station. He was short and stocky, bald but for an unruly fringe of white hair around his ears. His eyebrows, as if to make up for the lack of hair on his head, were wild and wiry, mixed black and white. He wore a worn blue terrycloth robe and slumped in the chair, looking tired. He straightened a little when he saw me and looked up at me with bright hazel eyes under his inimitable eyebrows.

"Hey, there, pretty lady. That's an elegant robe you're wearing."

I liked his smile. "Thank you," I replied. "It's good to have something to cover those rear-view gowns they give us here."

He chuckled and patted the chair next to him. "Would you like to sit a minute, take a load off your walker?"

"Sure." I sat down beside him.

He held out his hand. "Lenny." His clasp was warm and strong.

"Clara."

"Good to meet you, Clara. How did you come to stay in this elegant hotel?"

"I was taking a hike in the high country, got caught by a storm and hit by lightning. Not a direct hit, fortunately, but it knocked me over and left me paralyzed for a while. The mountain rescue team brought me down day before yesterday."

"I see you're moving now."

"Yes. Thank goodness. How about you?"

He tapped the left side of his chest. "Heart attack."

"Oh. Did you have to have surgery?"

"Yup." He pulled his robe open and showed me the long red incision on his chest. "They got me all bypassed and fixed up and say the old ticker should last a while longer."

"That's good. They're telling me I should be okay, too. I may even be able to go home tomorrow."

"You like to hike in the high country, do you? Where were you?"

"Up above Sapphire Lake."

"That's real pretty up there. I like to hike, too, but I haven't been that high for a long time. Lightning, huh. Whew. Looks like you got a knock on the head, too."

"That happened when I fell."

"How are you feeling now?"

"Better. I still have a headache and my limbs feel kind of clumsy, but I'm so grateful I can move again. Being paralyzed was scary."

"I bet. But you're moving well now. I was watching you coming down the hall, standing so straight, not all bent over like the rest of us do with our walkers."

He smiled at me again, cocked his head, and raised his left eyebrow. I almost laughed at the comical effect of all that wiry hair taking off at an angle. I managed to contain my amusement to a smile.

"How are you doing? When was your surgery?"

"A week ago. I'm doing okay. Weak. It frustrates me to be so weak. They're sending me off to rehab, tomorrow probably. The doctor is going to check on me today and decide."

The crisp young nurse came up to us. She nodded to me and turned to Lenny. "Mr. Barrett, you need to come back to your room now. Dr. Walton is here to see you."

"Speak of the devil," Lenny said. He pulled himself up slowly onto his walker. "Nice chatting with you, Clara." He started down the hall, then turned back. "Stop by and see me the next time you're meandering the corridors. I'm in room 204."

"I will." I watched him go, suppressing a giggle at the way he'd spaced out his syllables when he said "meandering." I made my way back to my room and rested. So easily tired.

In the late afternoon I took another walk down the corridor. Greg had come to visit and brought me the cane I used after my hip replacement, and I wanted to try it out. My legs were doing better. I walked along, getting into the swing of it. The doctor had told me I could go home the next day. I was looking forward to it. Also curious. Would all the work I had done in the house and garden during the fold in time still be there? Or would everything be in the neglected state I had left behind when I climbed the mountain so slowly on my eightieth birthday?

I was thinking about this when I noticed the room I was passing was number 204. The door was open. I stopped and looked in. Lenny was sitting in his easy chair reading, glasses with leopard-print frames perched on his nose.

"Lenny?"

He looked up, pulled off his glasses, and smiled widely. "Clara! Come on in. Sit down. Look at you wheeling around with only a cane."

"My son brought it to me. It's a lot freer than the walker, and still helps with my balance." I went into his room, pulled up a chair, and sat opposite him. "How's your day been?"

"Okay. I've been lazy, snoozing and reading. They're sending me to rehab tomorrow and the doc tells me they'll work my ass off, so I thought I'd better take advantage while I could. Hey, I'm real glad you dropped in." He set his book and glasses aside and beamed at me. "What've you been doing today?"

"Resting, mostly. I had a long visit with my son, Greg. And my doctor came by and said I can go home tomorrow."

"I bet you're glad. Do you live alone?"

"I do. Greg will stay with me a few days until I can get organized enough to take care of myself. After that my younger son, who lives nearby, will stop in and check on me. I'll be okay."

"Your head still hurt?"

"Yes. But that's how it will be for a while, I guess. There was the lightning strike and the concussion as well as this beautiful lump." I touched my right brow.

"Who are you going to whine to, living all alone, when your head hurts and the going gets rough?"

I laughed. "Mostly I try to whine only to my journal. I don't like my kids to worry."

"That's not good enough. Your journal doesn't commiserate. Tell you what. I'm going to be living alone, too, when I get home. How about I call you up every so often, or you call me, and you can whine to me and I'll whine to you, and then we can talk about other things. You look like an interesting person who'd be fun to talk to. We can check in on each other. How about it?" He raised his left eyebrow and looked at me questioningly.

I tilted my head and considered. It could be nice to have someone to whine to. Lenny had a warm energy. "Sounds like a good deal," I answered. "A telephone shoulder to whine on."

"Great. That's settled." He pulled himself up out of his chair and took a few steps to his night table, fumbled in the drawer, and handed me his card.

My mouth fell open. I looked up at him. "Certified Curmudgeon?" He chuckled.

"Is that your life work?"

"Now it is." He waggled both eyebrows and I couldn't help laughing. "I was a journalist for most of my life." He eased himself into his chair.

I looked at the card again. "Leonard Barrett. That's you! I used to read your column a while back. I was sorry when my local paper stopped running it. You had an interesting angle on things and a great sense of humor."

"Oh, well." He cleared his throat, looking embarrassed and pleased. "I retired seven years ago. Keeping up with this crazy world got to be too much. So I just settled on being a curmudgeon."

He had me laughing again. "Certified Curmudgeon. What a concept. Who certified you?"

"Oh, there's a special board." He tilted his head back, laughing with me. "Now you. What does your card say?"

"I'm a certified massage therapist. But I see only a few clients now. I also used to teach dance and yoga."

"Dance and yoga. I figured you were into something like that, the way you walk."

A nurse came into the room pushing a cart with trays, not the crisp young nurse, but a middle-aged woman, dark haired, heavy set. She picked up a tray, checked the card on it, and set it on Lenny's tray table. "Here's your supper, Mr. Barrett." She turned to me. "You're Ms. Norwood, aren't you? You should go back to your room now. We'll be bringing in your supper."

"No, no." Lenny waved his arm. "Bring her tray here." He paused and looked at me. "If that's all right with you. Let me start over. I would be honored if you would take your supper with me." He tilted his head, his left eyebrow up again.

I laughed. "I would be delighted."

"Good. Bring her tray down here," Lenny ordered the nurse. "And a table or something for her to set it on."

"All right, Mr. Barrett." She went out, and we heard her voice in the corridor. "Bring Ms. Norwood's tray down to 204. Mr. Barrett invited her to eat with him."

Another nurse's voice. "I saw them talking in the hall this morning. Aren't they cute?"

We looked at each other, grimaced, then laughed.

Over supper, we learned we had both grown up in Massachusetts and both attended Boston University, although he'd been a few years ahead of me.

"My father taught there," I said. "Sociology. He would have been there when you were, in the College of Liberal Arts. Did you know him? William Norwood?"

"I did know him. In fact I took three classes with him. He was an excellent teacher, a fine man. There was a clarity about him."

"He was a fine man. I still miss him. He was my first love, and as I found out later, a hard act to follow."

Lenny nodded, his eyes compassionate under his bushy brows. "I should think he would be. Well, it's a small world, as they say. Here we are, far from Massachusetts, in a Colorado hospital, and find we both went to the same university and even that I had your father as a professor."

We went on to speak of our lives, our marriages and children. He'd had only one wife who died of cancer eight years ago. He moved to Boulder after her death to be near his daughter and her family. He also had a son who was married and lived in Boston, and four teenage grandchildren.

We commiserated about the terrible food and laughed a lot. Then suddenly I was exhausted, my head aching so intensely I could no longer ignore it.

"Lenny, I'm crashing. I have to rest again. I've really enjoyed having supper with you." I got up unsteadily and reached for my cane.

"Wait a minute." Lenny drew his eyebrows together. "You do look beat. Let me call a nurse to walk back with you." He pushed his call button. "Sit down until she comes." I sat down again. My head was swimming.

"May I have your phone number?" he asked. "I'd like to check in on you tomorrow, see how you're doing at home. Maybe whine about rehab."

"Sure." I gave him my number. He wrote it on his napkin and folded it into the breast pocket of his robe.

The nurse bustled in. "You called?"

"Ms. Norwood is tired. I want you to see her safely back to her room."

I got up again. "Goodnight."

He patted his pocket. "I'll call."

Chapter 12

The Fold in Time

"How does my garden look?" I asked Greg as we drove home from the hospital.

"Okay. I've been watering for you. You've got some pole beans coming in, lots of tomatoes. I found a big zucchini hiding under the weeds."

A small moan escaped me. "Weeds?"

"Well, yes, Mom. I know it's hard for you to bend over to pull them. I'll clear it out some while I'm here."

Greg turned into my driveway and helped me out of the car. "Let's get you settled. You'll need to lie down after all the nonsense they put you through checking out. Dr. Martin says the best way to heal a concussion is to rest a lot." He took my arm and led me toward the house.

"Wait a minute," I said. "I want to look at my garden."

He stood still, frowning. "Come in now. You can visit your garden later."

"I want to do it now." I set off with my cane, first around back to the vegetable garden. There were the pole beans ready to pick, lettuce, tomatoes and kale, and the big zucchini. But it was a mess, all the work I'd done in the last year erased by the fold in time. I started to bend over to pull some of the grass around my carrots, but it was too hard. I wobbled, leaning on my cane, and felt like crying.

I limped back to the patio. The flower gardens were the riotous jungle they had been when I first came back from the mountain a year ago. Bewildered, I stared at what had been perfect order and beauty only a few days before. How could it all be undone?

Roses were blooming in the midst of the tangle. I picked a blossom off the pink rose, sniffed it deeply. The pink rose had the sweetest fragrance of them all. That at least was unchanged.

Greg had gone into the house with my bundle and come back out again. He stood on the porch. "Stubborn woman."

"I'm coming." The porch steps were hard for my legs. I had to pull myself up with the railing.

In the house, I put the rose in a vase and walked around, opening cupboard and closet doors. Everything I had cleared out was back again, the closets cluttered, the shelves full. My shoulders drooped. All that work for nothing. Could it have been a dream after all? A lightning-induced delirium, as my children believed?

As I turned away from the front entry closet I almost stumbled over my pack. It was leaning against the shoe shelf, my staff and boots beside it. I eased myself down onto the floor and opened it.

Tucked in the top was the silver blanket. It was real. They had slipped it under my cheek after they folded time and left it with me, gift of their love.

Hands shaking, I pulled it out and shook it open. Light and iridescent color filled the entryway. I laid my face against the silken fur, warm with an unearthly radiance that I had known only when the Elirians embraced me. It seemed almost, not quite, as if I could hear their song when I touched it to my cheek, the way you hear the sound of the sea in a shell taken far from its source. Loss and gratitude poured through me. I gathered the blanket into my arms and pressed it against my heart.

Greg squatted beside me. "Mom?"

"See, here's the blanket." I held out a corner to him. "Feel how silken it is. Isn't it beautiful?"

He touched the corner, ran it between his fingers. "It is. It's very unusual. Where did you get it?"

"I told you. The Elirians gave it to me."

He pressed his lips together and frowned. "Let's get you to your bed. You're looking pale."

He helped me stand. I gathered up the blanket and followed him. As I walked through my office on the way to the bedroom, I saw that the calendar on the wall said 2011. My engagement calendar lay on the table beside my desk. It, too, said 2011. Beside it was a list of phone messages I needed to return more than a year ago. My head ached and swam. I leaned on the back of my office chair.

"Mom, are you okay?"

"Just tired."

"Well, yes. Are you *now* ready to rest?" He took my arm and led me to my bed, pulled off my shoes, helped me lie down, and covered me with the silver blanket.

I lay quiet, holding a corner of it against my cheek, still reeling from the realization that all I had done in the past year was erased. But it wasn't a dream. The warmth of the blanket comforted me. I took a long breath, remembering the words of my Buddhist teacher, "Do not be attached to the fruits of your actions."

In the next few days, I began to transition into life as an old woman. It was hard at first. I kept starting to jump up as if I could. I almost fell down the porch steps, forgetting to hold the rail, expecting to be able to run lightly down. My limbs were still heavy, my head ached all the time. But the worst was how weak I was. The least effort exhausted me.

I poked at the things in my cluttered cupboards. How am I ever going to get this all cleared out again? I asked myself despairingly.

Greg stayed with me for five days, watching over me, helping me as I began to take up the tasks of my daily life. I moved slowly around the house, using my cane for balance. Often I would start something, then need to ask Greg for help. The basket of wet laundry was too heavy to carry down the porch steps, the pile of dirty dishes on the kitchen counter too overwhelming. After each single effort, I needed to rest.

"I don't know why I'm so tired," I complained to Greg.

"Mom," he said, standing over me as I sat slumped in my rocking chair, his voice edged with exasperation. "You took a very long hike. Then you got hit by lightning, fell and bonked your head and got a concussion. Then you lay soaked and paralyzed all night with temperatures below freezing. Any other woman your age would be dead. You're doing great. You just need to heal."

I looked up at him, tears of frustration running down my cheeks.

He squatted in front of me. "Hey, Mom. It's okay. You're really doing great. You're going to get strong again. You're already able to do more today than you did yesterday."

❧

Lenny did call, the first night I was home. "How's it going?" he asked.

"Pretty well. My son is here helping me get oriented. How's rehab?"

"Brutal. I should have warned you, curmudgeons don't just whine. They have sometimes been known to bitch."

I laughed. "Bitch away."

"They wore me out. No sooner did I get settled in my room than they had me in their gym doing exercises on their machines. It's hard to lift my arms; it pulls on the scar. Then they had me walking on a track that must be ninety miles around. After I had lunch, they made me do it all again. I'm wiped. I hate being so weak."

"I do, too. Any other bitches?"

"The elastic stockings strangling my legs. Do you have to wear those?"

"Not this time. But after my hip surgery I did. When they said I didn't have to wear them any more I made a celebration out of dropping them in the trash can."

"I'm going to burn mine—slowly."

"They'll stink."

"They sure will. Oh, God, here comes that nurse with all her gear to prick and poke and pump me. Gotta go. Take care, pretty lady. I'll call you tomorrow. You didn't bitch much. It'll be your turn next time."

"Who was that?" Greg asked when I hung up.

"Lenny. A man I met at the hospital."

"You picked up a man at the hospital and he's calling you your first night home?"

"I didn't pick him up. I met him."

"How old is he?"

"Older than I am, I would guess. Though it's hard to tell. He'd just had heart surgery."

"How'd you meet him?"

"We met in the corridor getting our exercise with our walkers."

"You pick up this old guy the minute you're out of bed? You don't miss a beat, Mom. What kind of guy is he?"

"He's nice. A former journalist." Greg's face was a study. I started laughing. "And I don't know what kind of car he drives, since I only visited with him in the hospital, or what kind of shoes he wears, since he was wearing slippers."

"What are you talking about?"

"Those were the questions you asked me about Zachary."

"Zachary?"

"Never mind."

Four days after my return from the hospital, Greg took me for a trial drive to the grocery store. I found my old driver's license in the back of my desk drawer. The driving went fine and I managed well enough in the grocery store.

Satisfied that I could take care of myself, Greg prepared to leave. "I've gotta get back, Mom. You're gonna be okay now. Rob'll be by to check in with you this afternoon. Just remember to rest." He threw his bag into the back of his car, hugged and kissed me. I stood in the driveway and waved as he drove away.

As long as Greg had been there, I had relaxed into the comfort of his presence, his talk, his caring. I hadn't asked myself how I was. After his car disappeared around the corner, I turned up the walk to my back garden, my cane tapping on the flagstones. I lay on the grass under the maple tree, looking up at the sky between the leaves, watching the sun flash off the wings of birds flying over me.

How am I, I asked myself, compared to how I was the morning of my eightieth birthday? It was hard to remember. Even though time had folded and my children remembered nothing of what had happened in the fold, for me it had been a year. I was weaker for sure. My knees were swollen. But they would have been anyway, I reminded myself. They always were after a long hike, sometimes for a week or more. On that morning my head had not ached as it did now; that was the result of the lightning and the fall. But my heart had been unsteady and now it wasn't. That was a big plus. I sent a prayer of thanks across the galaxies to Kiria.

I sat up slowly. Maybe I'm not so bad off, I told myself. The headache will eventually heal and I will get stronger. Before I got old gradually, one misery at a time, this time all at once. I must be patient. I will get used to it.

Some weeds were poking up in the ice plant along the edge of my flower garden. I hitched my way over to them, pushing with my hands, sliding on my bottom, and began to pull them out. I can get this all cleaned up again, I promised myself. A little at a time. Maybe I'll hire some help. A strong young person, like I was, who can dig and carry and help me clear out my house, too. At least I remember what I did. I won't have to make all the decisions again.

Lenny stayed in rehab five days, and we talked several times. Once he got home he started calling me every night around nine. I could tell he was lonely and struggling, as I had been at first. We exchanged bitches, then chatted. He always made me laugh. I looked forward to his call, to sharing my day, and to having someone say goodnight to me.

I often thought of the Elirians, treasuring the memories of them, hearing in my heart the echo of their songs. I must write the story, I thought. But I didn't feel ready yet. There was more to come that might help me understand the whole better. How will it end? I remembered the smile in Merilea's eyes as she had told me there was another piece to my *ulada*.

In small increments I found my way back into yoga, beginning with the simplest stretches, coaxing my still-sluggish limbs into bending and lengthening. There were postures I would never do again, never again the glorious wheel with hips pressed up to the sky and fingertips touching heels, but many that I could do. I knew I would gain more with time, as I had after my hip replacement.

The five back porch steps presented a daily challenge. I felt a sense of triumph each time I discovered how to overcome what had initially seemed physically insurmountable. I figured out how to carry grocery bags in—set them two steps up, walk up to them, and lift them to the top step. How to set the laundry basket on the top step of the porch, walk to the bottom, then reach back and swing it down. There was always the option of the dryer, but I loved hanging the laundry, reaching up to pin it to the line, looking into the sky, gathering it in fresh and sweet-smelling from the autumn wind.

I could no longer squat in my garden, but I could sit and, thanks to the flexibility of years of yoga, reach across a bed. Or I could take a little folding canvas bench between the rows and perch on it to weed and trim. I could no longer mow the lawn running barefoot behind my push mower. I had hired a lawn company to take care of it, had canceled it when I was young again, and now wondered how that would be affected by the fold in time. My question was answered a few days after Greg left, when two men with their big, loud mowers came roaring through.

The pace of my life became gentle. I sank with relief into slow mornings, lying abed for a half hour or more after I woke, no longer pushed by the energy of a young body to be up and doing. I watched the sun come into the leaves of the cottonwood, counting each morning how many more had turned gold. Often I would get up, still in my nightgown, and wander into the kitchen for tea, then come back to bed to drink it, write in my journal, meditate.

The frequent rests I needed during the day, stretched out on my bed under the silver blanket, gave me time to return to those ineffable processes that had been interrupted for a year—dreaming, musing, sorting the experiences of my life as the old do, laying flower petals on the path toward death.

If at times I felt frustrated by my weakness and the awkward difficulty of accomplishing the simplest things, I comforted myself. It's only aging. Aging is never easy. It's the toughest challenge on top of all the challenges of incarnate existence, and comes at the end when, hopefully, we have accumulated enough strength of spirit to handle it.

I never regretted the choice I had made.

⌒ ⌒

There had been a story in the paper about my being struck by lightning on the mountain. When I got home there was a phone message from a reporter wanting an interview. I turned him down. The less said about the whole business the better, I thought.

Anne came, very concerned, and gave me a massage. She was full of questions. As I lay on the table, she drew out of me the story of the hike up the mountain on my eightieth birthday. I kept hoping as I spoke that she would remember I had told her all that before. But she didn't seem to. All the details were still vivid to me, even though it had been more than a year ago. I told her again how my knees had hurt and my heart had raced, how I had been overwhelmed by memories, how I had dipped in the stream to set intentions. She understood. She had walked that trail with me many times, had shared numerous dips in icy streams. She knew how I felt about my bathing cloth and commiserated with me over its loss.

"I'll give you a new one. I know it won't be the same, but I got some pretty ones when I was in Bali last year. You can have one of those."

I thought of the one she had already given me, the one I had used all summer but was no longer in my pack. I did not speak of it.

I went on to tell her about the lightning, the cold night in which I thought I was dying. Then I paused. Waiting.

"Everyone's amazed that you survived the night," she said. "You're tougher than you seem." Her skillful hands began working with my neck. "I'm glad. I'm not ready to have you disappear from my life. There. That's better. That should help the headache."

Clearly she didn't remember.

A few weeks later I began taking walks again, short walks at first with many rests, then longer ones as I grew stronger. One afternoon Anne came and we walked together around the lake. We'd visited several times since she'd massaged me. It felt odd being with her, knowing she didn't remember all we'd shared in the last year. That afternoon she was excited about a new psychic she'd consulted and what he had told her regarding the big shift that was to take place on December 21, 2012.

"Only three months from now," I said.

"No." Anne stopped on the trail and looked at me sharply. "A year and three months. You've done that before, getting mixed up about what year we're in. Is it the lightning?"

I stopped, too. "Anne," I blurted out, "what would you think if I told you that between the lightning strike and the time they brought me down the mountain, I lived a whole year? That's why I'm mixed up. I keep forgetting that they folded..." I couldn't go on.

"What?"

"I need to rest. Can we sit down?"

"Sure."

We went a little farther to a place where some big rocks jutted out at the water's edge. The lake was still, reflecting the clouds, the hills, the trees just beginning to turn.

"What do you mean, you lived a year?" Anne asked as we settled.

I slipped off my sandals and put my feet in the water. Cool and soothing. "Just that. And you and I shared a lot in that year. It's so strange you don't remember."

She shifted so that she could sit looking into my face. "I was with you in that year?"

"Yes. What do you make of that?"

"I don't know." Her eyes were kind and concerned. "I've heard accounts," she went on, speaking slowly, "that people near death can move into some kind of parallel time. They come back and tell about having been taken to other places and having experiences that would take far longer than the two or three minutes they were actually gone. Like with dreams. A dream can last only a few minutes, yet a long story unfolds for the dreamer. You were alone there all night. You must have walked far on the *bardo* path."

"I wasn't alone. I would have died if they hadn't come."

"They?"

I was silent. It was ridiculous, but I felt betrayed that she didn't remember all I had told her of the Elirians.

She must have seen the shadow on my face because she touched my hand where it rested on the rock beside me. "I don't know how such things work, what they mean, but I'm curious. What did you experience? How did it change you? I've felt ever since you came back that you are changed. And I've been noticing there's something different about your eyes. Please tell me."

So once again I told her how the Elirians had rescued me and about the year that followed. She listened attentively, compassionately, interrupting from time to time to question and marvel, but as I continued my story, I could tell that she didn't believe it had happened in real time. I turned my face away to hide my disappointment. I had hoped that she of all people would believe me, even if my own children hadn't. She did understand the experience was real for me and had changed me. In the times that followed I could speak with her about it, and she would know what I was talking about. That at least was a comfort.

❧ ❧

The autumn unfolded with an uncanny confluence of two autumns that were both the autumn of 2011. Outer events happened exactly as they had in the fold in time, but my personal relationship to them was vastly different.

Heavy snow came in October, just as it had before, and the trees, still leafed out, bent under its weight. Only this October it was a struggle for me to get out to shake my maple tree. I staggered in the deep snow, got dizzy looking up, and had to hold onto the trunk to keep from falling. Finally I retreated to the porch and threw snowballs at the weighted branches. My aim was lousy.

When I felt stronger, I went to the Avalon for an evening of tango. All the same people were there that had been there the first time I went after becoming young. I realized that, without planning to, I had come on the same date. This time I created no stir. I sat and chatted with Sally, danced with Tim and Steve and Roberto. Marco didn't ask me. My dancing was better than it had been before. The skill I had gained taking classes and especially dancing with Zachary almost every night for four months was still with me. But soon my knees began to ache and I was tired. I sat and watched a while, then went home before ten.

By the end of October I felt able to start practicing massage. Martha came for a session. She said nothing about the young woman who had massaged her for a year. As before, she referred her friend, and soon the other clients I had worked with in the fold in time contacted me. My hands ached after a session and I was only able to see two or three clients a week, but I was glad to be able to do my work again.

One day in November, walking on the mall, I passed the kite shop. There in the window was the dragon kite. I had forgotten how beautiful it was. Of course I would buy it. The children had loved it so last year.

On the following Sunday when I went to visit Robin's family, I gave them the dragon kite—just as I had before. I opened it up and spread it out on the dining room table for the children to see.

Colin jumped with excitement. "Look at his teeth!"

Katie stroked the long golden tail. A misty look came into her eyes. "I had a dream about a kite like this."

I caught my breath, alert.

"When did you dream that?" Alice asked

Katie tilted her head. "A while ago." Her face lit up. "It went really high and its golden tail flew on the wind."

There was a strange pause. My heart was beating fast.

"Let's go," Colin burst in. "Let's go fly it."

"Are you up to taking a short walk to the park?" Alice asked me.

"Yes, I'm walking much better now."

"Okay, kids," Robin said, "get your shoes on and we'll go." I rolled the kite up as the children scrambled for shoes and jackets.

In the park Robin unfurled the kite. I watched, remembering how I'd raced along the creek with its string in my hand a year ago—was it the same day as this, the same sunny afternoon in November?

This year I sat on the bank by the creek, resting my legs while Robin and the children ran with the kite. I bought that kite, I puzzled, last fall when I was young, and bought it again now that I'm old, a year later, but not a year. My head ached as I tried for the umpteenth time to figure it out. Only the now is real, Kiria had sung. So I sat in the now, the afternoon sun warm on my back, the kite flying above, the children's shouts.

Lenny had a hard time that fall. Not long after he got home from rehab, he went out for groceries and picked up a flu. Soon he was back in the hospital with viral pneumonia. I sent him a card and flowers but wasn't allowed to visit because of contagion. For a week or so he hung in the balance. I was terribly worried about him. I checked with the hospital every day, but, since I wasn't kin, they would give me only general information.

Then one evening, to my great relief, he called, well enough to talk and needing to bitch. He still had his sense of humor, but when we got to laughing it set him coughing and our call ended abruptly. The next time he called he was at his daughter Bette's house, being cared for and irritated by all the noise and confusion created by her teenage sons. Then he was home.

"My apartment's not a fancy place," he said, "but it's quiet. I can have my own way again, and don't have to spend all my strength restraining myself from yelling at those kids."

He began calling every evening again, and I realized how much I had missed our daily connection. Then one night he said, "I'm feeling like stepping out. How about dinner?"

I was delighted. It was refreshing that everything about Lenny was new, not shadowed with images, like and yet unlike, from folded time.

"That would be lovely," I replied. "You know we talk every day, but we haven't seen each other since that one day in the hospital. Do you think we'll recognize each other without our bathrobes?"

He chuckled. "For you," he said, "I'll wear something different."

He picked me up at my house two evenings later. He was standing straighter than when I had last seen him, definitely thinner, looking quite dapper, dressed in a black suit and tie, a black beret set at an angle. His eyebrows were as formidable as ever. I, too, had dressed with care in some of my more modest tango attire— a close-fitting gray lace top, a purple velvet skirt, and long purple earrings. With some help from uplifting underwear I still had a good figure, although a little fuller than young Clara's had been.

"Wow!" he exclaimed, looking at me over from head to foot. "You're gorgeous. This is even better than the green silk robe."

"You look nice, too," I said, feeling suddenly shy, but pleased with his appreciation.

As I took my coat out of the closet, he looked around my living room. I'd had the wood stove going that afternoon, and the coals still glowed through the glass door. "Nice little place you've got. I love a wood stove."

He helped me on with my coat, gave me his arm as we went down the front steps, and opened the car door for me.

An old-fashioned gentleman, I noted inwardly as he went around to the driver's side. I loved it.

We went to John's, a small, fine restaurant in a little old house out on east Pearl Street. There were no shadows. I had never been there with Zachary.

Lenny ordered wine and we toasted our healing bodies.

"It's so good to get out," he said. "It's taken me a while. And what a treat to sit across the table from such a beautiful woman."

"I'm happy to be with you. So glad you're finally getting well."

"Believe me, me too."

Our conversation flowed easily. Although in our phone conversations we had usually spoken of daily events and the latest with our bodies, over time we had come to learn a good deal about each other.

As we ate, he regaled me with stories of his journalism career. I'd forgotten how much fun it was to watch his eyebrows as he talked. He began his career in New York City, but at the end of the sixties moved to San Francisco to report on the human potential movement. Dan and I were also in California at that time with our young children, though farther south. I taught dance and yoga at a growth center just east of San Diego and sampled all the New Age modalities that came through. Lenny and I had known many of the same charismatic leaders of that period and we had lots of fun swapping tales about them. Later he moved to Washington, DC, and covered the Reagan, Bush and Clinton years. It was columns from that period that I remembered reading and enjoying. He was solidly liberal, with a trenchant wit.

"When the second Bush got elected for the second time, I quit," he said. "I just couldn't stomach the insanity anymore. Now I play chess."

It was a delightful dinner. We laughed a lot and lingered over dessert and tea until we both realized at the same time that we were tired.

After our dinner, we began meeting each other every week or so, for an afternoon movie, a walk around the lake, or tea by my wood stove. I appreciated his intelligence, his thoughtfulness, his perspective. And he was always gallant, gracious, and fun.

❧ ❧

The days shortened and Christmas drew near. Robin came and helped me hang the lights. I bought a small Christmas tree, created a wreath for the front door, and set candles and greens around the living room.

That year, Lisa had no trouble recognizing me when I picked her and her family up from the bus. Robin and his family came over, and soon the house was full of talk and laughter and racing children. I loved having them all there, but they wore me out. As we moved through the Christmas rituals, I often needed to retreat to my rocking chair, thinking wistfully of the year before when I'd had boundless energy. Sometimes Colin came and snuggled in my lap.

Lenny spent Christmas with his daughter and grandsons but called me Christmas night. When I got off the phone, Lisa asked, "Who was that?"

"Lenny. A friend of mine."

"Is that the guy you met in the hospital? Greg told me you were wandering around the corridors picking up old men."

"Greg exaggerates. It was just one man. Lenny. And I did not pick him up. We met and conversed."

"And now he's calling you. Is it a romance, Mother?"

"No, not a romance. A good friendship."

When at last the celebrations were over, when Lisa and Phil and Jocelyn had gone on to visit Phil's mother, when Robin and Alice and the children had returned to their usual lives, I wandered aimlessly around the empty house, exhausted, picking up a stray bit of wrapping paper, a hair tie left behind by Jocelyn. I opened the refrigerator, surveyed the crowded shelves, and wondered what to do with all that food. I'll ask Lenny to come for a feast of leftovers, I decided.

❧ ❧

When New Year's Eve came I was not the least tempted to go to Denver to dance. I spent the evening in my rocking chair by the wood stove, looking over my journal for the last year. It flowed smoothly form January 2011 when I was still seventy-nine to the entry the night before my eightieth birthday. After that it became a hodge-podge.

When I picked up my journal for the first time after I came down the mountain an old woman, I found to my dismay that all I'd written of my thoughts, feelings, and experiences during the year I was young had been erased. In the four months that followed, I had described events and feelings as they occurred and also tried to recapture what I had written during the fold in time. Back and forth. As I read, my head spun. One year? Two years? Would I ever comprehend?

I laid my journal aside, tilted my head back, and shut my eyes, gathering in the whole year, from birthday to birthday, putting all the details and emotions in order.

My thoughts lingered over the summer in the mountains, cherishing the images of that magic time. Whatever else happens in my life, I thought, I had that summer—that magnificence, that strength to go high and far.

Finally I picked up my journal, and, skipping the flashbacks, read again of the months just passed as I slowly healed and adapted to being an old woman, the puzzle of the fold in time, the friendship with Lenny. Is it romance? I asked myself. I don't know.

I thought of the Elirians and wondered if they had returned to their planet by now and sunk in to be renewed. I remembered their soft fur, their luminous eyes, their gentle hands, their love, lost again in the wonder of them and how they had changed my life. They told me to write my story, I remembered. I must start while the details are still fresh. Much of it is here in my journal, but I'll have to unscramble it.

At last I sighed and looked at my watch. Ten thirty. Past my bedtime. But I should think of at least one intention for the new year. I'll start writing my story tomorrow, I decided. I'm ready now. Even if I don't know the ending, I can begin.

I wrote my intention, closed my journal, and went to bed. I was sound asleep when the phone rang at midnight.

"Happy New Year!" It was Lenny.

"Happy New Year," I responded sleepily.

"Sounds like I woke you up. I called to tell you my new year's resolution. I want to see more of you. Will you come to tea at my place tomorrow?"

New Year's Day was the first time I visited Lenny in his apartment. The smell of fresh baking greeted me when he opened the door.

His place was neat and spare—and dark. His door opened off a corridor, there were apartments on either side, and only one window in the single bedroom in the back. A tiny kitchenette in one corner opened into a main room which was living room, dining room, and office in one. A big desk with a computer took up another corner. There was a worn lounge chair with a leg rest and an end table beside it piled with books and papers. A television. A small table with two straight chairs pushed up against the counter that separated the kitchenette from the main room. A boom box on the kitchen counter. The only touch of luxury was a tall oak bookcase, filled with books, taking up one whole wall.

"It's small," Lenny said as he took my coat, "but it serves me. I shed most of my stuff when my wife died and I moved out here to Colorado. Stuff's heavy to move, and in the end, you know, you can't take it with you." He cocked his left eyebrow.

"Now sit here." He pulled out one of the chairs by the table. "I made muffins for you." The tea kettle whistled. He bustled into the kitchenette, poured the tea, and took the muffins out of the oven. "Raisin bran," he said as he set them on a plate. "Good for the heart."

We sat at the little table with tea and muffins.

"Did you make any New Year's resolutions?" he asked.

"I'm always making resolutions," I answered. "But I did make one last night."

"What did you resolve?"

"To write a story. I started this morning."

"What kind of story?"

"It's about an experience I had."

"Would you tell me?"

I sat silent, head bent, fingering the handle of my teacup. A wave of yearning surged up in me. I wanted to tell him. I longed to tell someone who would believe me, who would understand, who might even be able to help me figure out the fold in time. But he might not believe me. No one else had. He might think I was nuts, and that might spoil our friendship.

I raised my head and looked at him. He had drawn his brows together and was watching me with compassionate eyes. Just waiting, present with me.

"It feels like an important story," he said at length.

"It's huge. It's this extraordinary, I mean *truly* extraordinary, thing that happened to me on the mountain. The lightning was only—"

I broke off and looked into his eyes again.

"Tell me."

"I'm afraid you won't believe me; you'll think I'm crazy."

"Clara, I know you well enough to know you're not crazy. You're clearly a sensible and grounded woman, as well as being delightful and beautiful."

My hesitation broke. "It's kind of a long story."

"We have all afternoon. Hey, I'm a journalist. I love stories."

So I told him my story. The winter afternoon faded into dusk and then darkness before I finished. Lenny listened with rapt attention. Occasionally he exclaimed or asked a question. "That Zachary," he growled at one point. "Don't ever let me meet him. I'll take out his knees." But mostly he was silent, listening, I felt, with his heart.

I finished by telling him how I'd seen the spaceship disappear into the sky. "And then they brought me down, and the next day I met you in the hospital corridor."

"That was a good day, when we met."

I smiled at him. "It was a good day." He reached out his hand to me. His clasp was warm and solid. I felt vulnerable, having spilled it all. "Do you believe me?" I asked.

He nodded slowly. "I do."

I bit my lip, hope struggling with incredulity. "You do?"

"I do," he repeated. "It's a strange story, but I believe you. I haven't told you this, but between California and DC. I spent some time running around Northern Arizona and New Mexico following up on tales about alien visitations."

"*Really?*"

"Really. I never got any solid evidence, but I heard enough stories to make me think there must be something behind them. But mostly I believe you because you're you. How about some more tea?"

"Yes, thank you." Suddenly I was smiling all over my body.

Over the fresh cup of tea, I shared with him my confusion about the fold in time, how none of my children or my friends remembered what we had experienced together in the year I was young, how the two autumns had blended, how just sitting with my journal the evening before had made my head spin again. I sighed. "I don't even know how old I am."

Lenny drew his brows together into one wiry line above his eyes. "It's a very interesting puzzle. I'm going to think on it."

I realized that it was growing late and I was tired.

"I need to go," I said. "It's been a lovely afternoon. Thank you for the tea and muffins, and for listening to my story." I got up slowly, stiff from sitting so long.

"You look kind of worn out. You lived it all again. Do you want me to drive you home?"

"That's sweet of you. But then I wouldn't have my car tomorrow. I'll be okay."

He helped me on with my coat.

"Thank you for believing me," I said. "I can't tell you how much that means to me."

"Of course." He gave me a brief, warm hug, before I stepped out into the winter night.

On a Sunday afternoon in January, I opened my email and saw an announcement of a tango dance at the Avalon. I'll go, I thought. It will be good to dance an hour or two, see my friends. So that evening I went, all unguarded. I changed my shoes in the dressing room, greeted several of my friends, settled in a chair at the edge of the dance floor, and looked around.

Zachary was there. I caught my breath and froze. He hadn't seen me. He was across the room by the refreshment table absorbed in a young woman with long, dark hair and lovely long legs, dressed in a very short red dress and very high red heels. I quickly lowered my eyes. In my lap a single white hair lay curled on the deep purple of my shawl. I plucked it off.

That's right. I took a long breath. I'm old now. It's okay. He won't recognize me.

Still I kept my eyes down as a new *tanda* began. Before long I saw his feet in the shoes he had worn in all our dances together, moving by, intricately intermingled with the red high heels. After they'd passed I looked up. Roberto was smiling at me. I nodded. He came to me and we danced. Then Tim found me. After that I sat and wrapped myself in my shawl. I'd learned that if I rested after every two *tandas* I could last longer. As my resting *tanda* ended I glanced around for a new partner. Zachary was staring at me. He tilted his head, and I nodded.

He started across the room toward me, his blue eyes intense and Elirian. Oh, my God, I thought. He's coming to dance with me. Why did I nod? I should run. But I didn't. I felt as if moved by fate. He came and waited in front of me, smiling, his left hand extended. I stood up and stepped into his embrace.

It was as if I had never left it. I fit perfectly, my brow nestled against his cheek, our hearts touching. As we started to dance, I felt him begin simply; then as I followed his slightest cue, he gradually increased the complexity of his lead. I knew his ways. I followed him faultlessly. As we neared the end of the song, one we both knew and loved, he led me through his most intricate maneuver and gave a small exclamation as I matched his every step.

Between songs, he looked at me in wonder. "You're a fabulous dancer. I've never had anyone follow me like that."

At the end of the *tanda* he asked, "*Uno más?*" It was too uncanny. I should have answered "*No, gracias,*" and fled. But I did not. The music began and I stepped into his arms. Lost in his embrace I was young again, tasting the sweetest delights of tango. When the third *tanda* ended, I struggled to keep back my tears. If he had kissed a tear off my cheek…

"Come, sit with me." He took my hand and led me to a table. "May I get you something to drink?"

I nodded, biting back the words about no alcohol. I had to change something. Our meeting was unfolding almost exactly as it had before. I watched him weaving between the dancers crowded around the refreshment table, seeing again his elegance and grace.

"Déjà vu, déjà vu," I muttered to myself. I looked down at my hands resting on the table, the dry, fragile skin, the knuckles gnarled from years of body work, the brown spots, the blue veins standing out. It's not the same. He appreciates my dancing, but sees an old woman.

He was soon back with refreshments. He sat down and held out his hand. "My name is Zachary."

"Clara."

"Clara. That's a pretty name. I think I knew someone once named Clara."

I broke out into a light sweat.

He leaned across the table. "You're an incredible dancer, you know. You must have been dancing tango for a long time."

He's seeing the old woman, I told myself. I smiled and nodded.

He handed me a glass of wine, lifted his. "To tango. The most beautiful dance of all. And to you."

"To tango and to you," I replied. We clinked our glasses and sipped our wine.

At least it's not sparkling cider. Something is different.

He leaned toward me again. "You have beautiful eyes. They remind me of something. I know—it's this really strange dream I had when I was knocked out after skiing into a tree. You want to hear it?"

Shivers ran through me. I nodded.

"It happened last December when I first got here. I moved here from Seattle a couple of months ago. I'd been out skiing, way out alone in the backcountry. I like to get away from all the people. Anyway, I got out of control and ran into a tree. I must have been knocked out for a while, like I said. I had this dream that these furry creatures from outer space came and rescued me. They had eyes kind of like yours, real big and beautiful. In my dream I'd gotten seriously destroyed by hitting the tree. They carried me off to their ship, a round, silver thing, and fixed me and put me back down by the tree I had hit. I was okay when I came to, which is kind of weird because my skis were toast. But I guess I was just lucky. I was fine to hike out. Strange, huh?"

I sat quietly taking slow, deep breaths.

"I'd almost forgotten that dream. Your eyes reminded me."

I looked down at my old hands. Another breath. Then, risking everything, I lifted my head, looked into his eyes, and asked, "Are you sure it was a dream?"

He stared at me, his mouth half open. Then he rubbed his brow and said, "Of course it was. Stuff like that doesn't really happen." The music for the next *tanda* began. "It's a *milonga*. Let's go." He took my hand and led me out onto the floor.

It was a fast, playful *milonga* as only Zachary could lead it. I loved it. My feet flew. I laughed with delight. And at the end of the *tanda* I was completely exhausted.

"Thank you," I said breathlessly. "That was really fun."

"Another?"

"No, no thank you. I need to rest."

He took me back to my chair. I wrapped myself in my shawl and leaned back, struggling to steady my breath. Soon I saw him dance by with the long-legged girl in the red dress. When my breath finally calmed, I got up and slipped out.

I sat in my car in the parking lot, leaning my brow against the steering wheel. "Crazy, crazy," I muttered. "Oh, God, I'm exhausted. Just let me get home."

I gathered myself and drove home, bathed, and got in bed. No sleep. Finally I sat up, pulling the silver blanket around me. It was too cold to get out of bed and sit on my pillow.

My mind reeled. If Zachary skied into the tree only last month, then what year is it, when is it? How could he have just done that and I have old hands? Maybe—maybe if he hit the tree just last month, then it's the first year. Maybe the Elirians are still here. Hope surged up in me. *Kiria!* I cried out from my heart. I felt my call spiral out into the galaxy, fade in the vastness of space. There was no answer. *It is too far*, Rosiri had sung sadly. They were gone.

My head pounded. I could not hold such divergent realities any longer. I slid down under the silver blanket and slept at last.

In my dream I saw two banners floating in the sky, one above the other. In the upper one, brightly-colored images, like tiny movies, portrayed all the events of my life in the fold in time. In the lower one, the images portrayed my life since I had come down from the mountain as an old woman, all the way to dancing with Zachary that very night. The rest of that banner waved in the air, open and blank. As I watched, the two banners began to merge. In a burst of light they became one— and then were gone. Only the light remained, and I understood that the light was Now.

Lenny

After the dream, the shadows were gone. I felt clarified, present in a way I hadn't been before. My life was now. One moment, one day at a time. I felt a renewal of energy. Even my headaches began to ease as if part of them had been my struggle to understand.

I realized I was stronger even than I had been on the morning of my eightieth birthday. I could shovel the snow when it fell, take long walks around the winter lake, and enjoy my outings with Lenny. My heart remained steady, only slowing and accelerating as was appropriate to my activity. I knew that made a huge difference.

One evening I invited Lenny to come over for dinner and a movie. He arrived on a late February afternoon. The days had begun to lengthen, but that afternoon was dark and cold with heavy clouds.

"Smells like snow," Lenny said as I took his coat.

"Oh, is it supposed to snow? Have you heard a forecast?"

"I never bother with forecasts. They say a flurry and we get a foot. They say a foot and nothing happens at all." He handed me his beret and sat down to take off his boots. "I trust my nose more, and I'd guess by the smell that we'll have snow before morning. Ah, the wood stove." He went over to it, rubbed his hands together, then turned his back and stood up close to it. "You have such a cozy home. It's a pleasure to come here."

I smiled at him. "It's a pleasure to have you come."

"Can I help you with anything?"

"No, it's ready. Come and sit down." I turned down the overhead light and lit the candles. I'd roasted a chicken with all the fixings.

He sniffed appreciatively. "I'm one lucky dude to have a woman friend that's such a good cook. What movie are we watching tonight?"

I started slicing the chicken. "*Harold and Maude.*"

"*Harold and Maude.* I haven't seen that one in thirty years. It was about a young boy with a fascination for suicide falling in love with an old woman, wasn't it? A good story and really funny, as I remember."

"Yes, it's one of my favorites. I haven't seen it for a long time either. Maude's a wonderful character. In the end, she's the one who commits suicide, on her eightieth birthday, because she wants to die while she's still full of life. I've always thought there was something to that."

"Now don't go getting any ideas."

"No danger. I've already had my eightieth birthday—twice—and I'm still here."

"I'm curious," he said a little later as we cleared the dishes. "What's behind that door off the dining room? You've given me the tour, but never showed me that."

"Oh, that's the master bedroom. It's got its own bath and a big closet. I used to rent it out, but when my last housemate moved on, I didn't bother to get another. I keep it shut off to save on heat. When my kids come to visit it becomes a guest room."

"Hmm. Did you like having a housemate?"

"Yes and no. I've had good people come and go, some not so compatible. I guess I always hoped for more companionship, but my housemates were so busy with their own lives that I'd only see them passing through. Finally I decided that if I were going to be alone most of the time anyway, I might as well save myself the hassle of adapting to a new person. I do get lonely sometimes. It's nice to have you come for dinner."

After we'd washed the dishes together, I stirred up the fire in the wood stove and we settled side by side on the couch to watch the movie.

"Come here," he said. He moved close to me and put his arm around me. Then he bent his head to look into my face. "Is that okay?"

"It's lovely." I nestled up to his warm body. So lovely to be held.

We both thoroughly enjoyed the movie, the touching parts, the funny parts, all the more for sharing them. I loved feeling his deep chuckle vibrate through both our bodies.

When it was over, he stood up and stretched. I felt a pang of loss as his warm body moved away from mine. "Great movie," he said. "Well, I guess I'd better be moseying along."

In the front entryway, he sat down to pull on his boots. I handed him his coat and beret and turned on the porch light.

When I opened the door, a gust of wind blew swirling snow across the threshold. "Whoa!" I exclaimed, stepping back. "You were right about the snow."

We peered out together. It was coming down hard, big flakes driven by a strong wind. There were already several inches on the porch.

I closed the door. "Why don't you stay here tonight?" I suggested. "I don't like the idea of you driving all the way across town in that."

"I don't like it much either. Thanks. I'd like to stay." He smiled at me. "Then we can have breakfast together tomorrow morning."

"The bed in the guest room's all made up. Or…" I was still warm all through from his arm around me as we watched the movie. "Or… if you like… we could share my bed, keep each other warm." I blushed down to my toes at my impulsive boldness.

Lenny's eyes softened. A strange look crossed his face, almost as if he might cry. "That's the sweetest invitation I've had in many a long year," he said. He reached out his hand and I went into his arms. He held me close. "I would love to share your bed and keep you warm. Only, Clara… I don't want you to be disappointed. My old man"—he set me away from him and gestured downward—"doesn't stand up very well anymore."

"Oh!" I touched his cheek. "I won't be disappointed if you'll just hold me. It feels so good to be close to you."

"I can hold you. And I can still kiss. My lips work just fine."

"My lips work okay, too."

"Let's see." He drew me back into his arms and kissed me. Gentle kisses on my face, then my lips. Sweet kisses. Age only enhances the sweetness of a kiss.

We stood in the entryway, lost in kisses. Then, just when my knees began to complain so much they distracted me, Lenny said, "Let's find that bed of yours. We're too old to be standing up for as long as I want to kiss you."

We were shy at first of revealing our old bodies to each other. I got into bed in my big flannel nightgown, he in his long johns and T-shirt. But once we started kissing again, stroking and caressing each other, our shyness melted away. We shed our garments and lay skin to skin, moving slowly, taking time to discover each other.

My body was awake with an intensity of passion that had no imperative, only the ecstasy of the moment. Then Lenny said softly, in wonder, "Clara, you're a miracle woman. My old man's standing up!"

I slid my hand down his body and found that it was true.

⁓ ⁓

A month later, Lenny left his small, dark apartment and moved into the guest room in my house. So began the happiest year of my life.

My solitary world was transformed. I had not let myself realize how lonely I had been until he came to live with me. Our days began with early morning cuddles, tea in bed while we shared our dreams and planned our day. No longer the solitary decision of "I" but the companionable exploration of "shall we?" and "let's…"

Over breakfast we passed the sections of the morning paper back and forth and shared amazement, outrage, or laughter over the various stories. The journalist in him was still awake, and often I would receive an impromptu column about a current event, with his undimmed wit and insight.

We went on adventures, a trip to Denver to visit the museum, a week at the hot springs, movies and concerts, things I had given up doing on my own.

Walks together were a delight. How lovely to share the swift uplift of a flock of geese, the changing color of water and ice on the lake, the stark outline of the foothills against the sky, the shy gaze of a deer, and, with the spring, the lyric song of the meadowlark.

In long, rich conversations we covered everything from politics to the meaning of life. Lenny was a lifelong professed agnostic, but in many ways one of the most spiritual people I had ever known, approaching all of life with a sense of wonder and respect. He loved nature as deeply as I did, and was passionate about human rights and the plight of the dispossessed. After a while I learned that the reason he lived as frugally as he did was because he gave the major part of his income to progressive causes. "You can't take it with you," he often said, cocking his left eyebrow. "Might as well have it do some good."

There were also times apart. I still saw a few clients. Sometimes I went off for a visit with Anne, or a walk alone, or an evening of tango. Lenny was an ardent chess player. He met his chess buddy, Humphrey, at a local cafe several times a week. Sometimes Humphrey would come to our house and they would sit hunched over the chessboard in silent concentration, broken only by an occasional moan or exclamation of triumph. Whenever we met again after a time apart, Lenny's face would light up, and mine would, too.

We laughed a lot. He had a wry twist on almost everything, from the way a bee wiggled its butt as it delved into a blossom, to the expression of a dog we met on the trail. But mostly we laughed because we were so happy to be together.

Touch nurtured my days—his arms around me from behind as I worked in the kitchen, his hand in mine as we walked, our bodies curled together for afternoon naps.

Never in my life had I felt so loved and appreciated. I blossomed with it, returning his love with all my passion and devotion.

Spring came and Lenny worked with me in the garden, clearing out dead leaves, trimming back the perennials, planting seeds for our summer vegetables. The flickers trilled their mating song, and Lenny reduced me to tears of helpless laughter with his ribald translations of their calls.

When summer came I wanted to show Lenny my special place. I longed to go there myself and thought I might be strong enough. We warmed up with some shorter hikes, then went to the Silver Lake trailhead. He had walked that trail before, but not for several years. We walked the wide, level path beside Silver Lake comfortably, but the last steep ascent to Sapphire Lake was almost too much for Lenny. He struggled to breathe, and when we finally reached a resting place on the grassy slope beside the lake, he dropped to the ground. "That's it, Clara. Can't go any farther." I could see that it was true. We lay on the soft grass together and watched the sky.

"I did so want to show you my special place," I said, unable to hide my disappointment.

He turned his head, rousing from his exhaustion to wink at me. "I've been to your special place lots of times."

It took a long time going down and Lenny did not recover for several days. It was the first portent of what was to come.

The summer moved on with roses blooming and our vegetable garden offering fresh treats each day. We ate our meals on the patio, relaxed in lawn chairs under the maple tree, puttered in the garden, and took shorter hikes at lower elevations.

On my eighty-first birthday—or was it my eighty-second?—I went alone to my special place. My heart was steady, but still it took a long time. I was careful to keep my balance, and though my knees complained and I had to rest often, I made it. All was as it had been when I came there in my young body the year before—the great lichen-covered boulder, the shining pool in the curve of the stream, the vivid green grass, the new growth on the krum tree. I was not able to kneel as I had done then, but, filled with the same reverence for the spare, sacred beauty of that beloved place, I spread my arms and bent my head. That year there seemed nothing to let go of; my life was rich and full. So I dipped only once with the intention, "May I live in gratitude." Then, wrapped in the bathing cloth Anne had given me, I sat a long time by the stream as memories flowed around me like the moving water. It was twilight when I came home to Lenny's hug and kiss and dinner waiting.

When fall came, we mulched the shrubs, raked the leaves, and tucked the garden in under layers of compost. We ordered firewood, stacked it together, and lit the wood stove in the evenings.

The days grew short and cold and Christmas approached. The house was warm and festive with the wood stove glowing and Christmas carols playing, as Lenny and I arranged greens and candles and trimmed the tree together.

The week before Christmas our families descended. Lenny's son Jason came from Boston with his wife and two daughters. They stayed with Bette and her sons, but came over frequently to visit us. Lisa and Phil and Jocelyn arrived, Robin's family came over, and our little house rocked with children and grandchildren. Christmas Eve, we hosted a huge potluck for both our families.

On Christmas morning, in a precious quiet time before Lisa's family came upstairs, Lenny and I sat cozily in bed having tea together. Lenny reached into his bathrobe pocket and drew out a small, velvet box. Inside was a slender gold ring set with a deep blue-green sapphire.

"To match your beautiful eyes," he said. He took my left hand in his. "I'd like to put it on your ring finger as a… " He paused, seeking the words. "As an outward and visible sign of my commitment to love, honor, and cherish you… till death do us part.

Lenny looked deep into my eyes. "May I?" he asked.

Deeply touched by the look on his face and the familiar marriage words, I answered, "Yes. Oh, yes!"

He slipped the ring on my finger, and I spoke my vow. "I will wear this ring as an outward and visible sign of my commitment to love, honor, and cherish you till death do us part."

With a gentle hand, he caressed the tears off my cheek. Then he raised his left eyebrow, a twinkle in his eye.

"People don't usually get married in bed," he said as he set the tea tray aside and took me in his arms, "but it makes the consummation very convenient."

Later as we rested in each other's arms, he asked, "Would you be disappointed if we didn't do all the legal stuff and have a big wedding?"

"No," I said, relieved. "Not at all. What we just did was perfect."

So we were married in that sweet, simple ceremony witnessed only by God.

The rest of Christmas was a whirlwind. We took Lisa's family with us and visited Robin's home. After presents and dinner we went to Bette's home for more of the same. A few days later, when it was all over and our visiting children and grandchildren had left, we spent several days recovering, mostly in bed.

"Gotta love 'em," Lenny summed it up. "But it's more energy than an old man can sustain."

⌐ ⌐

As winter moved on, I became concerned about Lenny. He tired easily and had increasing difficulty breathing. One morning, as we cleared a light snow from the driveway, he stopped and leaned on his shovel handle. "Gotta quit," was all he said, but I could hear how his breath labored. I helped him into the house. As I pulled off his boots, I saw that his ankles were swollen.

"Lenny," I said. "I'm worried. Let's get you an appointment with your doctor."

"Women. They always want to take you to the doctor."

I set his boots aside and began massaging his ankles. "Statistics show that married men live longer because their wives make them go to the doctor."

"Oh, all right."

For the next two weeks we did doctor appointments. His family doctor referred him to his cardiologist. His cardiologist, the same Dr. Walton who had cared for him after his heart attack, ordered a series of tests. The tests were hard on him. They barely started the stress test before he gave out, and it took days for him to recover. My worry increased. When all the test results were in, we went again to see Dr. Walton.

I remember the day. It was early March by then. Gold and purple crocuses were blooming in the garden. The sun was warm, the last of the snow melting. Dr. Walton's office had a view of the foothills.

His face was grave. After the pleasantries of greetings, he said, "I have hard news for you."

I reached over to hold Lenny's hand.

"Out with it," Lenny said.

Dr. Walton shifted in his chair, adjusted his glasses. "Your diagnosis is congestive heart failure."

"What does that mean?" I asked.

"It means," Dr. Walton said, still speaking to Lenny, "that your heart's worn out."

"Treatment?" Lenny asked.

"Some lifestyle changes may give you a little more time, but it's pretty far along. If you were a much younger man, we might consider a heart transplant, but it's a long wait for a donor, a serious surgery, and the body does not always accept the new heart. At your age—"

"I don't want any of that," Lenny interrupted. "I'll keep my heart."

I was trembling inside, trying not to let my hand in Lenny's shake.

"Prognosis?" Lenny asked.

"A month, maybe two."

Lenny's hand tightened around mine. We sat still in shocked silence.

"I'm sorry," Dr. Walton said gently. "I'm afraid there's really not much more we can do. You have time to get your affairs in order." He turned to his desk and handed me a leaflet. "Here's information about hospice. They'll be able to help you."

When we got home, I helped Lenny off with his coat and boots. We sat down on the couch, holding each other, still in shock.

"A month, maybe two…" Lenny whispered. "God, Clara, I sort of knew the old ticker was running down, but… so soon!"

I couldn't speak, grief clogging my throat.

"How can I bear to leave you?" His voice turned fierce. "They're not taking my heart. No transplants." He thumped his chest with his fist. "This heart of mine is full of love for you. I'll keep it."

"What will we do?" I asked, turning my face into his shoulder.

He held me close. "We will live every single moment we have left together so deeply each one will be an eternity."

❧☙

And so it was. I put aside everything else in my life to be with him and care for him. We entered into a depth of intimacy and love beyond all I had dreamed possible.

As much as we could, we spent time outdoors. Rocky Mountain spring times can be fickle, intercepting balmy weather with sudden frosts and snowstorms, but that spring was unusually mild. Lenny liked to lie on the grass under the maple tree. The branches were just beginning to swell with buds, and the sun came through, warming him.

One afternoon, as I worked in a flower bed near where he lay, I looked over at him. He turned his head toward me as if he felt my glance and smiled at me. I smiled back, my heart aching with love. As I returned to my weeding, realization flooded me. I remembered Merilea saying there was one more piece to my *ulada*. It was Lenny. At long last, after a lifetime of disappointment in love, I had found him, and learned to love in a way that would not end in bitterness.

I set down my weeder and went to lie beside him. He turned on his side and stroked my body with his gentle hand. Gratitude poured through me. I touched his cheek, his lips. We looked deep into each other's eyes. The immensity of what lay ahead loomed between us.

"Lenny, what do you think will happen? Where will you go?"

"I don't know, Clara love. I don't know. I walk into the mystery. But strangely I'm not afraid. I thought I might be, but I'm not. I'm awed. And curious. Maybe I'm not afraid because the love I have for you feels eternal. And if that's eternal, then maybe I am, too, in some way. Maybe it's only that I sink into the earth, like your Elirians, and become part of all that is, the trees, the grass, maybe a rabbit that nibbles the grass, then maybe a coyote." He raised his eyebrow. "I could be a coyote."

"You could. Or maybe I'll look up into the sky and see your eyebrows waggling at me in the shapes of the clouds."

"Maybe." We laughed and then were silent, touching each other, dropping into the eternity of touch.

Our quiet days were interrupted by a visit from Lenny's son. Jason was a city man, a lawyer, who drank numerous cups of coffee a day and carried that hyped-up energy into all his conversation and movement. He was hard for me, but I knew it was important for him to be with his father. He had also come to make final arrangements about Lenny's financial affairs. I escaped into the garden while they sat at the dining room table poring over folders and papers.

On the morning of the third day, Jason left in his rental car to catch a plane back to Boston. From the porch I saw him standing in the driveway with Lenny. He said goodbye, threw his briefcase into the front seat of the car, then turned back.

"Dad—"

Lenny held out his hand. "Yes, it's really goodbye, son. I love you. Have a good life."

Jason hugged him fiercely, briefly, then drove away fast, as if he could leave his grief behind. Lenny came slowly down the walk to me. I went to meet him and held out my arms. He came into them, resting his head against me. "The goodbyes are hard," he said. "So many goodbyes. Goodbye to everything."

He grew steadily weaker and the day came when he could not get out of bed. He did not complain much—the situation had become too serious for playful bitching—but I knew by the way he drew his brows together that he struggled. I called the hospice people and they visited each day, good people, skilled and comforting. Bette came and sat with him sometimes. The grandsons came once. They stood in his room, shifting from one foot to the other. Lenny didn't have the strength to joke with them as he used to, and they soon fled.

A few days later the hospice nurse moved into the house, covering the essentials so I could stay with Lenny. He hardly spoke any more, but we no longer needed words, our touch communicating all that words could not express.

On a soft, spring day, he drifted away, eyes closed, his slow, rasping breathing the only sound in the quiet room. Bette came and we sat with him together. She cried and talked, breaking the silence. At last she left. Night fell. I undressed and lay in the bed beside him, touching him, feeling the pulse of his life fading.

Sometime in the night, he stirred. "Clara?"

"I'm here."

I put my hand on his heart. He laid his hand over mine, then sank back into himself, his breath loud and labored. In spite of myself, I slept again.

I startled awake with morning light. The room was silent. His heart under my hand was still.

Cold shock immobilized me. My own breath stopped. Finally I leaned up on my elbow. His eyes were closed, his brow smooth, his face peaceful. Peaceful. I drew in my breath. His body was still warm, still soft. I put my arm around him, laid my head on his shoulder.

Through the open window, I heard the flickers calling their love song, one to the other.

Epilogue

It is summer now. The high country is open.

I walk through the empty house. Only a few of my possessions are left, just what I need for daily life. The rest I have given away.

Lenny's daughter and her sons came after his death and took all his things. They tried to give me something to remember him by, but I wanted only the little ring he put on my finger on Christmas morning. Nothing more. "You can't take it with you," he often said.

I have finished my story. Yesterday I printed it out. It sits in a box on my desk where Robin will find it.

This morning when I was picking peas in my garden, my heart suddenly went awry. I had to sit down while it raced and pounded, stopped and raced again as it hadn't done since Kiria first laid her hand on it. Then I knew. Kiria said she would give me a steady heart until my *ulada* was complete.

I will leave a letter for my children, saying goodbye. They will grieve, but they will understand.

All is in order. I wonder who will live in this little house when I am gone, who will tend my garden. I hope at least Robin and Alice will come and harvest the vegetables, smell the roses. But I cannot be concerned about that. It is time to let go.

It is time.

I must go soon before I cannot. I must go early, for I will be slow now that my heart is unsteady, and it may take me a long while to find a place where I can sink in. I will pull on my knee braces and carry my staff. Perhaps a van full of small boys will spill out around me as I begin and a young man will walk a short way beside me, asking me how far I'm going. I don't know how far I can go. I will go as far as I can. Somewhere on the mountain I will find him, tall, black-robed and hooded, and he will open his cloak and fold me in.

Tomorrow I will go.

Also from Heather Starsong

Leaves in Her Hair

The Purest Gold

Song of Eliria

www.heatherstarsong.com

About the Author

*H*eather Starsong grew up in New England and graduated summa cum laude from Boston University in 1957 with a Bachelor of Arts in Comparative Literature.

She has been a dancer since childhood, especially fascinated with the connections between healing, art, and spirit. She has explored and taught many forms: creative dance, liturgical dance, dance therapy, yoga, ceremonial dance, Rolfing® and Rolf Movement,® Continuum, and most recently Argentine Tango.

Although her career has been focused on body language, she has loved and told stories all her life. In 2007 she began to write her stories. *Leaves in Her Hair* was published in 2009, the first edition of *Never Again* in 2015, *The Purest Gold* in 2017, and *Song of Eliria* in 2019.

She is presently semi-retired from a long career of teaching dance and yoga and practicing Rolfing. She lives in Boulder, Colorado, and enjoys writing, dancing, hiking in the high country, and spending time with her grandchildren.

Find out more about Heather Starsong on her web page:
www.heatherstarsong.com